1980

Larrie

Spring of Violence

DELL SHANNON

Spring of Violence

WILLIAM MORROW & COMPANY, INC.
NEW YORK   1973

Library of Congress Cataloging in Publication Data

Linington, Elizabeth.
   Spring of violence.

   I. Title.
PZ4.L756Ss [PS3562.I515]   813'.5'4   73-9723
ISBN 0-688-00209-9

1   2   3   4   5   75   74   73

Spring of Violence

I'd be a dog, a monkey, or a bear,
Or anything but that vain animal
Who is so proud of being rational.
                    —JOHN WILMOT, Earl of Rochester
                    (*A Satire Against Mankind*)

3rd Fisherman: I marvel how the fishes live in the sea.
1st Fisherman: Why, as men do a-land; the great ones
            eat up the little ones.
                    —*Pericles*, Act 2, Scene 1

One

Policewoman Wanda Larsen was the first one into the Robbery-Homicide office on this first Monday in March. If Policewoman Larsen ever heard any criticism of any LAPD officer, her response was indignant and immediate; privately, however, she told herself that men were men, and the best of them would make messes for women to clean up.

The ashtray on Sergeant Higgins' desk was overflowing; lately Rich Conway, on the night watch, had taken to smoking little brown cigarillos and the big glass tray was full of the butts. Tom Landers, for a wonder, had emptied his ashtray; Schenke didn't smoke and Galeano was trying to quit —he had left his ashtray littered with bits of foil from chocolate drops. Wanda cleared everything away and dusted energetically. She had got to her own desk just inside the second communal office they'd acquired when Robbery and Homicide got merged a couple of months ago, and was just taking the cover off her typewriter when Detective Shogart came in, with Sergeants Hackett and Higgins at his heels.

"Anything new gone down?" asked Hackett.

"I don't think so—no reports," said Wanda. Something new would probably show up today; the routine at Central Headquarters was seldom static. As of now they had the hit-run, that heist job at a bar last Saturday night, the unidentified body dead of a probable O.D., a couple of cases ready to be stashed in Pending.

Sergeant Lake came in, said, "Morning," and sat down at the switchboard. Glasser and Piggott drifted in together.

"I don't know what to get Prudence for her birthday," Piggott was saying. "It's on Friday."

"Girls always like cologne," suggested Glasser. "Anything new gone down?"

It was Sergeant Palliser's day off; he wouldn't be in.

"Excuse me—"

Wanda looked up from her typewriter. Standing hesitantly in the doorway, just past the switchboard, was a youngish woman. She was very shabbily dressed in a sagging brown skirt, limp pale-blue sweater, no stockings, ancient canvas shoes once white. She hadn't any makeup on, and her skin looked gray; she had the beginning of a black eye and a cut on one cheek. She looked at Wanda and the men, unsure and timid. "I didn't know there'd be a lady here," she said. "They told me downstairs to come up here." She had a flat near-Southern accent.

"Yes, what can we do for you?" asked Wanda. "Mrs.—"

"Easely," she supplied. "I'm Lorna Easely. I got my neighbor lady, Mis' Stevens, lookin' out for the kids. She's been awful good to me. I didn't tell her, and I didn't say nothing to the kids, but I got to tell you how it was—he said he'd kill us all." She looked at them piteously and the slow tears ran down her cheeks.

Behind her Mendoza came in briskly, and stopped on hearing that. As usual he was dapper in gray Italian silk, snowy shirt and discreet dark tie. His hairline moustache was neat, and he was carrying the inevitable black homburg.

"He said he'd kill the kids, see. They always bothered him, the noise and all. I put up with everything else from him— I didn't know what else to do. And I never lived in a big town before, we're from Tennessee, we come out here last year. He'd bring his women home—trashy women—I got to fix dinner for 'em and all, and never a night but he got drunk,

[8]

less he didn't have no money to. He'd beat me up before too, but when he said he'd kill the kids and me both—I just had to. I just had to. I waited till he was passed out, an' I got the big iron skillet and I hit him till I knew he was dead."

Mendoza came up to her quietly. "Mrs. Easely," said Wanda, getting up, a little bemused at the woman's dull tone reciting facts, "this is Lieutenant Mendoza—if you want to make a formal statement—"

"I want to do what's right, 's all. I knew it was wrong, but I had to do it account of the kids. I didn't let them see—I took 'em out the back way to Mis' Stevens."

Mendoza nodded his head at Hackett. "What's the address, Mrs. Easely?" asked Wanda.

"Oh, it's Park View—"

"So I'll go look," said Hackett, taking down the address.

"If you'll come into my office—" Mendoza took her arm. But she turned blindly to Wanda.

"Please, could you come too? I—I'd like another woman—"

"Surely I'll come." Wanda didn't add that she'd have come anyway, to take down the statement.

"People, people," said Glasser.

"You've got a two-eleven out on Beverly," said Sergeant Lake from the switchboard. "Something offbeat, what I got from the black-and-white answered the call. It's a pet shop or something."

"A *pet* shop?" said Shogart.

"I'll take it," said Piggott. As he got up, Detective Jason Grace came in. His regular-featured chocolate-brown face wore a slightly worried expression.

"Sorry I'm late—we've been up with the baby, she's running a little temperature."

"They do that for nothing," Shogart reassured him. As the father of nine he could be supposed to know.

In Mendoza's office, Wanda started to take down Lorna Easely's confession. In a way, this was an offbeat one too: a homicide coming to them rather than vice versa.

* * *

[9]

It was a shop called Scales 'n' Fins, out on Beverly Boulevard. When they got there—Glasser had decided to come along—the black-and-white was gone, back on patrol.

"We're from headquarters," said Piggott, pulling out the badge. "You've had a robbery here, we—"

"Oh, my God!" said the tall, bald old fellow hurrying up at the sight of them. "All my Regal Angels! All eight of them! I have a regular routine of feeding, and they're at the back on the left wall, so it wasn't until I'd worked my way back there I noticed—All my Regal Angels! All of them!" He looked ready to weep.

"Er—what are they?" asked Piggott. This place was full of aquariums, big and little, sitting on long shelving on all sides of the store. All the aquariums were full of fish.

"Oh, dear, of course you wouldn't—I'm Dave Duff. I own this place. And if they had to steal anything, the Regal Angels are the last ones I'd have wanted—My God, when I think of it—"

"What are they?" asked Glasser. "Fish? Somebody stole some fish?"

"Well, of course they're fish," said Duff. *Pterophyllum scalare*, to be exact. Angel fish. The very newest developed color—and they're all gone! And damn it, the females are all ready to spawn! It's a little tricky, the temperature's got to be just right—and the feeding—"

"What are they worth?" asked Glasser. Piggot had wandered up the aisle in the middle of the store.

"Well, call it twenty-five bucks each," said Duff mournfully.

Glasser suppressed an exclamation. "That much?" he said mildly. At least that made it more than petty theft: two hundred bucks. "You haven't got an alarm system here?"

"My God, Officer," said Duff, "in a place like this? I know the crime rate's up but it never occurred to me things'd get so bad robbers would come after tropical fish! I haven't looked at the door—"

"Well, we'd better," said Glasser. "Hey, Matt?"

Piggott was standing in front of a large square aquarium, staring at the occupants. "Say, these are the prettiest little things I've ever seen," he said. "They're just like little rainbows."

Duff came up. "You like my tetras? They are pretty—nice little fellows too. Kind of tricky to breed, but nice little fish."

"I never saw such colors," said Piggott. "I didn't know fish came in such colors."

"Some even prettier than these."

"Look," said Glasser, "let's get with this, Matt."

"Are they hard to keep?" asked Piggott. "I mean, people keep them at home?"

"Oh, sure—big hobby now, home aquariums. They kind of hook you, these little fellows. Hundreds of different kinds, most of 'em pretty. But hardly anything," said Duff, remembering his loss, "prettier than angels—"

"What do they look like?"

"There's some there—ordinary angels, not like my Regals but the same shape, of course."

Piggott stared at the indicated aquarium. The fish sailing serenely around in it were shaped rather like triangles, with a tall pointed fin above and what looked like streamlined antennae below. They were about five inches long, and colored pale amber with distinct black vertical stripes. They were as graceful as swans. Piggott could see a hazy reflection of himself in the glass, unremarkable, sandy, medium-sized Matt Piggott, and he said seriously, "It's a funny thing, Mr. Duff. We're supposed to be the noblest work of God, but He certainly made a lot of things more beautiful, didn't He?"

Duff laughed. "He sure did. But when I think how my Regal Angels—and all ready to spawn—"

"Hey, Matt. Over here."

Reluctantly Piggott turned away from the angel fish. Glasser was squatting at the front door. "Break-in, all right —marks on the jamb, something metal I'd guess. Did you come in this way, Mr. Duff?"

"No, I always come in the back—I park behind the store."

"Well, he got in this way. Forced the door open with a jimmy or something, and broke the lock. Have you had any customers this morning?" Duff shook his head. "Well, they might not have noticed anyway, the door just unlocked—you hadn't come to unlock it yet?"

"I was late coming in—I wanted to get the feeding done first."

"This is the damnedest thing," said Glasser. "How could anybody steal fish? I mean, how would they—"

"Well, I suppose he'd have his own carrying cans," said Duff. "And nets. And that's another thing—changing them into different water can be very dangerous sometimes—if whoever it is doesn't know about— But it's got to be an aquarist, doesn't it? I just hope—"

"A what? Oh, you mean somebody who likes tropical fish? Knows about 'em. I'd say so," said Glasser. "Somebody who couldn't afford twenty-five bucks for one. That still seems—"

"I suppose because they're special, Henry," said Piggott. He was wandering around again. "A lot here for half a dollar, seventy-five cents, a dollar."

"That's so," said Duff. "As more are bred and the supply goes up, the price comes down, but right now these Regal Angels—"

"Well, I suppose we'd better have the lab print the door —and the tank they were in," said Glasser. "He just might have left some latents, but it's a million to one he'll be in anybody's files even if he did. An aquarist, for God's—"

"Oh, my!" said Piggott. "What kind are these, Mr. Duff?"

"*Copeina arnoldi,*" said Duff. "Characins. Lovely little things, aren't they? Nice fish for a communal tank too, very peaceful little fellows."

"I can't get over all the colors," said Piggott. "How much does an aquarium like this cost?"

"Well, I've got various sizes at different prices—"

Glasser had sought the phone to call the lab. When he came back he found Duff showing Piggott a new empty aquarium and talking about filters. "Look, Matt—"

"Well, I was just thinking, Henry, it'd be nice for Prudence's birthday."

Hackett and Higgins had gone over to the address on Park View to find their new corpse. It was a shabby street in a shabby neighborhood, and the house was old and ramshackle. Mrs. Easely had said forlornly that the door was open. Inside, it was sparsely furnished and rather dirty. The corpse was on the bed in the front bedroom, a big hulk of a man, unshaven, with head wounds that had bled copiously; the iron skillet lay beside him.

"Not much need for lab work," said Hackett. They had called the lab nevertheless; she might recant on the statement. They tried the house next door and found Mrs. Stevens, a comfortably fat middle-aged woman who let out a small scream when they introduced themselves, told her why they were there.

"For the Lord's sake! She *murdered*— My Lord! She never said a word, just would I look to the children— Oh, that poor soul! And the poor children—"

There were, it seemed, seven kids, aged nine down to the baby.

They left Duke and Scarne out of the lab truck dusting and taking photographs, went back to the office and told Mendoza about it.

"I mean, talk about drastic," said Hackett, lighting a cigarette. "Why didn't she just leave him? Silly question, I suppose."

"Human nature," said Mendoza, "doesn't seem to change, Art. She did tell us she has a set of parents. In Tennessee. So at least the kids won't clutter up Juvenile Hall for long. I wonder if the lab got anything on that heist on Saturday night."

"Early to ask—you know the lab," said Higgins. He and Hackett together dwarfed Mendoza's office. "What I'm thinking about—"

"That was a very pro job," said Mendoza meditatively.

"In and out, quick and easy. And don't tell me, I know how many experienced heist-men are on file and out of jail. ¿Pues y qué? What are you thinking about, George?"

"That hit-run." Higgins looked angry. Well, awhile back Steve Dwyer had nearly been killed by a hit-run driver; but that hadn't been all bad, considering that it had finally stirred Higgins up to asking Mary Dwyer to marry him. These days, he was still getting used to his firsthand family, nearly-six-months-old Margaret Emily. "You know we'll never get him." There had never been much hope of finding the driver who, last Friday afternoon, had killed ten-year-old Kevin McLeod, dead at the scene in the twisted tangle of his bicycle.

Mendoza's phone buzzed and he picked it up. "I've got something for you, I think," said Lieutenant Carey of Missing Persons. "No body, but from all I've got on it I think the woman's bound to be dead. And it's a little mystery."

"That sounds a little vague," said Mendoza. "I don't like your things, Carey—they're always all up in the air. Unless there's evidence of homicide it's nothing for us."

"Well, I'd like you to hear the story, see what you think of it anyway."

"¡Vaya al diablo!" said Mendoza resignedly. "All right, all right."

"After all, you're supposed to be the expert on homicide."

Mendoza laughed. "For my sins? Well, I'll listen to your story."

"Say in about an hour. I'll have some people with me."

Mendoza put the phone down, and Grace poked his head in the door. "New two-eleven just in—apartment over on Miramar. Neighbor just walked in and found this old lady beaten up, place ransacked. I've called the lab. If Virginia calls—"

"Somebody'll take the message," said Hackett. "Don't fuss, the baby'll be all right, Jase."

"Well, you can't help worrying," said Higgins. "What about the Easely woman, paperwork all started?" The de-

tectives from the old Homicide bureau had been much gratified to find, when they got merged with Robbery, that they
had acquired a secretary to type reports for them.

"Our efficient Wanda—initial report typed and warrant
applied for. Murder two."

"What do you bet it gets reduced to manslaughter?" said
Hackett pessimistically.

"No bets," said Mendoza sardonically. "It probably will.
But I don't think she's all that dangerous, Art. I'd like to get
those heisters. They didn't hesitate to take a shot at the bartender when he didn't hand over as fast as they wanted.
Which reminds me—" He picked up the phone. "Jimmy, get
me the lab. . . . Did you get a make on that slug you picked
up at that bar Saturday night? . . . Oh. Oh? Thanks. . . . It
was a Colt .45, an old one."

"A big gun for a big man," said Higgins. They had rather
vague descriptions of the three heist-men from the customers
and the bartender: all three Negro, all fairly big, one of them
with an Afro hair style, the other two with moustaches. And
that was all they had, and all they were likely to get, unless
and until those boys pulled off another job. Which was all
too likely; they'd only got about ninety bucks on that one.
R. and I. had turned up names, of course, names picked by
the computer fed those vague descriptions, and at the usual
routine they were looking for those men, picking them up
for questioning when they were found. The bartender said
he could make a positive identification.

Shogart had gone out on that, and Hackett and Higgins
divided the latest names they had and went out on it too. At
least it was nice weather, and the usual little March heat
wave hadn't arrived yet.

"I wonder what Carey's got?" said Hackett idly.

"Something up in the air, just like Luis said. Those M.P.
reports usually are."

As they went out they passed Piggott and Glass just coming in. Piggott was saying, "The prettiest little things I ever

[15]

saw—like little rainbows. And those small size aquariums aren't too expensive, the five-gallon ones—"

"Those damned fish," said Glasser.

When Lieutenant Carey came into Mendoza's office at ten o'clock, he had two women with him. "Mrs. Eldon, Mrs. Donahue, Lieutenant Mendoza. Now I tell you, we've got something funny here, Mendoza."

"Funny isn't the word for it," said Mrs. Eldon. "I won't say Mina couldn't 've done such a thing, but to just disappear—" She was a woman at least in her late seventies, a thin white-faced old woman in a worn black crepe dress. But her eyes were bright and her tone direct. "And what with one thing and another it's been four months about. She'd have written to Charlie, and she'd have let me know where she was, if she was able."

"So let's take it from the top," said Carey. His round snub-nosed face looked serious. "We're talking about Mrs. Mina Borchers, she's eighty-six and a widow with one son—he lives in Chicago. She lived with Mrs. Donahue here, on Bonnie Brae over by the park—"

"I'm sure we tried to please her," said Mrs. Donahue agitatedly. She was about forty, a plain thin dark woman dressed untidily in a drab navy-blue suit. "She came to us six years back when Mother was still alive—before I married Jack, you know. We don't have a license, it's not a regular rest home like, we just have two or three old folk with us—that can't look after a place of their own or cook for themselves any more, you know—we've got, I mean we had, Mrs. Borchers and Mr. Gadden and Mrs. Pruitt now, and I will say, Mrs. Borchers could be kind of difficult to please, but we—"

"Mina's a cantankerous old witch," said Mrs. Eldon roundly. "And she always was. I've known her for nearly seventy years and I know that, make no bones about it. But tell you the the truth, I'm sorry for her. My son says, why on earth bother with her, but she'd driven everybody away from her, I'm the only person knows her ever did go to see her, just once in

[16]

a while, be a little friendly. She nagged her husband into his grave thirty years ago, and her son only writes her a letter now and then out of duty—of course she couldn't abide the girl he married, and just as well he got transferred back east." She sniffed. "You see, I nearly died last November—took bad the day before Thanksgiving, and they never thought I'd live. Pneumonia it was, all that flu going around. And while I was getting better, I never gave a thought to Mina—she'd never bother to come see me. But a week ago last Wednesday was her birthday, and as long as I'm back on my feet again I thought I'd just drop by and say hello. So my son drove me, and that's when Mrs. Donahue told me—"

"We don't know where she went! Or why! I just can't make it out, or Jack either!" Mrs. Donahue wrung her hands. "It was November— I don't recall the exact date, it was about two weeks before Thanksgiving, she just went off—and then—"

"Mmh." Mendoza regarded them both from over his steepled hands. "She's active? Get's around all right?"

"Well, she's got arthritis in one hip, but she can walk all right—not very far, I guess. She used to take the bus and go uptown a couple of times a week, maybe go to a movie."

"What was she living on—pension, Social Security?"

"Well, that's one of the funny things," said Carey. "She wasn't getting either, and we can't turn up a bank account for her either. Her husband died over thirty years ago, and he wasn't in any regular job, by all we can hear, and never paid into Social Security. And since then—"

"I can tell you this," said Mrs. Eldon. "He was a gambler, that man. I wouldn't doubt he might've left her pretty well-off. She nagged him about it, but he was a gambler."

Mendoza smiled. "And they die broke as a rule."

"You should know," said Carey.

"Well, he was a lucky one, I guess. I don't mean cards and such, maybe that too, but what he said—we didn't see so much of them then, just once in a while—like land, and property. My husband always said there was something likable about the man, kind of hail-fellow-well-met if you know what I mean. I do know, he used to go off for spells and then come back, and Mina—secretive she's always been, she'd never say about that. But she's never had to work, earn a living, since he died. All this time."

Mendoza sat up. *"Interesante,"* he said. "But if she had money, what was she doing living down here?" He flashed an absent smile at the women. "Not to imply you live in a slum, Mrs. Donahue."

"That's all right, sir, I know it's not the fanciest part of town. But we own the house clear—that is, Mother did, she left it to me of course—and it's too big for just Jack and me. It seemed best just to go on like Mother and me had for all those years, with the old folks, it was a little money coming in and I've got used to doing it all since Mother died. Mr. Gadden's on the state pension, he gives it to us all but ten dollars a month, for room and board—and Mrs. Pruitt's on the Social Security, she pays ninety a month—and Mrs. Borchers was paying a hundred."

Mendoza looked at Carey. "Not much of a take. But where did the hundred come from? How did she pay it, by check?"

"It was always cash, sir. And she could be sort of mean and always complaining, but I'd've thought if she was going to move she'd've told us. And we never knew where she went—"

"It wasn't till I came round asking," said Mrs. Eldon, "that I heard about it, and it seemed funny. I wrote off to her son Charlie, thinking he'd know, you see. And he wrote back that the couple letters he'd wrote her since then, they'd come back, and he was wondering about it too. He said, maybe go to the police about it. So I—"

"What about her belongings?" asked Mendoza. "She just went off—no car, no taxi?"

"That's the funniest thing," burst in Mrs. Donahue shrilly. "She went to the doctor that day—she went to him about every couple of months—and she couldn't get very near there on the bus, he's up on San Vicente, a Dr. Franken. She'd usually go as far as she could on the bus and then take a cab, but that day Jack—my husband—drove her in our car, it was when he was out of work a spell. And when she come out of the doctor's, she asked him to leave her off at The Broadway downtown, so he did, and she never come back at all. We were worried when she didn't, we called the police then, case she'd been took bad on the street or something, but she wasn't in any hospital or anywhere. And the next day there was a woman come and said she'd been asked to fetch Mrs. Borchers' things, she had her keys—Mrs. Borchers always kept her room locked when she went out—and if you please, there was everything packed up in her two suitcases all ready to go! So she must've planned to—"

"*¿Por qué tanta prisa?*" said Mendoza. "Why the hurry? That's a queer little tale, Carey, but nothing at all says homicide. She's evidently competent, age or no, and where she goes is her own business."

"Look, she was eighty-six and taking prescriptive medication for dangerously high blood pressure," said Carey. "Why didn't she tell the Donahues she was leaving? Tell them where to send her mail?"

"What about the woman who picked up her luggage? Find her and chances are you'll find all the answers."

"Fat chance. Vague description, could be anybody."

"She looked like a hussy," said Mrs. Donahue. "She had on one of these awful short skirts, and her hair was bleached blond. And she—well, she'd had some drinks, you could tell."

"Funny is not the word," said Mendoza, "as a presumed associate of Mrs. Borchers. I gather she wasn't given to—"

"Oh, Mrs. Borchers is a strict teetotaler," said Mrs. Donahue. "That's what was so—"

"Mainly because drink costs money," said Mrs. Eldon wryly. "Mina's the worst miser there ever was. That's the main reason she stayed with Mrs. Donahue, carp and complain though she would. It was cheaper than she could've got took care of anywhere else, a rest home or such. She kept a little old cheap room over by Echo Park till it got to be too much for her, cook and so on. But she heard about Mrs. Donahue's place somewhere, and she said to me it was cheaper than paying rent and buying groceries."

"So what do you think?" asked Carey.

"It's up in the air," said Mendoza. "You've got nothing. Put out what you've got to NCIC, and hope you find her in a rest home in Hollywood—or Tampa, Florida. What about the son—he have any theories?"

"Well, he's the one filed the Missing report."

"But he hasn't come rushing out here to hunt mama?"

"You needn't think he's not a dutiful son," said Mrs. Eldon tartly. "But it's a wonder to me he still bothered to write her once in a while, send her a little money when he could—the way she nagged him all his life, and things she said about his wife. Mina's a real contrary, cranky one, anybody knows her could say, and queer things she might do but I don't see her just disappearing like this."

"Up in the air," repeated Mendoza. "You don't want me, Carey. Nobody's really missing the woman."

"But where did she go—and why?" asked Mrs. Donahue plaintively.

"I would really like to know," said Carey. "It looks to me for eighty percent sure she's dead, Mendoza."

Mendoza shook his head at him. "Do your homework over. She could be living three blocks away from Bonnie Brae, going to a different doctor. Or—"

"Uh-uh. New doctor'd have asked the other for her records."

"I'll give you that," conceded Mendoza. "All the same, you've got nothing for me. The only thing that intrigues me, what was she living on? Paying out the cash?"

"There's more than that that bugs me about it," said Carey, getting up. "You won't take a hand?"

"There's nowhere to go on it," said Mendoza. "Give it to

NCIC." The National Crime Information Center had been of enormous help to all police forces since its inception.

"I already have," said Carey gloomily.

The peculiar little problem stayed at the back of Mendoza's mind as the day wore on—what had Mina Borchers been living on? Otherwise, he was inclined to think that Carey was overly pessimistic. The cantankerous widow could be almost anywhere, still breathing.

His two senior sergeants came back presently with two possibles for the heist job, and he helped to lean on them, questioning, with no results. Nothing but their rap sheets said they could be Saturday night's heisters.

At lunch at Federico's up on North Broadway, Glasser and Piggott joined them, and they heard about the tropical fish. "It's an offbeat one anyway," said Glasser. "Breaking in to steal fish, I ask you. Worth twenty-five bucks apiece, I also ask you. There were a mess of latents on the door, a few liftable, but it's not likely we'll catch up that way."

"Fish? That's a queer one all right," said Hackett, brooding over the menu; as usual he was trying to diet. Grace came up and said the baby was all right, Virginia had just called. New parents would fuss; the County Adoption Agency had only relented and let the Graces have little Celia last Christmas, and she was special to them.

"And you've just got no eye for beauty," said Piggott to Glasser. "Those pretty little fish— Oh, and Duff called back about an hour ago. He remembered this customer that came in yesterday, a man interested in those angel fish. Tried to beat him down on the price. Young fellow about six feet, blond. Not that it does us any good, I don't suppose we'll ever find out who it was. Not a pro, anybody with a record, just somebody interested in tropical fish. What they call an aquarist."

"Of all the outlandish things," said Glasser.

"I'm getting some for Prudence's birthday. A five-gallon aquarium, and Duff said those red-white-and-blue ones 'd get along fine with some angel fish—tetras, he called the others —and maybe a couple of those glass fish too, chanda something. I never saw such pretty little things."

"¿Y ahora qué?" said Mendoza. "Tropical fish—what next?"

Hackett, Higgins and Grace went back to tracking down the possibles on the heist job. A new body turned up at two-thirty, probably another overdose: teen-age male Caucasian, in a rooming house on First Street. Piggott went out on that. Five minutes after he left the office they got an identification on the body found yesterday. The autopsy report had been on Mendoza's desk when he came back from lunch: overdose of H. It now appeared that it was one Danny Riordan, twenty-one, with a pedigree of possession, pushing, inciting to riot, identified by his prints.

"No loss," said Mendoza. He wondered again, idly, what the cantankerous old witch Mrs. Borchers had been living on. That was the only mystery Carey had.

He glanced at his watch. Three-forty. He rather wished it were time to go home. After a misspent bachelor life, entering late on matrimony and parenthood, he had been surprised lately to find the obstreperous twins turning suddenly into small human beings possible to communicate with. Alison's inspiration about Christmas presents, those McGuffey primers, anticipating the small private school, had certainly wrought a change. Though what such unlikely genes—Weir, McCann, and Mendoza—might produce was debatable. At least they hadn't got Alison's red hair.

The phone buzzed at him and he picked it up. "Mendoza, Robbery-Homicide."

"You won't believe this," said Glasser tersely. "We've got another hit-run. Just like the one Friday—boy on a bicycle. About ten—no I.D. yet, the ambulance just left. Critical condition, I'd guess by his looks. But there are witnesses, all pretty clear—it's a residential neighborhood, Columbia Avenue, but there were a couple of people out on front porches and they all say it was deliberate—intentional. Car aimed for the kid, ran him down on purpose. Consensus is a medium-sized car, Dodge, Chevy, a sedan about five years old."

"*¡No me diga!*" said Mendoza incredulously. "Deliberate? How could—"

"Well, by what they all say nobody could have helped seeing the kid, and the car was gunned straight for him. I know it sounds impossible, but—"

"It sounds worse than that, but I'll listen to the witnesses," said Mendoza. And he thought, that hit-run last Friday— He rummaged for the reports on that.

Two

"I know what I saw, is all," said Mrs. Claudia Salbeck. "Nor I couldn't believe it either, like I told this officer, but that driver meant to knock that boy down! I saw the whole thing, I was out in front feeding my roses, and I saw the boy riding down the street—no, I don't know his name, but I know he lives in the next block down somewhere, he goes past all the time—" The traffic men were tracking down the parents. "And that car, it sort of looked as if it was following him, going slow, and then all of a sudden it speeded up and went right *at* him—it was awful!" She was still looking shaken; but she was obviously a level-headed woman, and she was the third witness who'd said the same thing. Old Mr. Allen admitted his close vision wasn't too good, but claimed he saw clear enough at a distance; he'd been sitting on his front porch across the street from Mrs. Salbeck's house. Mrs. Allen, who'd just come out to ask him to run up to the grocery store for her, backed both stories firmly.

"*¡Imposible!*" said Mendoza. "A boy on a bicycle—what possible reason—" But there it was. Hackett and Higgins were back by then, and had left another couple of possibles for the heist waiting in interrogation rooms, to hear about this. By the time Mendoza had listened to the witnesses, the boy had been identified, one Robert Saldivez, and the parents located.

Mendoza had reread the initial report on Kevin McLeod, but there wasn't any similarity. Three witnesses said that the McLeod boy had ridden from the sidewalk between parked cars into the street; the only odd thing about it was that if the driver had stopped he probably wouldn't have been charged.

"What the hell, Luis?" said Hackett. "There's no rhyme or reason to it. An adult in a car—unless the boy, oh, maybe knew something—or somebody had a grudge on the parents—"

"That is really reaching, Art," said Mendoza. "Offbeat— *Dios*, am I having a hunch? First those damned fish, that really is outlandish as Henry called it, and now—I wonder if we're in for another little spate of queer ones."

"My God, I hope not," said Glasser. As a rule the kind of business occupying the detectives at Central Headquarters was very routine, not to say dull—because the violence they dealt with they were used to, and it was mostly irrational, random violence. Just now and then there came along the oddities, the queer things. And sometimes they could be very damned odd. They hadn't had any of that kind come along in a while.

"I want to see the parents," said Mendoza abruptly. "It could be something like that, I suppose—a grudge." The day watch was ending; he called Alison to say he'd be a little late, and went over to Central Receiving.

The parents had just been reassured that the boy would recover; he had a fractured skull, a broken leg and numerous bruises. Richard and Patricia Saldivez looked at dapper Mendoza and told him those witnesses had to be crazy. Robert was usually careful with his bike, but boys did forget the rules sometimes, and there couldn't be any reason for anybody wanting to hurt him—riding him down with a car, that was just crazy. Nobody had any reason to dislike them or Robert, they hadn't had any trouble with anyone ever, they got along with their neighbors, it was just an awful accident. Richard Saldivez worked for Sears, Roebuck, his wife stayed home and took care of their four children. There just wasn't any sense in it, they told Mendoza, those people were all wrong, just an accident.

The boy wasn't conscious yet. Ask him, when he was?

No rhyme or reason, thought Mendoza irritably. Just a queer thing. He went out to the big black Ferrari in the lot, clapping on his hat, and started for home and dinner.

Piggott called Prudence to say he'd be late and drove out to Scales 'n' Fins on Beverly. He found Mr. Duff and a lanky, dark teen-aged boy huddled together over a small tank on the counter. "You don't think it's a fungus, do you?" the boy was asking anxiously.

"Doesn't look like it. Maybe she got nipped. Keep an eye on her, keep her isolated, but I wouldn't worry too much, way she's taking brine shrimp." Duff looked up to Piggott. "Well, you got any line on who took my Regal Angels?"

"Not yet, Mr. Duff. I want to hear more about that customer you mentioned, and—"

"Sure. Oh, this is Ron Babcock—Ron's my steadiest customer if not the best paying, you might say."

"Guess so," said the boy a little shyly. "I been fooling around with exotics since I was a kid. I was sure sorry to hear about those Regal Angels—they are really the most. You a cop, sir?"

"That's right," said Piggott. "What about this customer, Mr. Duff? You know him?"

"I don't know his name," said Duff. "He's been in here before, but not very often. He's an aquarist all right—knows his stuff. And every time he's been in, call it half a dozen times, he's been after something pretty rare. I got the idea that when he's in the market, he shops around, see. I told you what he looks like, but I don't suppose that's much use to you."

"Not much." Piggott peered into the nearest tank where a school of gaily colored little fish were darting about. "Say, Mr. Duff, your little fish are the cutest things I've ever seen.

My wife's got a birthday coming up, and I think I'd like to get her some—you know, just a little aquarium and some of these pretty ones."

Duff looked at the boy and they both smiled. "Oh, my, he doesn't know what he's getting into, does he, Ron? I can show you some tanks, sure—" Duff went on talking about tanks, and fish, and Piggott heard, to his surprise, about water aerators and filters and fluorescent lights and the best plants for tanks, and the amount of water surface necessary per fish, by size. When they got round to the fish, he said he wanted some of those angel fish: he'd noticed that the ordinary ones were only two bucks each. "Well, you were talking about a five-gallon tank—if you want angels you'd better make it ten, they like room to move around—"

"And some of these patriotic ones," said Piggott, pointing out the red-white-and-blue ones. "And that's a pretty one too," pointing out a graceful green fish alone in the next tank.

"Well, I wouldn't advise it," said Duff dryly. "That's a *Moenkhausia oligolepis*. Put that in a tank with other fish and pretty soon you just got one fish left—that one."

"You mean it'd eat them?" said Piggott, horrified. The fish looked so peaceful. There seemed to be a bit more to keeping the pretty things than met the eye. Now Duff was talking about water; it seemed you had to take along some of the water they were already in for a new tank. "Well, I'd like to get it set up as soon as possible."

"Look," said Duff kindly. "I've got a ten-gallon tank just about set up for fish, with plants and so on, for another customer, but he won't want it till next month and I guess I can let you have it, Mr. Piggott. It's not filled yet, of course. Suppose you take it home and set it up and start to fill it, and I'll have a nice selection of fish for you to pick up tomorrow. Now mind, you add the water gradual, water from the tap, but you got to warm it up to about seventy-three degrees. And just fill it halfway, and put it somewhere out of strong light. You'll get the rest of the water along with the fish. Oh, and you'll want a thermometer, you've got to keep the water temperature more or less steady, between seventy and seventy-six."

Piggott reflected that it sounded like a little work; but they were such cute, happy-looking little fish—"Could I have some of these?" he asked.

"Oh, the red killys, yes, they're peaceful little guys. I'll make you up a nice selection," said Duff. "Lessee, you could have about twenty-five small fry and the angels. Should look very nice. And you'll want an aerator too, increase the oxygen supply for those angels. I might put in a few paradises—"

Driving home, Piggott wondered uneasily if Prudence would appreciate the lovely little fish, if it involved some labor.

Hackett went home and told Angel he hoped Luis wasn't having a hunch. "About another round of offbeat ones. But those fish—and those witnesses have got to be wrong about that hit-run. That's just silly."

Angel eyed him, her cheeks flushed and brown hair slightly ruffled from the heat of the oven, and didn't ask if he'd weighed today. "Tell me about it at dinner. I'm blessing Alison these days—and that McGuffey primer. Mark really picked up the basis of phonetics in no time, and he's poring over that primer instead of television."

"Well, we've got a bright one, reading at four and a half."

"It's largely the quality of the primer," said Angel. Hackett went to find the kids, his darling Sheila now a bit steadier on her legs at nearly two.

Higgins went home to find Mary arguing with Steve Dwyer. "But I want to bake a cake tonight, Steve."

"Aw, you can do that after I go to bed! It doesn't give me any time at all when I have to go to bed at eight-thirty! Honestly, Mother—" They broke off to appeal to Higgins as umpire, and the little Scottie Brucie pawed at his legs.

"That darkroom," said Higgins meditatively. A couple of

months ago he and Steve had explored the possibility of home-developing snapshots, only to find that it was practically impossible for the amateur to develop color film, and more expensive. Higgins was still using the Instamatic; but Steve, a convert to *Modern Photography* magazine, had acquired for all his savings a very secondhand Eastman Medalist and was going in heavily for artistic composition shots in black and white. He was good about cleaning up after himself, using the kitchen as a temporary darkroom, but Higgins had been thinking about somehow adding a real one to the garage.

"It'd sure be great if we could, George! Would it cost much?"

"I don't know, Steve. You'd want electricity run in, for safelights—there's a water line on the side of the garage, we could—well, we'll think about it."

Laura was practicing loudly on the piano. "And how she can through that I don't know," said Mary, "but the baby is asleep. If you wake her up—"

"Well, I can go look at her, can't I?" said Higgins meekly.

The night watch drifted in man by man—Conway, Landers, Schenke, Galeano. Galeano had a bag of chocolate caramels with him and Landers kidded him about that. "Everybody always puts on weight when they stop smoking. Now I know why. Listen, you'll ruin your teeth."

"The hell with my teeth," said Galeano. "It's my thrifty peasant ancestry. I said if cigarettes went up another quarter a carton I'd quit. And you," he added to Conway, "can stop trying to convert me to your damn Mex cigars."

"They aren't cigars," said Conway. "I wouldn't be caught dead smoking a cigar. Did the day watch leave us any jobs?"

"Apparently not, but Jimmy left us a note. He says the boss has a hunch that we're in for some more funny ones. God, what a thought. Of course it does break the monotony," said Schenke.

[29]

"Is it just out of the blue or does he have a reason?" asked Landers.

"Well, it seems this pet shop or something had some tropical fish stolen. That's a funny one all right."

"How're you doing with that blonde, Tom?" asked Galeano.

"Oh, making a little progress, I think," said Landers. His blonde was also an LAPD officer, trim little Phil O'Neill down in R. and I., and she had a good deal more common sense than blondes were reputed to have. She was still telling Landers she was making up her mind about him, and they hadn't known each other a year yet. At least, he reflected, he'd be going off night watch next month, get back to a normal routine when he could take her out to dinner now and then.

The first call they got was at nine-forty, a two-eleven at a liquor store on Wilshire. There were three witnesses, the owner and two customers, and as Landers and Conway listened to them, it added up in their minds.

"Three of them there was, three big colored guys, and two of 'em had guns—they come in real fast and just said, this is a stick-up, give us the bread—"

"I've got a game leg," said the owner; he was still looking shocked and scared. "I can't move so fast, and when I didn't get the register open right away, this one fellow swore at me and fired a shot—you can see it hit right there, didn't miss me by a foot, broke all those bottles of gin—"

"They all looked mean as hell, like they'd shoot all of us for one wrong move—"

"Well, we said we'd probably hear of them again," said Conway. "I'll see if I can find the slug." He started gingerly poking around in the mess of broken gin bottles on the shelf, and presently found the place at the back of the wall where the slug had hit. He dug it out with his knife. "Wonder if it's the same gun. Lab can say, probably." He dropped it into an evidence bag.

"Did any of them touch anything in here, you remember?" asked Landers. But the consensus was that they hadn't. Just come in fast, and taken the money from the register and all the men's wallets, and gone out fast. None of the men had heard a car start up outside, but with the mid-evening traffic on Wilshire that said nothing for sure. "Can you tell us how much they got?"

The witnesses consulted and the owner looked at the register tape. "About four hundred from the register, and I had nearly fifty on me." The other two men had lost around twenty apiece. There wasn't anything more the detectives could do on it tonight but write a report, but that sounded like a carbon copy of the heist on Saturday night.

They got back to the office about ten-thirty and Landers was typing up the report when another call came in. A body this time. Schenke and Galeano went out on that.

It was Commonwealth Avenue over past MacArthur Park, a dark side-street of mixed small apartments and single houses. The black-and-white was sitting in front, doors open, and one uniformed man waiting for them. "It's round in back. Looks like murder one to me." They followed him down the narrow driveway.

This was a four-family apartment, a little shabby; nothing was very new down here. "Guy who lives here just came home and found him. Made him for you—a Kenneth Jowett, also lives here."

The finder of the body was an elderly man, ruddy and white-haired, and in the little light from a rear apartment and the uniformed men's flashlights he looked completely shocked. He kept saying, "But who'd want to hurt Mr. Jowett? He's a nice young fellow, always very pleasant to me—who'd want to—" There were several heads crowding at the kitchen window of the two rear apartments, occupants suddenly aware something was going on.

Schenke squatted over the body. It was just outside the line of four garages behind the apartment; the garage farthest

[31]

to the left had its door open, and there was a car inside. Schenke went into the garage and looked at the registration on the visor. "His," he said to Galeano briefly.

"Yes, yes, he works at night," said the elderly man. "He works for the Water and Power company, I know that. I think he usually goes to work about this time— What? Oh, yes, my name is Durban, James Durban, I went to the movies tonight, I just—"

The body, in fact, was still warm; he hadn't been dead long. "What do you think?" asked Schenke. "We'd better get the full treatment on this, Nick."

Galeano agreed resignedly. He went out and used the black-and-white's radio to call in and ask Headquarters to rout out some lab men for the overtime. Photographs and a general look around the body. They left the uniformed men to guard the body until the lab truck arrived, and went into the apartment; Durban said Jowett had been married.

They had a little difficulty finding his wife. She wasn't in the right-hand apartment upstairs with the name beside the door. After five minutes they turned her up in the apartment across the hall, and broke the news to her.

She was a pretty woman, about thirty, ash-blonde and slim, and she didn't seem to take it in at first. "Ken—" she said. "But I don't—he just left for work at the usual time, he had supper like always and kissed me and left. And I came over here to help May mark this hem for shortening, she—" She was still holding a blue skirt in one hand.

The other woman, Mrs. Walling, younger and plumper, was quicker on the uptake. "This neighborhood!" she said. "Running down—it isn't safe for even a big strong man to be out at night— Oh, Rose, you poor thing—"

"But Ken—you aren't—you aren't telling me he's—" She began to cry weakly, and the other woman put an arm around her. They couldn't question her much, and by all that they could forget about her anyway: she had a solid alibi, even if it hadn't been what it obviously looked like, the simple act of violence for robbery.

They went back downstairs to see what the lab men were getting. Scarne cussed them out for calling them back on overtime, but added, "I don't doubt you'll be calling your boss out too. I remembered that other case because it was a real offbeat thing."

"What other case?" asked Schenke.

Scarne smiled. "We took some pictures for you, and then we had a closer look at him." They had portable lights up now, and the body lay in a little glare. "Have a look yourself. He's been knifed—I'd have a guess, in the back." There was a pool of blood seeped from under the body on the cement drive. "But there's something else too."

Galeano squatted over the body. Jowett looked to have been in the early thirties, a big man and good-looking, with dark hair and a firm jaw. He lay face up. He was wearing a tan jumpsuit with the city's Water and Power company label stitched on the breast pocket. His pants pockets had been pulled out, emptied. But there was something half protruding from the breast pocket. Galeano lifted the flap and edged it out carefully. A moment later he said explosively, *"Dio mio!* I don't believe it! For God's sake, offbeat! Look at this, Bob."

Schenke bent to look. It was a little sheet of paper, torn out of a small tablet or memo pad, and across it in straggly ballpoint ran a nearly illegible message: *god bless tha parool bord.*

"Jesus H. Christ!" said Schenke. "I don't believe it either, but I think we'd better call the Lieutenant, Nick."

Mendoza, still muttering about impossibilities, had been soothed and stimulated by his household. Coming in the back door of the big house on Rayo Grande Avenue in Hollywood, he was confronted by their hairy sheepdog Cedric slurping water from his bowl in the service-porch; he offered Mendoza a polite paw. In the kitchen, Alison and Mrs. MacTaggart were busy amid various appetizing smells. "Good day, *amado?*" asked Alison as he kissed her.

"A funny day," said Mendoza. "I have the awful feeling my hunch is right, *cara*. Where are the offspring?"

"Just where you might expect. And what an inspiration that was," said Alison. One of the twins' Christmas presents had been those first primers of the set of McGuffey Readers, now reprinted and in use at a number of private schools. The twins had never looked back after discovering the first picture in it to be a fat tabby cat, and by now, having with Alison's help mastered the basic phonetics, were reading the easy words and eagerly pursuing knowledge. Oddly enough, confrontation with the printed word and only English words had eliminated some of their confusion between Spanish and English, which was all to the good.

Mendoza found them in the nursery, which was a term they objected to vigorously. Dark heads close together, they were bent over Terry's primer. "Like our *el pajaro*," Johnny was saying. "He's got eggs in the nest and he's afraid the bad cat gonna steal 'em."

"Well, *niños*, you learn any new words today?" asked Mendoza.

Terry flung herself at him first. "I can read bird, Daddy! I can read bird 'n' tree 'n' eggs 'n'—"

"I showed her how," said Johnny firmly. "I could read first."

Mendoza regarded them interestedly. From being occasional nuisances and responsibilities, the twins were growing up into new personalities. Just lately, they'd been making him feel some alarm at how time sped by. They'd be four in August, which seemed unlikely; only awhile ago they'd been keeping their parents awake all night, howling, until Alison had given in and found Mrs. MacTaggart.

Hostages to fortune, he thought. That was another thing, the money. The money nobody knew the miserly old man had, until he died. And Luis Rodolfo Vicente Mendoza, growing up in the slum streets down there, had done without much money before and could again; but he was just as glad there was the money, now, on the twins' account.

They climbed into his lap to vie with each other in proving what they knew. A benevolent Bast, the Abyssinian, was curled up on Terry's bed; the other three cats would presently be winding about feet under the dining table, Sheba talking loudly, Nefertite hooking claws in stockings, El Señor silent unless there happened to be fish.

When Alison called him to dinner, he contemplated her across the table and said, "I remember my grandmother saying it, but it never sank in until the last couple of months. You don't look any older than when we were married."

"*Gracias, amado.* Saying what?"

"How much faster time goes as you get older," said Mendoza. "Damn it, before we know it they'll be ready for college—it was only yesterday you were saying I told you so about it's being twins." He sounded plaintive.

Alison laughed; she did look absurdly young, with her red hair in its short feathery cut. "Well, there's not much we can do about time. Speaking of which, you know that bird hasn't shown up, and I'm wondering if something's happened to him. Our mockingbird. Ordinarily, he and his latest missus would be building a nest by now."

"I can't say I'll lose any sleep over that," said Mendoza. Their mockingbird, rescued from a bout with an asphalt machine and fed on Mendoza's rye, had been a confounded nuisance.

Mrs. MacTaggart got the twins settled down; reading or no, they still demanded their favorites of her old Scottish songs at bedtime.

Mendoza was wandering around half-undressed, and Alison sitting up in bed reading a biography of Rubens when the phone rang, at midnight. Mendoza went out to the hall to answer it.

A minute later he said loudly, "*¡Diez millón demonios desde infierno!* I don't believe it!" Alison put her book down. "All right, all right, I'm interested! Yes, I want to look at it. What's the address? I'll be there in twenty minutes."

"Now what?" asked Alison.

"The damn offbeat things," said Mendoza, picking up his tie. "I had a hunch, all right. Something in Pending just turned active again, is what. ¡Condenación! And it is just impossible!"

He drove down to Commonwealth Avenue and met Schenke and Galeano; the lab truck had gone. He looked at the body of Kenneth Jowett; the ambulance was standing by, waiting to take it in. "I still don't believe it," he said.

"Neither did we," said Galeano. "There's not the slightest damn similarity. Well, the violence, but that's about all. Yes, we had the lab out, you'll get pictures."

"And give that thing to Questioned Documents. Whatever the hell they can tell us about it—they didn't give us much on the other one. I do not like this one damned bit, Nick."

"I didn't think you would," said Galeano.

He sat at his desk on Tuesday morning and told all the day men how much he didn't like it. There were other things for them all to be doing; there was this new heist job bearing all the marks of the other, and the old lady beaten up and robbed—Grace had been on that, and he was off today: to balance that they had Palliser back. There wasn't much to do on the two other offbeat ones, the fish and the hit-runs.

Palliser scratched his handsome straight nose and said, "Mrs. Ellen Reynolds. I went out on that some. We never turned up any lead at all."

"Here's all the paperwork on it," said Mendoza; he'd had Wanda look that up the first thing. "I've been over it, and there's nothing in it. Nada absolutamente. You're welcome to look."

"Take your word," said Hackett. He leaned back and the chair creaked under his bulk. "I did some work on that too. It was just after New Year's—"

"January third," said Mendoza. They all kept up in a general way with the current cases being worked, and they all remembered Ellen Reynolds.

She'd been thirty-one, a divorcée living in a little rented house behind a bigger house on Carroll Avenue. She was a legal secretary for a firm of attorneys on Spring Street, and she had a clean record: a very respectable young woman. Everybody who knew her said she lived very quietly, seldom took a drink; attended an Episcopal church every Sunday; had no current boyfriends, steady or otherwise. Her ex-husband was a mining engineer and at the time on a job in Peru. She'd been found by her landlady one morning, and what evidence showed up said that somebody had broken in the back door of the little house, beaten and raped and killed her. She had fought him, but evidently had no chance to scream; nobody had heard anything. She'd been dead about twelve hours when she was found. And whoever had killed her had left a crooked little note at the scene, with the nearly illiterate message scrawled on it—*god bles th parol bord.*

"And I do not *like* it," said Mendoza. "It makes me *muy desgraciado,* boys."

"It's funny," said Palliser. "It doesn't fit, some way. But there it is. We never gave anything to the press or anybody else, about that note. So that says it's got to be the same X, doesn't it?"

"But look at the discrepancies, John," said Higgins. "A sex crime—attack and rape—on a woman, and then a man knifed for what he had on him. Reynolds was beaten—no knife used. And—"

"Look, all of you know as well as I do," said Hackett, "you get the violent ones, it's any kind of violence. Depending what weapons they find to hand, or happen to have on 'em. I don't think that says anything, George. What that note says is, all right, it's the same one killed Reynolds. And he's a nut."

"*Cómo sí,*" said Mendoza sadly. "And the slightly different misspelling says nothing—an illiterate wouldn't write the same way twice."

And all of them had been detectives long enough to know

what slogging routine this indicated; they felt depressed, thinking about the routine on Ellen Reynolds and what that had turned up.

They had, of course, gone down to the non-investigative LAPD department known as Welfare and Rehabilitation, and got lists of men recently paroled from all California prisons. They had tried to find and question all the sex offenders from that list, first, and then just any men from that list. There had been two hundred and sixty-nine men paroled in California in the previous six months, and seventy-four of them were resident in the L.A. area. They had found most of them eventually, and there was nothing at all to tie any of them to Ellen Reynold's murder. No latent prints at the scene, no leads on that X at all. And eventually, they had put the file in Pending and gone on to new problems.

"See what Questioned Documents has to say about the note," said Higgins now.

Palliser said, "Just what they said before." Questioned Documents, examining the first note, had said apologetically that whoever had penned it was so nearly illiterate that there were no distinguishing marks about the writing, and a ball-point pen didn't show shading or angles of pressure. The paper had been from a cheap memo pad sold in ten thousand places.

"What the hell do we do with it?" asked Hackett. "It isn't as if we'd ever had any definite lead to any of those very loosely possible suspects. If we had, look again and see if the same ones show here. But—"

"Routine!" said Mendoza savagely. "Go back and look at them all again. At least we've already got the list made up. Who wants to start on it?"

Piggott said, "Well, there's this new thing Jase had yesterday—the old woman beaten up. Hospital said we can probably talk to her today."

"So go and see her. My two stalwart senior sergeants can start the routine on Jowett."

"Oh, hell," said Higgins. "Of all the thankless jobs. You know we'll get nowhere, Luis."

"Negative thinking, George. Of course, as I said at the time, nothing tells us that this X got paroled in California. The population tends to be mobile these days."

"That's a very helpful thought," said Hackett. "Do we start asking eight states around for lists of parolees?"

Mendoza flicked his desk-lighter. "Wind up with fifteen thousand names. Look at ours first."

"I swear to God," said Hackett bitterly, "you called it down on us, Luis. You and your hunches about the spate of funny ones! And these heisters running around pulling a job every forty-eight hours, and no damn lead at all—they'll end up killing somebody—"

"*Muy posible*," said Mendoza. "You picked the job, *compadre*."

"I don't know why the hell," said Higgins crossly.

Palliser sighed. "Don't we all sometimes wonder. But there it is, we'd better get on it."

"I just had the thought," said Piggott slowly, "you know we looked for the husband. I mean, till we found he was in Peru. The ex-husband." Piggott was a highly moral man, and a firm fundamentalist; he disapproved of divorce. "It could've been something private, and that funny note just a blind. To make us think it was a nut—a halfway nut—just paroled."

They looked at him kindly. Matt Piggott was a plodder, not a Sherlock Holmes. "Questioned Documents said definitely a near illiterate, Matt," said Hackett.

"It was just a thought," said Piggott.

"And what is our brilliant lieutenant going to be doing while we go round in circles, *compadre?*" Hackett got up, automatically reaching to adjust the shoulder holster.

"Ruminating," said Mendoza. He had opened the top drawer and got out the cards. The domesticities had ruined his deadly poker game; these days he didn't sit in at draw four times a year, but he still thought sharper with the cards in his hands. He began to stack the deck systematically for the crooked deal. "All I know is, I don't like Jowett. I don't like that note. *No tiene pies ni cabeza*—there's no sense in it."

"Run around on all the damn routine and get nothing," said Shogart disgustedly.

"That's about it, E.M." Hackett shrugged.

And Sergeant Lake put his head in the door. "You've got a bank job now," he said tersely. "Savings and loan on Beverly. The Feds are called."

"Hell and damnation!" said Mendoza.

Three

Mendoza, Hackett and Higgins got to the Federal Savings building on Beverly at the same time as three F.B.I. men. Inside, the place was in an uproar, with an excited knot of tellers all talking at once in the middle of the one big bank-like office, and an agitated middle-aged man trying to quiet them. Three curious customers stood gaping a little apart.

At sight of the badges, the man exclaimed, "Thank goodness someone set off the alarm! I don't know who—Ada, did you set off the alarm? Who set off— Now quiet down, it's all over now and these are police officers, they want to ask questions—"

Instantly they all stopped talking. But it dawned on the three customers for the first time what had happened, and they started gabbling excitedly. Mendoza and the Feds got them quieted down and the man introduced himself as Ray Dettin, the manager. "Now I'd like to know what happened here myself—I was in my office. It wasn't till I heard Ada scream that I realized—this is Ada, Ada Gibbon—"

"Miss Gibbon?" said one of the Feds. "Were you the one he held up?"

She stared at them as if she were hypnotized, mouth slightly open. She was a plain girl about twenty-five, with lank brown hair to her shoulders, and brown cowlike eyes. She closed her mouth and then opened it again and said in a thin voice, "I couldn't say a word. Not a word. I was never so surprised in my life. Never. I swear to God. Even after—after I handed over the money, I couldn't *move*. I just watched—I was never so *surprised*. It wasn't till she went out the door I could make a sound. And I screamed."

"That's when I realized what must have happened," said another teller eagerly, a slim blonde. "I heard her, of course, and saw her looking out the door, and I realized she'd been robbed and I stepped on the alarm—"

"Which was pretty stupid," said a third. "With Ada, she might've screamed for any reason—"

"She?" said Mendoza and the Feds together. "It was a woman?" said Mendoza. "Was she alone, or could you—"

Ada nodded slowly. "I never saw a gun so close before. It looked awful big. And she had the nicest smile!" She started to cry. The Feds looked at Mendoza.

"Would you recognize her again? What did she look like, Miss Gibbon?"

"Oh, oh," said Ada, "she was the sweetest little old lady you ever saw! Really little, not as tall as me, and thin, but she had on a kind of trim little blue suit and a white blouse and her hair was real white and she had it done in a big knot on her neck—long hair I guess—and she looked like—she looked just like the kind of sweet old grandmother anybody'd like to have! I was so *surprised*—"

"*¡Dios!*" said Mendoza. "It seems I had a hunch. A sweet old lady bank robber. What did she say?"

"Oh, oh, she didn't much, she came up to my window and leaned right in and took the gun out of her purse and she said, oh, oh, she said I want all your money, my dear, and I was so *surprised*, and then I just—I just gave it to her, and she had a big red handbag and she put it all in that and walked away."

"And you just stood and watched her walk out—if you'd yelled then," said the blond teller, "one of the men might have grabbed her. But an old lady? That sounds—"

"Now, I'm sure Ada did her best," said Dettin. "How much did you hand over, do you know?"

Ada wailed aloud. "We'd only just opened, Mr. Dettin, it was only five after nine, she was the first customer in and I'd just counted—it was three thousand dollars."

"Well, well, it could have been worse," said Dettin.

"Did she touch the counter?" asked Hackett. Ada said she might have. The Feds had some lab equipment with them and went to dust the counter for prints. Mendoza, Hackett and Higgins asked questions of everybody else, and found only one woman besides Ada who had even noticed the sweet old lady. She gave them substantially the same description. On a very long chance they took Ada back to Parker Center to look at some mug shots. Hackett settled her at a table down in R. and I. and explained matters to Phil O'Neill, who had fetched in some books filled with the females in their records.

"But she looked so *nice*," said Ada. "You'd just never dream, looking at her—"

"Well, you see if you can spot her anywhere here, and tell Miss O'Neill if you do. I'll be back—we want a statement from you." Lady bank robbers yet, he thought in the elevator. The offbeat ones turning up again. No way to guess if the old lady got into a car, alone or with accomplices, or strolled away on foot. But the Feds would be on it too, and they had more files to look at.

On top of this Jowett thing. That was just impossible, but some work had to be done on it.

Mendoza left Hackett and Higgins at the routine on that and went down to the Welfare and Rehabilitation office, which housed the parole officers. He had with him the list they'd made up last January, of the men then six months or less on parole, in this area, with records of violence. There were twenty-three men on the list.

That office was usually busy too, but they let him see a Sergeant Ballard they'd talked to before, on Reynolds. Mendoza remembered that Sergeant Ballard had callously enjoyed the whole thing, not having to deal with it himself; and now he stared at Mendoza and began to laugh incredulously.

"You don't mean to say it's happened again? The same kind of note? I will be damned! That is really one for the books. Get anything from Questioned Documents?"

"Probably not. But they're both murder one, I'd remind you," said Mendoza shortly.

"Oh, I know, I know—not really funny. But a strange one all right. What help can I give you on it?"

"This list." Mendoza handed it over. "The priority list we weeded out of your files the first time. I'd like to talk to their P.A. officers."

Ballard nodded. "The only thing is, we've got such a caseload here, they don't really have a chance to spend all that much time on individuals. I'll look them up for you. They'll know a little more about these men than anyone else would, of course."

And they'd done this before too, or started to just before it went into Pending. It had turned out that several of the men had had the same P.A. officer; they could say something about them, but nothing conclusive. But it was a thing to do. Ballard got hold of all of them and managed to set up appointments with Mendoza over the next two days.

More or less at random he then went to see Mrs. Rose Jowett. She'd been crying, and he didn't think she was a very intelligent or imaginative female anyway, but she seemed open enough. "Of course Ken didn't have any *enemies*— that's silly—he got along fine with everybody—it's just all these judges letting criminals out of jail all over, just like May says, nobody safe on the street—"

But of course the note took it out of the personal realm. He went back to the office, feeling vaguely dissatisfied. The warrant, murder second, had come in on Lorna Easely. After they'd got her statement yesterday she'd been formally arrested and jailed, the children taken to Juvenile Hall, and a teletype duly sent back to the little town in Tennessee to inform her parents. If there was any money, which he doubted, they might want to pay a defense attorney. No autopsy report yet on Easely; Bainbridge and his assistants were usually busy too. But he called Bainbridge now.

"Your latest corpse. Kenneth Jowett. Have you had a look at him yet?"

"Very briefly," said Bainbridge. "He was stabbed in the back three times. I'll tell you more about the knife when I've looked inside. Otherwise looked like a healthy specimen."

Questioned Documents hadn't looked at the note yet. Mendoza swore mildly and was about to ask Sergeant Lake where everybody was when one of the Feds came in and introduced himself as Joe Valenti. He was new to this area, just transferred from back east. "Thought you'd like to know we didn't get any latents off the counter. But this is really one for the books, isn't it, the little old lady. Come to California and see life."

"One for the books," said Mendoza dismally. "You should see some of what we've got going here. Of course there's nothing to do about those fish, and I don't know that I believe those hit-run witnesses."

"Fish?" said Valenti.

There was an inquest scheduled today on Kevin McLeod, the ten-year-old killed last Friday. Everybody seemed to have forgotten it, and Lake reminded Palliser about it as he passed the switchboard, five minutes after Mendoza, Hackett and Higgins had taken off. "Somebody's got to cover it, and you were on that."

"Oh, thanks, Jimmy, I will." It was Grace's day off. "That thing Jase had yesterday—I'd better do something on that too."

"A Mrs. Kowaljic, they said we could talk to her today." Lake handed over the address.

"And the other boy," said Palliser. "Two birds with one stone." He'd have just time before the inquest. When he got to Central Receiving, he asked about the boy first.

They had let his mother stay with him. He was a nice-looking boy, Robert Saldivez, and he stared at Palliser's badge with interest. "You find whoever it was hit me?" he asked.

"Not yet. Do you remember much about it?"

"Gee, no. Just bam, and when I wake up I'm here. But Mom keeps saying it must've been my fault, and it wasn't. Honest, it wasn't! I'm always real careful."

"But, Bob, you must have been careless somehow—unless," she said doubtfully, "it was a drunk driver, I suppose, but in the middle of the afternoon—"

Palliser didn't remind her that they got the drunk drivers at all hours. "Remember where you were when it happened?" he asked.

"Sort of. I *was* being careful, honest. I was on my right side of the street and there weren't any parked cars right there— just nothing—and all of a sudden, wham, and that's it." He moved uncomfortably; they had one leg in traction.

"Well, thanks," said Palliser.

"I sure hope you find him, Sergeant."

Grace had, yesterday, after calling the lab on the Kowaljic robbery, sealed that apartment door and left it. There hadn't been a lab report yet. When the nurse let Palliser into the four-bed ward where Mrs. Kowaljic was, she said, "She really was knocked around severely, Sergeant—it's a wonder she wasn't hurt more badly."

But Mrs. Kowaljic faced him brightly enough, pleased at the attention. She was in her seventies, a wrinkled brown old lady with thin gray hair and very white false teeth, a splinted arm and bandages on her head.

"Can you tell me what happened?" asked Palliser gently after introducing himself. "How did the man get into your apartment, Mrs. Kowaljic?"

"I will tell you," she said, nodding once. Her eyes were rueful. "It is that I am in America too long. I have been lying here thinking about that, and it is true. I must remember to tell my sons—they come to see me tonight. I am in America too long! In the old country, people they are afraid and suspicious, they know are bad people all around—thieves, and revolutionaries with bombs, like at home before we came away. But in America—hah!—fifty-two years I'm here, and never in America is any reason to be afraid! Sure, you lock your door, you got any sense, but people act nice, friendly, you don't get suspicious about them. And he said he was from the phone company. The robber."

"Oh," said Palliser.

"Knocked on the door, I open it, he's a nice-looking young fellow, none of this funny-looking long hair or nothing. He says there's some trouble on the phone line, he's got to look at my phone. So I let him in. He had a, what's the name, a little bag with him."

"I see. Like a tool-kit?"

"Yah. And the minute I shut the door he knocked me down. Hit me hard."

"Knocked you unconscious?"

She nodded. "Last I remember, till I wake up here." Palliser went on asking questions, and it emerged that there'd been less than twenty dollars in the apartment, but she had a few things he could have walked off with—a portable TV, a sewing machine, a few bits and pieces of jewelry. He wondered if Grace had got anything from the neighbors.

When he came out of the hospital, he had to hurry to make the inquest. It was brief and formal; he gave the coroner's deputy the police evidence on it, and it was brought in Accidental Death.

The McLeods were there, and the man came up to Palliser angrily when the deputy had gone. "I'd like to know what the hell they mean, call it accidental!" he said bitterly. "It was murder—just murder, a hit-run!" He was a bulky dark fellow in his forties, with a pugnacious jaw and dark eyes.

"I know how you must feel, sir," said Palliser, "but legally it was an accident—your son rode out from between parked cars, by what the witnesses—"

"It was murder!" said McLeod. "I don't know why it had to be my boy! I don't know why— And calling it an accident—"

"Oh, Kevin, don't," said his wife. She'd been crying; she took his arm. "It just makes it worse. Come home, dear—you can stay home with me for a while now, and we've just got to think it's God's will. Come on, Kevin."

Palliser watched them out, feeling sorry. It was eleven-thirty; he wanted to call Robin sometime, see how she was feeling. The baby was due in less than a month, and she'd been having what the doctor called false labor pains the last few days.

Shogart and Glasser had gone out on the routine hunt for the heisters; there were still unfound a number of men the computer had handed them. Glasser found one of them, Paul Huberdeau, at a bar about eleven-fifteen, and brought him in to question. The office was empty except for Piggott, who'd just come back from Mrs. Kowaljic's apartment; the lab team was there now. Palliser came in before they started to question Huberdeau, and brought them up to date on Mrs. Kowaljic. "Good trick to get in, you can see. She gives us a description of sorts. About thirty, blond, six feet and stocky. See what we turn up in Records. Who've you got here?"

Glasser told him. "His pedigree's right for it—four counts of armed robbery, burglary, assault with intent. He's on P.A."

"Why?" wondered Palliser.

"You tell me."

They took Huberdeau into an interrogation room and questioned him patiently. He conformed to the description of the heister with the Afro hair style. He was only twenty-seven now, had spent less than four years inside, and had accumulated charges from age thirteen of eleven felonies, mostly accompanied by violence. He didn't like cops, and he was sullen, saying as little as possible.

"I don't know nothing about it," he kept saying. He wouldn't tell them, or couldn't, where he'd been last night

[48]

or last Saturday night. But after three-quarters of an hour he suddenly said, "I guess I was home last night. I was broke, I dint have no bread."

"All right, anybody back that up?" asked Palliser.

"My old lady, she was there."

"Will she be there now? Your wife?"

He shrugged. "How'd I know? I ain't married to her. She ain't locked in."

"Suppose we go see," said Glasser. Huberdeau lived in a housing complex out on Seventieth. It hadn't been up long, but already it had accumulated smells in the halls and a general air of decay. Most of the tenants in a place like this had few personal standards, and when the rent came free— to them—there wasn't much reason to keep the property nice and tidy.

"It's the third floor," said Huberdeau. In the narrow hallway he opened the door and went in ahead of them. "Viney? You here?"

"You fetch back that bottle like I tole you?" She came from the kitchen, a big black woman in jeans and a man's ragged shirt. Seeing him empty-handed, she began to cuss. "I give you the welfare check to cash, damn lazy nigger— What the hell you want?" she added to the three behind him.

"They're pigs," said Huberdeau. "You tell 'em—" but Glasser cut him off.

"Can you tell us if he was here last night? From when to when?"

"Why the hell? He supposed to pulled something? Yeah, I can tell you that, pig. He was here. From about six to when he passed out a couple hours later, he finished the last bottle I had inna place. And I'm about ready to kick him out, so I ain't tellin' no lies, get him outta trouble, pig."

They left him there and went back to Palliser's Rambler. "Round and round," said Palliser. "The time we waste. I suppose you're as ready for lunch as I am."

They went up to Federico's on North Broadway and ran

into Mendoza. Everybody else was evidently hard at the routine. Palliser ordered and called Roberta from the public phone in the lobby.

"Don't fuss, John. No, I haven't had any today, but the doctor says it's just gas or something. Heavens, the way I look, I'd be relieved if it does come early," she said. "I'll never get back to size fourteen."

"And don't you fuss. Come to think, I'll be damn relieved to have it over too," said Palliser. "See you, love."

It was Landers' night off tonight, and he was taking Phil out to dinner. With all the Frascati restaurants closed, they'd discovered an interesting new place out in the valley, The Castaways, which had a magnificent view from high on a hill. Landers spent most of the day over an old novel. He'd get dressed and go to pick up Phil about seven.

He wondered what luck the boys were having on the various things they were working now. He reminded himself to tell Phil about those fish.

Grace was using his day off for some dickering. In the excitement of acquiring Celia Ann last Christmas, he had rushed out and bought a Polaroid camera. Higgins had warned him about it—it wasn't, he said, the initial cost but the upkeep—and Grace had found it was all too true. If you took many snapshots, the price of that film kept you broke.

On Tuesday morning he took it back to where he'd got it. They offered him ten bucks off for it on a new Instamatic. He went to three more places before he got an offer of fifteen, and closed the deal. With the Instamatic, you had to wait to see the pictures, but the price was a good deal more reasonable.

He went home, found Virginia giving Celia her bath, and used up the whole roll of film in the camera.

"I suppose we'll get used to having a family some day," said Virginia fondly.

The rest of Tuesday was singularly unproductive. Mendoza talked to one of the parole officers that afternoon, who said it was hard to say about any of the cases he was handling —or had been when Ellen Reynolds was killed. He was a rather prim, lanky fellow named Darwin, and he said, "One thought I might pass on, Lieutenant. These five men on your list that I've handled, and this type in general—and you asked about illiterates too, or nearly so—a couple of these men are, for a fact. That type in general too, time doesn't mean so much to them, they don't live by a routine."

"*Obvio*. What are you leading up to?"

"Well, it was just a passing thought. When whoever it was was still feeling, um, grateful to the board for letting him out, my guess would be that he'd been let out fairly recently."

"And that is a thought," agreed Mendoza. "You wouldn't have even a guess, on the men you know?"

"Nobody could say what's possible. It's too—offbeat. Queer," said Darwin, and paused, looking thoughtful. "Now you know—" He tapped the list. "Just as I said that, I thought of this Arnold Hahn. He is, a little. Queer, that is. Tends to be a loner, and he's said a few odd things to me."

"Such as?"

"Oh, well, for one thing, he's got a job in a pet shop. He came in to report to me, and I asked how he liked it, and he said fine, he'd always liked animals better than people. Now I thought that was—"

"Queer? *Al contrario*, I'm inclined to agree with him," said Mendoza, regarding Darwin coldly. "If that's all you can offer—"

And very probably Darwin went away with the opinion that Lieutenant Mendoza of Robbery-Homicide was somewhat queer too.

At the end of all the routine on Tuesday, not another possible suspect had been found on either the Reynolds-Jowett case or the heisters. They left notes for the night watch; sometimes these characters showed up at night in bars, and they had the names of a few associates, the names of some local hangouts some of them were known to frequent. And they went home.

Piggott had brought the aquarium home last night. He was really enamored of the little fish, and anxious to have Prudence see them. The thing weighed a ton even empty, but he managed to get it upstairs to the apartment, and after some debate they'd decided to put it in the living room, on top of Prudence's stereo cabinet—Duff said, not too much strong light, and that was a north wall. Piggott had brought home a book, too—*Exotic Aquarium Fish* by Dr. William T. Innes—and he showed Prudence all the color plates at the back. "But they're so tiny, Matt! Some of them only an inch and a half long! But what gorgeous colors!"

"You wait till you see them." Piggott looked fondly at her auburn head bent over the pictures. They'd half-filled the thing carefully, with warmed tap water, according to instructions, and even minus the fish it looked nice, with its green plants rooted in sand moving a little with the water, and the ornamental stones at the bottom. He hooked up the filter and tried the aerator thing, and it worked fine, sending a silent stream of small bubbles toward the surface.

When he left the office at six on Tuesday, he drove out to Scales 'n' Fins, and Mr. Duff had everything ready for him, fifteen good-sized cans with tops on them, and he helped Piggott load them into the car. "You just treat 'em slow and easy, don't dump them all in at once, and they'll be fine. Little work for you, lugging them in—you've got about forty pounds of water here. And I made up a list of what you've got, you'll soon get to know 'em."

It took him a while to carry all the cans upstairs, but it was worth it in the end. Having been warned that some of the fish might jump out, he was careful with tops and the little net. But with the nervous operation accomplished, and the plastic screen fastened back on top of the tank, he and

Prudence were both entranced at the pretty sight, all the colorful little fish darting about the greenery. It was Prudence who woke up to the fact that it was nearly nine o'clock. She bustled out to the kitchen to start dinner, leaving Piggott with the book in one hand and Mr. Duff's list in the other, trying to identify each of their new possessions.

The night watch didn't locate any of the suspects.

"You're going to be late," said Alison.

"I don't much care," said Mendoza, finishing his second cup of coffee. Sheba stuck her nose in the cream pitcher and was promptly put off the table. Nefertite and Bast were having second breakfasts in the service porch, crunching dry catfood loudly, and El Señor of the blond-in-reverse Siamese mask was brooding out the window at the twins and Cedric in the back yard.

"Of all your queer things I like the fish," said Alison. "Only I suppose you'll never get that one. But your grandmotherly bank robber's nice too."

"*¿Es ésa su opinion?* Nice. I can think of other words. And this Jowett thing—" Mendoza got up and stepped on Sheba's tail. Her yowls brought Mrs. MacTaggart to the door.

"You know, *achara,*" she said to Alison, "I'm that worried about that bird. You mind it showed up just around Christmas, early, and went off again, but it should be back nesting now. The weather opening and all."

Mendoza had picked Sheba up to apologize. "And that's another thing. All those louts on P.A.—the one we can cross off is Arnold Hahn. Or can we?"

"Yes, I know," said Alison to Mrs. MacTaggart. "I do hope nothing's happened to him."

"I'll tell you what might have happened to him," said Mendoza. "If somebody with an air-rifle handy was driven mad enough by listening to the first four bars of 'Yankee Doodle' repeated nine thousand times, he might have got a slug in the head."

"Och, the puir creature!" Mrs. MacTaggart was shocked at the idea. "I'll hope not."

"Well, I'm not doing any worrying," said Mendoza. He put Sheba down, reached for his hat and went out the back door.

When he got to the office, Wanda was typing energetically and Sergeant Lake told him they already had a new one. "Art just went out on it. Body found on the first-level ramp of the parking lot under Pershing Square. When they opened up."

"*¡Santa María!*" said Mendoza mildly. "Why I stay at this thankless job—"

Hackett looked at the body, feeling tired. It was the body of a white male in the mid-twenties. Its throat had been cut. "So we outlaw butcher knives," he muttered to himself. He squatted over it and went through the pockets. No I.D. There was a lot of dried blood all around; he had probably been killed right here. Sometime last night.

The parking-lot attendant who had found him was standing nervously about twenty feet away, looking green. "Listen," he called, "we got to open. This is a public place. You gotta take him *away* and Jesus, who's gonna clean all that up—"

"What time did you close last night?" asked Hackett.

"What? Nine o'clock, like always. Listen, we gotta *open*—just get that *outta* here!"

"All in good time." Not much point in photographs. The corpse was wearing a short-sleeved shirt and there were a few old needlemarks visible on both arms. There was an ambulance on the way. "He wasn't, of course, here when you closed last night." There was a three-level tier of parking here under the green of Pershing Square.

"Jesus, are you kidding? Acourse not!"

The ambulance came and Hackett dispatched the body to the morgue. See if his prints were on file.

He went back to the office and handed Wanda his notes,

told Mendoza about it. "Everybody else is out on something, the heisters mostly. You collect any ideas from those P.A. officers yet?"

"*Nada*," said Mendoza. He was swiveled around looking out the window at the clear rounded heads of the Hollywood foothills in the distance. He looked preoccupied.

Hackett called the lab and told them to send somebody down to take the corpse's prints. Then he went out looking for possibles on the heisters. When he passed the open door of Mendoza's office, Mendoza was on the phone, looking annoyed.

"I've got the son here now, Charles Borchers," Carey was saying. "And some of what he can tell us is a little bit interesting. I swear this Borchers woman's been murdered, and I'd like you to—"

"Look, I've got quite enough to think about already," said Mendoza. "You've got no evidence at all. She's a missing person, and as far as I'm concerned that's all, and she's your business. If you—"

"But he says it's possible she had a wad of cash," said Carey. "And she's been missing over four months. She was an old lady, Mendoza, settled into routine, it's not very damn likely she'd take off all at once without telling anybody."

"Call me back when you've got a body, or better evidence," said Mendoza firmly, and put the phone down and got out the cards.

He was still sitting there practicing crooked deals half an hour later when Scarne called from the lab. "I didn't have to do any comparing," he said, "because I remembered him. I happened to print him one time he was picked up. Your newest corpse, this is. I had the hell of a time coming up with his name, but there was a kind of unusual tented whorl, and I just turned him up."

"So who was he?"

"One Francis J. Delgado. It was a narco bust."

"Thank you so much," said Mendoza. "Jimmy, get me

Narco. . . . Is Callaghan there? . . . Well, Goldberg?"

The phone sneezed at him and he said, "How are the allergies, Saul?"

"Doing fine," said Goldberg thickly. "What do you want?"

"Anything you know about Francis J. Delgado."

Goldberg's tone sharpened. "Why? Don't tell me something's happened to him?"

"Would you care? Yes, it has. He had his throat cut last night. In the parking lot under Pershing Square."

"Oh, my God!" said Goldberg. "Oh, for—Pat'll have seven cat-fits, Luis. My God!"

"Why?" asked Mendoza economically. "A junkie—I haven't seen his record but Art said there were needlemarks—"

"My good God!" said Goldberg, and sneezed. "Well, it's got to be somebody in Vic Moreno's bunch, you can bet on that. Somebody must have blown Frank's cover, Goddamn it. Damn it, Frank was one of our few successes, Luis. He'd kicked the habit, he'd started going to church again, and he was feeding us a lot of useful information, undercover. Lately, on Moreno. Moreno's a supplier, has a string of pushers working for him, and Frank 'd been trying to get us something on a big delivery expected in this week. Goddamn the luck to hell! All I can tell you, his cover got blown somehow—"

"So we'd better have a look at what you've got on Vic Moreno," said Mendoza. "And associates."

"Associates be damned," said Goldberg. "They're tied up to the big boys, sure—tenuously as you might say—but it'll be some local thug in Moreno's bunch went after Frank. Oh, hell. Apart from anything else, I liked the kid, Luis—have to admire him for having the guts to straighten out."

"Mmh. I'll see your records," said Mendoza.

Piggott had been at the routine all Wednesday morning, out hunting for possibles on the heists. He found one, after a brief lunch break, at a bar on Second Street—Joe Bailey— and brought him in to question. It was Glasser's day off. The office was empty except for Lake and Wanda; Piggott stashed

Bailey in an interrogation room and Lake brought him up to date on the new body, interrupting himself to plug in the switchboard.

"Robbery-Homicide, Sergeant Lake. . . . Oh, yes, he's right here. Somebody wants you, Matt."

Piggott picked up the phone on his desk. Higgins came in towing a big Negro with a bushy Afro hairdo. "Detective Piggott."

Mendoza came in with Captain Patrick Callaghan of Narco, huge and redhaired and looking mad, on his heels.

"Oh, Mr. Piggott!" said Dave Duff excitedly. "The damndest thing—some of my Regal Angels are back! Quite all right, thank goodness—just one pair of them. I usually go out to the breeding tanks in back on my lunch hour, check on things there—and when I came back to the shop, there they were, on the counter, in a Hills Brothers coffee can— quite properly covered with netting, not that angels tend to jump much—"

"Well, that's funny," said Piggott.

"But the female's back to normal," said Duff. "They've spawned. Whoever it was, they've stolen the eggs. That's what they wanted."

"What?"

"The babies," said Duff. "It's certainly funny. But somebody's taken good care of them, thank God."

Four

Piggott passed that on to Higgins absently. "I've got one too," he added. "I haven't talked to him yet."

"So let's take 'em one by one," said Higgins. They were the only detectives in the office.

They started in on Bailey first, and of course they always made a good team, deceptively mild Piggott acting like the good guy, tough-looking Higgins the opposite. Joe Bailey didn't like either of them, and he said hurriedly that he was clean, hadn't got in no more trouble since he was out. "You got nothin' on me," he said. "What you think I done?"

"What about a couple of heists, Joe?" asked Higgins.

"Oh, no, not me—I never did no such thing."

"All right," said Piggott. "Where were you last Saturday night and last Monday night? From six on?"

Bailey sat up and looked relieved. "I was at work. Tom'll tell you. I was at my job, I got a part-time job nights, in a bowling alley, that's where I was. Tom Shaver, he's the boss, he'll say—plenty o' people see me there."

"O.K., we'll check that," said Piggott. Outside, he said to Higgins, "You mind checking on it alone? I want to run over and see Duff a few minutes." The alibi wouldn't take long to check: the bowling alley, by the address Bailey had added, was on Santa Monica in Hollywood, twenty minutes on the freeway.

Higgins went off, and Piggott got into his rather shabby Nova and drove out Beverly. Duff greeted him, still excited, when he came into Scales 'n' Fins. "Damndest thing I ever saw—look there—my Regal Angels! But no eggs. That's what he was after, the eggs."

Piggott looked at the returned pair of Regal Angels. They were four times the size of his little amber angels, and regal-looking all right; dark sable brown shading out to the palest of cream color on the tops of their fins. "They're pretty. But it seems so soon—I mean, if he expects the eggs to hatch, wouldn't they need their mother?"

Duff laughed and went on laughing for some time. "You'll have to learn more about fish, Mr. Piggott. It's safest to take the eggs away as soon as they're fertilized, even with angels —they aren't given to eating their eggs, but I've known 'em to do it. Best way is to take the parents out as soon as the eggs are dropped. Babies'll be swimming on their own in a couple of days, and from then on it's a question of getting the right food down 'em, how many you'll raise."

"Well, that's funny too," said Piggott. "You suppose he'll bring the others back when they've produced eggs?"

"I surely do hope so. But it's the queerest damned thing— and I tell you, I'm going to keep a sharp eye out from now on, and if he tries to sneak back and leave 'em I'll nail him. Find out who it is."

It wasn't, of course, worth a stakeout. "Wish you luck," said Piggott. "Oh, my wife thinks they're pretty too—she helped me get them all in the tank." He told Duff where they'd put it and Duff approved. "Only thing is, she says she'll probably get all behind with the housework, get hypnotized watching the fish."

"Doesn't work, eh? I don't approve of wives working. That's good."

"Well, she works at the church—we both do. Sunday school, and we're both in the choir." Tonight was choir practice, he reflected comfortably. "We finally figured out names for all of them, with the book. Prudence likes those little tetras best, the head-and-taillight ones, but I kind of like those feathertail tetras. Flashy little fellows, always on the move. You put in a couple of each, and they're really something to watch."

When he got back to Headquarters Higgins was just coming in; Bailey's alibi had checked out, and Shaver seemed to be a solid citizen, so they let Bailey go, and started to question Higgins' capture, he of the bushy Afro. His name was Bill Dortch, and he had a pedigree, but not as long or bad as most of those the computer had listed: one count of statutory rape, resisting arrest on a burglary charge, a couple of D.-and-D.'s. The latest count on him was nearly three years ago. He had been conditioned against cops, but also in spite of his size he was afraid of them; he didn't like Higgins at all.

"I haven't done nothing. What you think I done?"

"How about a heist job, Bill?"

"Oh, no, not me, mister, I never done no heist jobs, I never hadda gun in my whole life, I wouldn't do nothing like that."

"We'll believe you," said Piggott, "if you can tell us where you were last Saturday night and last Monday night. And will anybody back you up?"

This simple request got an unexpected response. Dortch was dumb, shifting on the hard chair before the little table. He looked from Higgins to Piggott nervously, and after a minute said, "Is it O.K. if I smoke?" Higgins gave him a cigarette and shoved the ashtray over.

"What about it, Bill? Where were you?"

"I was—I was—" But he didn't seem to be as frightened now; and then he looked even more scared at whatever was passing through his mind. "I was with my girl friend," he said almost casually. "Etta Mae Williams. She don't want to marry me account o' my record with you, she's a real nice girl, but I try show her I'm clean now, got a regular job and all. I was with her where she lives, her folks' house down on Fifty-six Street."

Piggott exchanged a glance with Higgins. "They'll say so? Fine, let's have the address. Anybody be at home now?"

Again they got silence. Dortch was thinking, and for him it wasn't a quick process. Higgins asked the question again, patiently. "What?" said Dortch, and then absently gave the street number. Piggott wrote it into his notebook.

"So you didn't help pull the job," he said softly, "but maybe you know something about it, Dortch?"

Dortch shifted uneasily. He smoked the cigarette rapidly and stubbed it out; passed a hand across his jaw. "I—I got into some foolishness, I'm just a kid, but my folks aren't bad, they was ashamed, try straighten me out, live right. I been doin' like that, try to. I work a regular job now, since a couple years ago, I don't get drunk no more. Show Etta—" He was silent again; now he was trying to make up his mind. They waited.

After another while Piggott said, "You know who pulled those heists, Bill?"

"I guess I do," he said, suddenly deciding. "See, it's account o' my sister. Ruth. She got married to this guy last year, guy from back east, and my folks don't like him and I don't like him. He's one mean nigger, man. Ruth, she won't say does he beat up on her, but—" He stopped again.

"Let's have it all, if you're going to talk," said Higgins harshly.

"I don't know who the other guys were. Just him. Ruth was scared, she come home last night—I moved back with my folks—and she told Mama. Didn't mean me to hear, but I did. How he told her that was him, piece in the paper about those places robbed. Showed her a whole wad of money."

Sometimes a thing broke like this; they could never count on it, but it happened. "So what's his name?" asked Piggott.

"Lonnie Epps. They live down One Hundred and Six, one o' those apartments guv'mint puts up for folks on the welfare. I wasn't going to say at first, I'm afraid o' that guy, he's a mean one, but Ruth oughta get shut of him and if you get him for that—"

"Thanks very much," said Higgins. "Tell us what he looks like."

"He's a big guy, maybe six feet two, three—and he wears his hair kind of bushier than me— Look, so I told you. That's all I know, can I go?"

They let him go, and he went thankfully. They followed him out and stood by the switchboard. Jason Grace came in, looking tired and annoyed.

"Shall we go look for him now?" said Piggott.

"Look for who?" said Grace. "Talk about rat races. I can't find anybody. You two are looking pleased—something break?"

"In spades," and Higgins told him what. "We're going out to see if we can pick him up."

Grace regarded them sardonically. "And you've both been cops awhile too." He brushed his neat moustache in unconscious imitation of Mendoza. "At an urban development center on One Hundred and Sixth Street in the middle of Watts."

"You have any objection?" asked Piggott.

"Yes, I damn well have an objection," said Grace. "You understand, it's not because I have any special affection for either of you. But we're shorthanded as it is, and if we lose two trained detectives, the rest of us will come in for the hell of a lot more work, that's all. If he was anything but a pro heist-man described as mean, I'd chase along with you to do the talking. As it is—uh-uh. I think I had better go and nose around down there. Cautiously."

"And you think we'd let you walk in there alone, I suppose?" said Higgins.

"It's a damn sight safer for me alone than you two."

"Well, that's a damn lie. You carry the same badge."

"So I do, but I blend better into the shrubbery down there. Come on, let's have the address."

"Don't you give it to him, Matt. You are not going alone, Jase—that's asking for it."

"So all right, we'll all go," said Piggott.

[62]

Grace wasn't satisfied, but accepted the compromise grudgingly. They took Higgins' Pontiac.

There were streets down here quiet and respectable, where people worked at regular jobs, kept their single houses painted and their lawns green. But there were different streets too, because people came all shapes and sizes and kinds, and forever would. The biggest contrast, perhaps, was between those nice little houses and the few new housing complexes. There was a bumper sticker Piggott had seen: *Slums don't make people, People make slums.* Shortly after all those big apartment houses went up, people filled them; and because most of the people knew no kind of living but slum living, they made it into a slum, and the minority of people who had any personal standards moved out in quiet despair.

This one, when they came to it, was nine stories high; on one side of it was an empty lot littered with everything from old mattresses to garbage. The block down from here was a block of ancient storefronts, frowzy and long unpainted. Grace argued at them to stay in the car.

"Now don't be a damn fool, Jase," said Higgins. "We're as much help to you here as back at the office. You go up there and show the badge, and if he's there and jumps you—Ballistics did say one of them's got a Colt .45."

"I'll tell you something, George," said Grace seriously. "I feel a lot more nervous walking in here with two white cops than I would going alone."

But—maybe it was the time of day—they didn't meet a soul in the lobby or the elevator. The halls and the elevator had obviously been used as latrines, and the paint deliberately chipped off the elevator door. "Do we know where we're going?" asked Grace. There were no names on the mailboxes in the lobby, no names in the slots beside each door.

"Number fifty-two on the fifth floor," said Piggott. The elevator landed with a thud and the door rolled back and stuck halfway. Higgins put one of his bulging shoulders to it and shoved it open.

Halfway down the hall they passed a fat black woman in a red dress. She stared at them but went on past quickly. Two doors down was the door marked with the stark numerals, no bell. Higgins knocked sharply on it.

After a dragging moment it opened hesitantly. A woman looked out at them. She didn't look like Dortch, but her general air of shyness might mark her as the sister. "Mrs. Epps?" said Grace in his soft voice.

"Yes, sir, that's me. What—what do you want?"

"We're looking for your husband, Mrs. Epps. Is he here?"

She shook her head. She looked at Higgins and said faintly, "You're cops. You found out about Lonnie. You—you want to be real careful with him, he's awful mean. You want to be careful." It was almost a whisper.

"We intend to be just that," said Grace. "Do you know where he is?"

"Most prob'ly where he is most afternoons. Drinkin' in a bar up Willowbrook. It's Randy's. Are you—gonna arrest him?"

Grace opened his mouth and two very black men came up the hall; they stared at Piggott and Higgins, and slowed, but finally went on past and turned into the cross-hall.

"I'm goin' home," she said suddenly. "But you be real careful." She shut the door.

They went back to the elevator. "So much for all your timid warnings," said Higgins in the Pontiac, lighting a cigarette. But when they located Randy's, up toward One Hundred and Eighth on Willowbrook, and he slid the car into a red-painted section of curb two doors down, Grace looked at the dingy store front and said, "This time I mean it, boys. I go in alone to see if he's there. If you come in, there's a little stir right away. Me, no. If he's there, it could be I can get him out to the street quick and easy, and we take him. If I have to show the badge, it just could make him cave in right away. If he tries to run you'll know it soon enough from right here."

He wouldn't back down, and finally they let him go. "I

[64]

don't care what he says, he'll stand out," muttered Higgins. Grace was nearly as dapper a dresser as Mendoza, and his well-cut gray suit, white shirt and patterned tie would certainly mark him apart from the expectable crowd of regulars at Randy's.

They watched the door. Five slow minutes crept by and then Grace came out again. He was holding a man by one arm lightly—and he fitted the description all right, all the descriptions: the one with the Afro hairdo, a big heavy man, in dirty jeans and a once-white sweatshirt. Grace was talking to him. Evidently he'd persuaded him out to the street without showing the badge; he was bringing it out now. Higgins and Piggott got out of the car.

Epps let out a sudden bellow and swung wildly on Grace, who dodged and reached for his gun. "Now just hold it, Epps—" But Epps was lumbering fast down the street, and if it wasn't a thickly crowded street there were enough people around that they would hesitate to use the guns.

Higgins pounded after him, his longer stride taking him past Piggott and Grace, and just as he was near enough to tackle him, Epps suddenly turned with a gun in his hand and fired blindly. Simultaneously Higgins brought him down with a heavy thud; and Piggott, whom they had known to utter a cussword on exactly two other occasions, said loudly, "Goddamn it, he got me!"

Higgins brought out the cuffs, got Epps's gun, clapped on the cuffs and hauled him to his feet. "Matt?" Piggott was leaning on the building front there looking mad, Grace bending over him.

"It's not bad—he got you through the arm. You're bleeding, we'd better get you in—let's not hang around for an ambulance."

Higgins couldn't have agreed more. Already a crowd was collecting, and a few men mechanically starting the name-calling they'd been so well-programmed to repeat. A brick came out of the crowd and hit the side of the Pontiac as they came up to it. He bundled Epps into the back seat where Grace joined him, and Piggott into the front, and manhandled the car in a U-turn, heading back uptown for Central Receiving. Piggott had his handkerchief padding the wound, and they added theirs. At the hospital, Grace got him out at the emergency entrance and flashed the badge. A couple of interns came up and insisted on laying him out on a stretcher; he'd lost some blood. "Say," he said to Grace a little faintly, "I'm sorry if I bled all over George's car. Somebody'd better call Prudence."

"Don't worry, Matt. I'll hang around."

Higgins found a phone and called up a black-and-white to ferry Epps the rest of the way to jail. He then called the office to let Mendoza know they could let up on that routine: it could be that Epps would tell them who the other two were right off, unwilling to take the rap alone.

"He's not here, George," said Sergeant Lake. "He and Callaghan had quite a bull session, and Callaghan came out looking ready to chew nails, and just a couple of minutes later we had another bank job and the boss and Art went tearing off on that."

"For God's sake!" said Higgins. "Same sweet old grandmother, you suppose? Well, I'll pass this on to you then—"

"How's Matt?"

"He'll live. You might apply for the warrant—start the machinery, anyway."

The doctor who bandaged Piggott said he'd been lucky, the bone wasn't touched. He'd be fine in a few days. "You know something," said Piggott, "maybe I've got a charmed life or something, this is the first time I've ever got a scratch on the job, in nearly ten years. It's my day off Friday anyway." He wanted them to take him back to his car, protesting that he was all right to drive home, but Higgins took him up to Hollywood in the Pontiac. "Well, so you can come up and see my fish."

Prudence fussed over him, but she was a sensible girl and

[66]

knew what she'd let herself in for, marrying a cop. "Couple of days and I'll be fine," said Piggott. "How do you like our fish, George?"

"Say," said Higgins after watching the tank a minute, "they're pretty, aren't they? Kind of graceful. They remind me of ballet dancers. Well, you take care, Matt. I'll let you know if we get anything out of Epps."

Mendoza and Hackett, unaware that they were presently to get the heist jobs cleaned up, had had a frustrating afternoon. It was Callaghan's opinion that Vic Moreno or one of his pushers had blown Delgado's undercover act and he'd been taken off on Moreno's orders. "And listen, Luis, we know there's a shipment due in—we think we know the drop —and if you go smelling around on a homicide and spook him they may cancel delivery."

"It's not a very usual M.O. for that kind of thing," said Mendoza. "A contract on him—"

"It wouldn't be that. No big deal. Moreno's not that big a man—no link to the Syndicate except that that's right at the top in any dope dealing."

"All right. I still say, one of Moreno's men would have been likelier to have shot him, not slit his throat."

"But it's the only reason anybody could have had to go for Delgado, that he was undercover for us—"

"We don't know that," said Mendoza. "He'd been a user. He knew the in crowd."

"Yes, but—just don't you spook Moreno," said Callaghan with a growl. "I want to nail that bunch." He knew where Delgado had been living, and Mendoza chased the lab out on it, handing over the single key found on the body.

Callaghan had only been gone five minutes when the bank-job went down. They started for that in a hurry, siren scream-ing on the Ferrari. It was a bank up on Sixth, not far from Headquarters, and Mendoza braked the Ferrari, double-parked in front; they ran in. That Fed, Joe Valenti, was right behind them with a couple of others. Inside there was uproar, but there hadn't been many customers in, and the first thing they heard was the girl shouting excitedly, "Mr. Shafter ran after her—I stepped on the alarm right away, she wasn't at the door yet, and I just pointed and screamed—Mr. Shafter took after her—"

And before they got up to her, an equally excited man came running in the side door of the bank, shortcut from west on Sixth. "She got on a bus!" he yelled. "I chased her, but she had a head start, she got on a bus a block up—are the police here yet?"

Mendoza got to him first. "Which bus? We're police—"

"Number Four—big yellow bus—going west uptown," panted the man.

"Come on!" said Mendoza. He and Hackett ran for the door with Valenti after them. They pushed him into the jump seat of the Ferrari, fell into the front, and Mendoza switched on engine and siren at once. "A bus!" he said bitterly. "Getting away from a bank job on a bus!— *¡Válgame Dios—eso ya es llover sabre mojado!* But it can't be far off—" He gunned the Ferrari and traffic halted ahead.

"Say," said Valenti breathlessly, "how come you rate a racer? For God's sake, Lieutenant—" as they sailed across the center line to pass bunched traffic, "watch it—a bus, for God's sake—"

"There it is ahead!" said Hackett. They caught it at Sixth and Vermont, a big yellow bus loudly emitting its belch and diesel smoke: it had its right-turn signal on. The surprised bus driver, belatedly realizing that the siren was for him, stopped in mid-turn, and all three of them piled out and made for the front door of the bus.

"Luis, we're idiots," said Hackett. "We don't know it's Grandmother—didn't hear a description—"

"You don't tell me there's two female bank robbers operating the same week on my beat," said Mendoza.

And Valenti stopped and uttered a wordless cry of rage. "Goddamn it, it's Number Five!" he said.

The driver leaned out the side window. "What's going on? Did I do something wrong? What's up, you chasing me?"

"¡Diez millón demonios desde infierno!" said Mendoza violently. "We want a Number Four bus—"

"Are you guys nuts or something? That's not a squad car! You want a bus, you wait where it's supposed to come by— it's against the law to use a siren unless you're cops—my God, I thought I'd met every kind of lunatic there was, but chasing a bus with a siren just because you missed it—"

Despite frustration, Valenti burst into mirth at this righteous wrath. "We're cops," said Mendoza, clawing for the badge. "The Number Four bus going this way up Sixth— does it turn off? Where?"

"Well, for God's sake," said the driver. "You are? Well, what the hell's it all about?" All the passengers were crowding at the windows to see the excitement, and asking loud questions.

"Just tell us! It must have been just ahead of you—did it turn off? About twenty, twenty-five minutes ago—"

"Oh, the Number Four," said the driver, enlightened. "Is that a real badge? Let's see it. Oh, yeah, that's not a local—I dunno where it ends up but it turns off north on Glendale Boulevard, back there downtown."

"All right, thanks, you can go on." They got back in the Ferrari. "Of all the Goddamned luck!" said Valenti, and then began laughing again.

Mendoza didn't even swear. "If it's headed for Glendale it's still on its way," he said. He moved the Ferrari up into a red-painted section of curb where a public phone booth stood on the corner. "Art, try for somebody efficient at the bus company. Get the route."

"Got you," and Hackett was out of the car.

"But how do you rate this—this hot rod?" asked Valenti. "My God, it's a Ferrari! I didn't think there were any LAPD men on the take."

"I hope not," said Mendoza, flicking his lighter. "My grandfather was an unusual man."

"Oh?"

"A gambler who didn't die broke."

"You man the desk at headquarters as a labor of love?"

"Well, it didn't turn up—all the loot—until I'd been riding a black-and-white for three years, and it got to be a habit. I hope to God Art doesn't get some stupid switchboard girl—"

Hackett did reasonably well. Inside of ten minutes he was back with some hasty notes. "It goes straight up Glendale past the Golden State freeway and skirts Atwater—jumps over to Brand Boulevard and up there to Glenoaks, and turns west. Goes all the way to Burbank, Alameda and Glenoaks, and starts back."

"*Bueno*," said Mendoza; he had the engine on already. "But he's got a head start, Arturo. Forty minutes or more. At least we know—or do we?—it's the only Number Four bus ahead of us on this route?"

"On the nose. It runs once an hour from both ends."

"Well, I don't often get to use my siren." Mendoza switched it on again; they made a U-turn and went screaming back down Sixth to Lucas Avenue, left on Lucas and ten long blocks up to where Glendale Boulevard terminated at Second Street. It was a long fast ride up Glendale, past Echo Park, past Alvarado, under one freeway and then another, the boulevard turning and twisting. Hackett and Valenti were staring ahead, watching for the bus. Under the underpass where the railroad marked the boundary of the city of Glendale, and then briefly onto San Fernando Road, and a right turn onto Brand.

"There's a bus—" Hackett leaned forward. But as they came up in the center lane, the yellow bus shearing obediently right, they all saw the card in the side window: *No. 6 N. Brand*. Hackett swore: a local bus. They swept on up Brand Boulevard, across the bridge over the Wash that led the Los Angeles River, occasionally tumultuous, through town, and turned left on Glenoaks Boulevard. They passed street signs posted in the middle divider-strip: Central, Pacific, Concord,

Highland— "That's got to be it!" exclaimed Valenti. The bus was stopped at the corner of Grandview, past the intersection. Mendoza cut the siren; they leaped out.

"What the hell?" The bus driver, startled, looked at the badge in Hackett's hand. "What's going on? What'd I do? Hey, that's not a squad car—"

Mendoza and Valenti had already discovered that their quarry wasn't on the bus. Not if she was the sweet old grandmother with the nice smile. Mendoza turned to the driver. "You had a passenger awhile back—she got on down on Sixth—" he proceeded to give Ada Gibbons' description, and the driver nodded.

"What *is* this? Yeah, I remember her—a nice-looking old lady. Dressed kind of trim and cute for all she had white hair. What about her?"

"Where did she get off?" demanded Mendoza.

"Oh, say, I wouldn't have any idea," said the driver. He looked over his shoulder at his cargo of passengers. "She got off, hah? I guess so—she's not here."

"But the passengers ring to get off—"

"Listen, Mac," said the driver, "I see 'em when they get on the bus, they get in the front door and pay the fare, no? When they want to get off they pull the cord, and I stop at the next bus stop and they get out the back door, yes? I don't know who got off where, what do I care?"

"*¡Condenación!*" said Mendoza, exasperated. There were only five passengers left, and it turned out that none of them, intent on their own affairs, had noticed where the old lady had got off. "But you do remember this woman? Small and thin, white hair in a knot? Has she ridden with you before?"

"Yeah, I remember her," said the driver. "What's up, anyway? No, she doesn't ride my bus regular, I never saw her before in my life. Listen, I've got a schedule to keep. What's going on, did she rob a bank or something?"

They went back to the bank and asked questions and took

down answers. Grandmother had got away with only about two hundred bucks this time. The teller gave them the expected description, adding, "I was never so surprised in my life! That nice old lady!"

On top of everything else, it was now likely that the press would take amused note of Grandmother and run some would-be-funny human interest stories.

They dropped Valenti off there and got back to Headquarters at six-fifteen, where they heard the news about Epps and Piggott. "Well, something accomplished at least," said Hackett. "Has he been questioned?"

"George and Jase went on at him for a while, but he hasn't come out with anything yet. E.M. took him over to jail. The warrant's applied for."

"Yes, and he'll be indicted sometime next week and bail set and first thing we know he'll be out again," said Hackett.

"Maybe not. I," said Mendoza, "am going home. I need some peace."

"That's what George said."

"What?" said Hackett.

"That there's another reason why the divorce rate's low for cops. Besides most of us being respectable citizens. He said a cop more than anybody appreciates a peaceful home and a good wife because of what he sees on the job. Oh, by the way, he said to ask everybody if they can do electrical work. He can't. He wants to build a darkroom for Steve."

"You know, he may have something there," said Hackett seriously. "About the divorce. I wouldn't volunteer to tackle any electricity. I wonder if Henry could help him out, he's pretty handy."

Mendoza picked up his hat. "And tomorrow is also a day."

Higgins, starting home at ten past six, was tired. It had been a full day. He noticed, getting into the car, that Matt had dripped a little blood onto the front seat. Try some cold water on it: not that it mattered much, the seat covers were brown and the stains would dry that color as old blood did . . . old blood. He remembered a little sadly that this car had once been registered to Sergeant Bert Dwyer. And he could conjure up that vision, with effort, from nearly four years past: Bert dead in that pond of blood on the marble floor of the bank. But it seemed a long time ago. And Bert had been a friend of his, but he thought Bert would be glad to know—as maybe he did—that he was looking after Mary and the kids, Bert's good kids Steve and Laura.

Steve a bright boy, and Laura with definite musical talent, said the teacher. He'd like to build that darkroom for Steve. . . . Some of the shots he'd got of the baby were pretty good, but you really needed color to show her off, her curly dark hair and the almost-dimple and hazel eyes.

That was a pretty girl of Matt's—first time he'd met her.

At least he was off tomorrow.

"I think," said Hackett, "George has got something there, my Angel. We see so much dirt. So much—randomness. We appreciate the orderly schedule." He hugged her soundly. "And the good cooking."

Angel laughed, but her mountain-pool eyes were serious. "Only natural, Art."

And the kids erupted into the kitchen, discovering that he was home, Mark yelling at the top of his voice and Sheila clasping the indignant hairy bulk of the silver Persian. "No, darling, let Silver Boy go—" Angel bent to the rescue.

"The domestic peacefulness," said Hackett.

Detective E. M. Shogart went home to his solid big house on Corralitas Drive in the Silver Lake area, to his plump wife Sylvia and the nine kids, fourteen down to the baby. He was a contented, maybe stolid man, Shogart. He'd never claimed to be brilliant, and if the truth was known he had slightly resented the merger of Robbery with Homicide, and the new boss, that reputedly brilliant—if caustic and mercurial—

Lieutenant Luis Mendoza. But Mendoza, he had to admit, seemed to be a sound man, a good and fair officer, if he did occasionally go off at tangents and have silly hunches.

It wasn't hunches that broke cases. It was slogging hard routine work.

"You have a good day, dear?" asked Sylvia as he came in.

"The usual. Matt Piggott got shot up, not bad." She wouldn't fuss; she knew the odds. "At least we've got one of those heist men."

"But you know, *enamarada,* I don't think it was," said Mendoza.

"Was what?" asked Alison.

"I think a small drink is called for. To celebrate Epps at least." Mendoza wandered toward the kitchen. The tangle of four cats on the sectional was galvanized as El Señor heard the word. He preceded Mendoza to the kitchen and leapt up on the drainboard, demanding his share. "Señor *Ridiculo,*" said Mendoza, and filled a shot-glass with rye and gave him an ounce in a saucer. He wandered back to Alison in the living room. "Moreno," he said. "Because it wasn't the economical, workmanlike way to kill him—that Delgado. Because he'd been working undercover for Narco. The beating up, the shooting, I could see. Not the throat cutting. That's —what do I want to say"—he swallowed rye—"*entusiasmado.*"

"Emotional—yes," said Alison thoughtfully. "I follow that."

"Pat Callaghan," said Mendoza, "is a logical man. For an Irishman."

"I don't follow that," said Alison. "The Celts are all cold-bloodedly logical."

The twins were long in bed, Cedric the sheepdog snoring gently in Mendoza's armchair.

"Sometimes," said Mendoza, finishing the rye. He eyed her thoughtfully. "Clichés are misleading. They're also supposed to be amorous, but Pat's been a widower for a while now, and he's only, what, forty-seven. All I'm thinking—"

"I know what you're thinking," said Alison amusedly, her green eyes dancing. "Clichés. Also about amorous Latins. Misleading?"

"*Posible.*" Mendoza laughed and reached for her purposefully. "But useful, except for some occasions—"

Five

It was raining on Thursday morning. "Damn," said Alison. "I was going down to the beach." In her spare moments she was an amateur painter. "I guess I stay home as an amateur teacher instead."

Mendoza left his hostages to fortune absentmindedly. He didn't head for the office but for Sherbourne Drive in West Hollywood where Victor Moreno lived. And as he drove, his mind moved from this to that. . . . Very much shorthanded they'd be today, with Hackett, Higgins and Shogart off and Piggott temporarily out of action. It was to be hoped that Epps would part with the names of the other two; until they knew, shut down that hunt and concentrate full time on the parolees. Though what evidence there'd ever be on that one— He didn't like Jowett: not at all.

Callaghan had sketched in backgrounds, yesterday. Delgado had been making small buys from a couple of Moreno's pushers, keeping them sweet, with supplied money. As a supposed user, he wouldn't be let in on any secrets, but one of the pushers, Alfred Lamb, was talkative, and Delgado had ostensibly taken up with Lamb's sister, excuse to hang around. He'd managed to overhear this and that, and by piecing together what they got from other informants, Narco thought a delivery was due in this week. If somebody had dropped on Delgado's cover, if he'd given himself away somehow, bang, said Callaghan.

"Pero as es asi," muttered Mendoza to himself. Not necessarily so. A bullet in the head, yes; but a slit throat, he thought, stemmed from something other than a concern for business profits.

It was a new and expensive apartment house; Moreno would be raking it in, even as a relatively small frog in the big pond. Mendoza left the Ferrari in a loading zone, and in the silent lobby searched the mailboxes. Moreno had never done any time, and as yet they hadn't much evidence on him. Upstairs: apartment twelve. The elevator was noiseless.

Mendoza pushed the bell. It was eight-twenty; he didn't think Moreno would appreciate an early call. After a minute he pushed it again; and a third time. After five minutes the door was yanked back. "And who the hell are you and what you want at this Goddamned hour?" Moreno was tall and thin, narrow shoulders and a narrow white face with a smudge of thick black moustache dividing it in half. He was tying a gorgeous-colored bathrobe around him; he stared at Mendoza, and squinted down to the badge in his hand. "What the hell—fuzz? What do you want?"

"Just the answers to a few questions," said Mendoza. "Lieutenant Mendoza, Homicide." Moreno wouldn't know about mergers of police bureaus. "We've been wondering if you knew anything about the murder of Frank Delgado."

"And who in hell is he?" asked Moreno. "I don't know any Delgado."

"Oh, we thought you might," said Mendoza vaguely. "He was a friend of Al Lamb's, you know him, don't you?"

"Listen," said Moreno roughly, "I know Lamb about as good as I know you—I run into him now and then because we like the same place for lunch." That was the cover, of course. "And I don't know anything about any murder, and you can go to hell." He stepped back and shut the door.

"Now I wonder," said Mendoza to himself. It would take him a little while to dress, though if he were alarmed or curious enough, he'd hurry. He went back to the Ferrari, drove back down Sherbourne to Sunset, made a U-turn at Horn

Avenue and parked facing back to town. From here he could look up the short length of Sherbourne to the apartment-house drive.

Five minutes later a tall figure in a black raincoat and hat came down the apartment steps and disappeared up the drive. A minute later a gunmetal-colored Mercedes backed out, slid down to the corner of Sunset and turned right. The Ferrari came gently to life and started after it, not too close. A Ferrari, of course, not the most inconspicuous car to use on a tail, but hopefully in the rain Moreno wouldn't notice it. Sunset turned into Holloway a block on, and the Mercedes only stayed on it until La Cienega crossed it, and turned right there for a block to get onto Santa Monica. He kept on that all the way out through Beverly Hills, to take Doheny down to Wilshire. Presently he slowed and turned into a parking lot attached to a smart block of colonial-fronted shops. Mendoza braked and caught the light at that corner, and looked back as he waited. The black raincoat was just going into the first shop this side of the lot. An ornate sign over the door said *Art Treasures of the World.*

"*Interesante,*" said Mendoza to himself. He looked at his watch; it was a quarter past nine. He found a parking place on the street and used the phone in the Ferrari to call the office. He talked to Callaghan first. "He's just gone into this place in Beverly Hills, on Wilshire Boulevard—"

"Art Treasures," said Callaghan. "That's the drop. I hope we'll get a search warrant on it today. Damn it, I told you not to spook him!"

"He's not my boy, Pat. He honestly didn't know who Delgado was. He was annoyed at finding a cop at his door, and he didn't like being connected with police business of any kind, but he isn't scared because he knows it's nothing to do with him. I think he's feeling very annoyed at Lamb—he must know he talks too much—and if you want my opinion, he's gone to find out who Delgado was and what he had to do with Lamb."

"The hell he is. He's going to call off the delivery, damn it, and you—"

"Want to bet? I'm Homicide, I said, not one word about Narco. He's mad at Lamb, and curious."

"My God, if I can get that warrant—why the hell you always have to meddle— Goddamn it, if you've spooked him into running—!" Callaghan hung up on him. Mendoza grinned to himself and got Sergeant Lake.

"What happened to you?" asked Lake.

"I'll be in—I've been poking around on Delgado. Anything new and what's going on?"

"Anything new, the man says. You can just be thankful we've got a few dedicated officers. George came in even if it is his day off, he said he couldn't do much about that darkroom in the rain anyway, and he knew Matt was off. The night watch left us one—it's the same boy on Mrs. Kowaljic, another old lady in an apartment on Burlington, a Mrs. Sutton. He told her he was from the gas company, a leak in the line, so she let him in and he knocked her on the head with a piece of pipe or something. She wasn't serious enough for the hospital, but when she came to and called us, he'd ransacked the place. Another portable TV, about forty dollars, a little jewelry. She gives us the same description."

"Mmh. So it might be useful to get her and Mrs. Kowaljic together—"

"John thought of that. Mrs. Kowaljic's being released today. He's going to set it up with the lab, get an Identikit sketch."

"*Bueno.*"

"Higgins went over to the jail to pry at Epps some more, and Jase is out looking for the parolees."

"Which is going to be the hell of a lot of use," said Mendoza. "I'm coming in."

Which could also be said of the A.P.B. out on Grandmother, such a very general description. Some men who had been on parole when Ellen Reynolds was killed were now off probation, and new men had been paroled. But what they knew for certain on Jowett—about all they did know for certain—was that that was the same X on Reynolds, and it didn't really matter when he'd been paroled.

It was still raining when he got downtown. As he came up to the elevator Henry Glasser joined him. "Wet," he said. "I've got it set up with that bartender, the one last Saturday night—on the first heist. He says he can make a positive identification of any of 'em, so we'll try a lineup with Epps. Set up for one-thirty. I made a detour and went to see Matt a minute. His arm's sore as hell, but he was damned lucky it wasn't worse. Say, you ought to see his fish."

"Fish?" said Mendoza.

"You know that funny one, the tropical fish stolen? Well, he went nuts over them, and got a tankful for Prudence's birthday, he said—they're pretty little things, all colors of the rainbow."

"I'd have said he was the last man to go for tropical fish," said Mendoza, amused. The elevator landed and they turned right into the Robbery-Homicide office. Lake was just manipulating the board; he looked relieved to see them.

"Well, welcome home. That was a new one—body just found. Sounds like a natural death, but somebody'd better go look."

"I'll take it," said Glasser resignedly. "Where is it?"

"At, of all places, the Biltmore Hotel," said Lake.

Mendoza went into his office. There were a couple of new reports on his desk: the autopsy reports on Easely and Jowett. He read them through rapidly. Nothing unexpected. Easely had been drunk, of course. The knife used on Jowett had been about nine inches long and very sharp. There were three stab wounds and two of them would have been fatal alone.

Jowett. It was such a simple case; and thus more difficult to do anything about. A simple motive: robbery. A simple death: stabbing. And the note that said it was the same X on Reynolds.

Suddenly he sat up and said loudly, *"¡Pedazo del alcorno qué! I am an idiot! We are all idiots!"* It didn't say any such damned thing—rather, it said that it was that same X, because nobody else had known about that note, but it said other things too. He sat thinking about them. Presently his eye was caught by the autopsy report again, and reluctantly he dragged his mind back to mundane duties and told Sergeant Lake to get Mrs. Rose Jowett. Getting her, he told her that her husband's body could be claimed now.

"Oh," she said. "Oh, yes, the other officer told me there'd have to be a—an autopsy, and then I could— Thank you." A muffled sob. "But when I think—he was only thirty-two —and just like I told the other officer, he wouldn't have had five dollars on him, just going to work like that. It isn't *right*, all these criminals running around! Well, thank you. I've already been to Forest Lawn, they'll— Thank you."

Mendoza offered her sympathy, evaded any questions about whether they'd found out who it was yet, and she thanked him again forlornly and hung up.

"Excuse me," said Sergeant Lake formally. Mendoza looked up. "This is Mr. Price. Mrs. Easely's father. Lieutenant Mendoza, Mr. Price. He'll tell you what you want to know."

He was a tall old fellow, somehow carrying his own rural atmosphere with him, even dressed in city clothes, an old-fashioned tweed suit with a vest and gaudy necktie. He had Indian-black hair and a hawk nose. He offered Mendoza a farmer's hard hand.

"The sheriff, he come and told us about it. Monday night. Just an awful thing. Mother'd have liked to come too but wasn't the money and she couldn't come alone. But we got to do everything we can, and there's the kids." He shook his head. "We told Lorna she'd regret marrying up with that fellow, but you know young girls. I had to come on the bus, my boys scraped together what they could, and— But now I want to know just how it all stands, sir."

Mendoza explained about the public defender, about the legal charge. She'd probably get a reduced charge, a couple of years' sentence. Yes, Mr. Price could see her, and take the children. He ended up, as Price seemed bewildered at the strange city, driving him down to the jail and then to Juvenile Hall.

When he got back to the office at eleven-thirty, he found Higgins sitting at his desk smoking. "Did you do us any good with Epps?" asked Mendoza.

"I did not. He's got nothing to say to cops. And where have you been, goofing off?"

"I've been out on some legwork of my own," said Mendoza. Glasser came in, wetter than ever. "What was the new one?"

"One of the guests at the Biltmore. Mrs. Natalie Cole from Boston. I don't know what she was doing here, nor does the hotel, but she knew some people here, by her address book." He brought it out. "People, I ask you. You'd think anybody would know better by now—and of course we wait to see what the autopsy says—but my guess would be, by what was left around, the lady had a few stiff drinks and then took some sleeping pills. Doesn't look like deliberate suicide."

"My God, you would think so," said Higgins, "but just as Art's always reminding us, it's half and half, what we run into—"

"The stupidity and cupidity," said Mendoza. *"De veras."*

Palliser had been to the hospital to see Mrs. Kowaljic. Her family was there—two sons, two daughters-in-law—tenderly readying her to go home. Or rather, she told Palliser, to her son Alexander's. "Big rich house he has to have, show he's a success. Hah! I like to be independent."

"Now, Mother, you know we've been at you for years, and after this I won't have you in that neighborhood any longer. We can bring all your things— Have you caught that thief yet, Sergeant?"

"We're working on it, sir. What I want to ask your mother—" Mrs. Kowaljic was interested to hear about her fellow victim, and delighted at the prospect of helping to get a sketch of the thief. He set up a tentative date at Head-quarters for tomorrow morning.

For a start on that, he and Grace had taken the description down to R. and I., and the computer had given them the usual discouraging list of men who met the description and had records of theft and violence. Yesterday, out on that, he hadn't found any of them: several had moved, with no for-warding addresses. Now, pending the sketch, he went back to the list of parolees. He struck pay dirt on his first cast, and brought him in: Werner Van Tine, pedigree of known vio-lence, robbery from the person, burglary. He was a sullen, rather dirty middle-aged man who told Palliser his P.A. officer could say he was clean, and said nothing else at all on the way in.

Palliser left him in an interrogation room and looked to see who was in. Higgins was talking to Mendoza, Glasser bending over Wanda Larsen's desk, and Grace had just come in, divesting himself of a wet raincoat.

"I've got one of the possibles on Jowett, who'd like to sit in?" said Palliser.

"Before you start on him," said Mendoza, hoisting one hip to Hackett's desk, "listen to some belated deductions by your uncle Luis." Palliser and Grace sat down and shared a match for cigarettes. "I must be getting old, I should have seen that before. And so should several other people. Now, the note, in the Reynolds case, was queer. An oddity—*de veras?*" They nodded at him. "All right. Some very simple, basic deductions. Ellen Reynolds was attacked, raped and killed by somebody who broke into the house at night—by the autopsy, between nine and twelve. The probability is that she was in bed at the time, by what the rooms looked like— bedclothes pulled off the bed, and so on. There were no lights on when she was found. She was in bed in the dark, probably asleep, when he came. If he turned on any lights, which is doubtful, he turned them off again. Are you with me?"

"So?" said Higgins, and then sat up and said, "Oh."

"Kenneth Jowett was going to work. At night. He left the apartment, long after dark, and went downstairs to the garage after his car. The garage was unlocked, which we deduce by the fact that his keys were in his pocket—the only thing left on him, incidentally, by what Schenke said—he hadn't got them out. Whether the door was open or shut, anybody could have been lurking in the garage, and evidently someone was. And attacked him from behind with the knife. He staggered around, maybe trying to strike back, and fell just outside the garage."

"In the dark," said Higgins slowly. "No light in the garage?"

"Not turned on."

"Oh," said Palliser. "My God, why didn't anybody see that before? No, you can't say, on Reynolds. He could have turned on a light there, in the middle of the night, and nobody saw it."

"I wonder," said Grace. "The landlady, I seem to recall, slept at the back of the front house—and anyway, he couldn't have known nobody'd see it. My God indeed. Are you saying—"

"That's what I'm saying," said Mendoza. "When Jowett was found the body was still warm. What all that says, my brilliant detectives, is that possibly in both cases, certainly in Jowett's case, that little note was all prepared and ready to leave behind."

"But that's crazy!" said Higgins. "Why?"

"That I don't know," said Mendoza. "But it seems to me that that indicates something more than a near-illiterate with a low I.Q. given to violence. When he's done it, probably, twice."

"But we know that he *is* a near-illiterate from what Questioned Documents said about that note," Palliser reminded him.

"Which makes it all the more interesting, doesn't it?" Mendoza lit a new cigarette. "I wonder what they'll have to say about this one. Let's see if any section of the lab's got any-thing for us." Those boys always took their own sweet time. He went back to his office, told Sergeant Lake to get him the lab.

"We haven't got to that yet," the technician in Questioned Documents told him. "I'm sorry, Lieutenant, we've had a whole stack of evidence in a blackmail case from Wilcox Street—old letters. We'll get to you."

Scarne, in another section of Scientific Evidence, said, "Oh, Lieutenant. Matt Piggott there?"

"He got shot yesterday. No, no, he's fine—nothing serious. Why?"

"Well, tell him, about that funny one he had—the stolen fish, you know? We didn't get any latents off the door of that place, but then yesterday he asked us to go and print a big coffee can, some of the fish were brought back in it and left—"

Mendoza looked at the phone. These fish seemed to be even a little queerer than they had looked at first. "Oh?"

"We got four good latents off it but they're not in our records. I sent 'em on to Washington just to be thorough. That's the damndest thing I ever heard of, stealing fish."

"We're having a few fish-stories here," said Mendoza. "Did you get any prints in that apartment on Miramar? I suppose it's too early to ask about the new one, or Delgado's place."

"Oh—just a minute. Yeah, I'll send you up a report—in fact Jimmy's just typing it now. Nil. Only the old woman's, the apartment on Miramar. There wasn't anything at the Hartford Street place but some personal effects—I'll send them over."

"I'd like to see those photographs you took of Kenneth Jowett sometime."

"My God, hasn't anybody sent you copies yet?"

"You will."

"I'll get on it right away."

Mendoza passed that on. "I don't like Jowett," he said

uneasily. "I don't like these damned notes. But the bird in hand—I suppose you'd better see what you get out of him." The phone rang on his desk and he went to answer it.

"We thought you'd like to know," said Goldberg, "that we've just got that search warrant. For the art shop and Moreno's apartment. In spite of your meddling—we put a stakeout on both places—he hasn't run, and we're just off to pull a raid. Pat says you can come along."

"What, at this hour, in the rain? Thanks just the same," said Mendoza. "I'm going to have lunch, Saul. Have fun."

They all went to lunch before Grace and Palliser tackled Van Tine. They didn't have a long session with him, because rather early in the exchange it emerged that Van Tine was something of an oddity himself, but the kind that turned up now and then. He had been a professor of chemistry at Stanford once, and started on the downward path through a combination of drink and a taste for low company.

Werner Van Tine couldn't have written those notes. Even in the state he was now in, drunk or sober.

They let him go, and separated again to get back to the hunt. Before he left the office Palliser called Roberta.

"I can't stop burping," she said crossly. "It's like the worst case of indigestion there ever was, and the doctor says all cheerful not to worry—hic—about it. Damn. I always said I disapproved of only children, but—" Palliser laughed and she told him he was heartless.

"Well, if the doctor isn't worried—"

Men still on parole, of course, would stay put, having to report to their P.A. officers. By three-thirty he had found three more of those on the weeded-out list, and talked to them without bringing them in: it didn't seem worth it. One of them was a young fellow who seemed to be really rehabilitated, in the jargon: he was on a regular job, and he had graduated from high school—if that meant anything these days, the half-educated kids they were turning out. The other two had records of violence but not of rape, and he found them together poring over a racing guide.

He went back to the office to see if Grace had done any better, or Higgins.

Grace was feeling very tired of the routine, and after lunch he debated with himself. Higgins, he thought, was a very good cop, and a good man. But no question, this race thing was a factor, and Grace got a little tired too of all the well-meaning people who kept saying there wasn't any difference among people. There damn well were differences—he'd hate to think there wasn't any difference between Jason Grace and the people in that housing complex. But the inescapable fact was, it just could be that he could get at Lonnie Epps better than George could.

It was better than wandering around in the rain, anyway. He went down to the jail on Alameda and saw Epps.

"Now you know, Lonnie," he said in his soft voice, "we've got the goods on you, and you're going up for a stretch. It doesn't make much sense for you to take the rap for your pals."

"I don't fink on nobody, man," said Epps with a growl.

"Well, that's just one way to think about it." Grace offered him a cigarette. "There you'll be, probably up at Folsom—no easy one for you, Lonnie, with a record of violence—for maybe a five-to-fifteen stretch, and your two pals on the outside where there's liquor and girls and a lot of things you won't find at Folsom. Look at it this way, Lonnie—suppose we'd picked up one of them, you think he'd keep quiet on your name? Either one? Or both, Lonnie."

Epps frowned. That was patently a new idea to him. "I—" he said. "What you mean, man?"

"Well, you know them—I don't." Grace shrugged. "I just wondered, Lonnie. What do you think?"

At two o'clock he came back to the office and handed Mendoza two names. "He told me," he said simply. "Epps. I thought he might. The two pals are Thomas Robinson and Clarence Barnard."

"*¡Qué hombre!*" said Mendoza. "Our sweet talker. Let's see what shows on them." They called down to R. and I. and the packages came up in fifteen minutes. Both Robinson and Barnard had records: Robinson had done time for armed robbery before, one count, and Barnard's said burglary, robbery from the person, assault with intent. Robinson was just out of Folsom, but not on P.A.—he had served the full time.

"And they might be anywhere," said Grace. "Epps says he doesn't know where either of them lives, they meet at a bar down on Washington."

"Any particular time?"

"They were going to pull another tonight, he didn't know where. He was supposed to meet them at eight—but if it's on the grapevine he's been picked up, and you know it will be, they'll never show."

"*De veras.* Well, it's a chance. We'll leave it to the night watch to stake out."

What they didn't know then was that the night watch would have other things to do.

When Palliser came into the office at ten minutes to four, he found two strange women sitting at Higgins' and Grace's desks and everybody else in Mendoza's office listening to him swear.

"I do not believe it! *¡Qué disparate—es el colmo!* The thing is ridiculous. Look, it's raining—it's a dark gloomy day—"

"What's going on?" asked Palliser.

"A pack of over-imaginative witnesses," said Mendoza.

"Look, it won't go away because you won't see it," said Higgins. "You said, a spate of the queer ones. We're getting them. This is one more, Luis. We've got another kid run down, riding his bike in the street," he added to Palliser. "Hit-run. Two witnesses say, deliberately run down."

[88]

"For God's sake, another? Like the Saldivez kid? How is he?"

"Not too good. I didn't see him, the ambulance had gone, but the Traffic man said he was bleeding pretty bad. At least we identified him right away—it happened as he left school, elementary school up on Lemoyne. Nobody around to speak of, he was late leaving—they let out at two-thirty on account of the rain. He was late because he had to fix a tire on his bike, we got that from the janitor. But one of the witnesses is a teacher at the school—"

"But there's no sense in it!" said Mendoza.

"Not much," agreed Higgins soberly. "He's Timmy Jordan, aged ten. The parents have been called. And I'm trying to get Luis to listen to the witnesses."

"All right, all right!" said Mendoza. *Es un cuento absurdo* —but we'll have to take statements anyway. Get Wanda in here."

The first witness was Mrs. Sandra Wahlsperger, fifth-grade teacher. No, Timmy wasn't in her class, but she knew him because his best friend Randy Fuller was, and Timmy waited for him outside her classroom door. She'd stayed after school correcting papers, and she was on her way to her car in the teachers' parking lot at three-twenty when it happened. The lot faced on Logan Street. She was looking that way, going toward her car, when she saw it. No, she wasn't carrying an umbrella, she had on a plastic rain hat. She saw Timmy ride out from the schoolyard gate there, and it was a quiet street, never much traffic, so she saw it all very distinctly. A car had come down Logan, going much too fast for a dark rainy day, and it hadn't skidded, or braked, she was positive, it had just been aimed at the boy on the bike, and knocked him down, off his bike into the street, and roared off. "And what kind of fiend would do such a thing—I don't think I've ever screamed before in my life, but I did then, and I ran— no, I couldn't see anything about the driver, he was on the opposite side of the car from me—and it was so far back to

[89]

the building where I could find a phone—he was bleeding so terribly! But this other woman, Mrs. Mularvey, was there then—"

Mrs. Mularvey was in her sixties, broad and normally a cheerful soul, but her round face was still white and drawn, her eyes shocked. She'd been walking up to the little independent grocery on Glendale Boulevard, she didn't mind the rain, and she'd been all bundled up against it with a thick wool headscarf on so she hadn't bothered with an umbrella. Like Mrs. Wahlsperger she had seen it happen, and that was just how it was, something deliberate. She didn't know the boy. She saw him ride out of the gate just ahead of her, she was on the same side of the street, and the car came at him on purpose, knocked him down and ran over his bike, and it was the most terrible thing she'd ever seen.

"All right," said Higgins. Wanda was taking notes silently. "What about the car?"

Mrs. Wahlsperger said apologetically that in her shock she couldn't say what it had been. "It was a sedan, medium sized," but two-door or four she couldn't say. "But it was a dark color, black or brown." Mrs. Mularvey agreed with that, but added that it wasn't new, and the other woman said that was her impression too. A car five, six, seven years old.

They were thanked, and Higgins, casting an enigmatic glance at Mendoza, said he'd drive them back to the scene.

"Now I wonder," said Grace gently. "We had witnesses—but they all admitted they hadn't been looking, till they heard the boy yell—who said the McLeod boy had been careless, caused the accident himself. I wonder if that was what they thought they saw because it's how a lot of accidents on bikes happen. If that wasn't the first one?"

"We do occasionally get the queer ones, Jase—not the impossibilities," said Mendoza impatiently.

"It's like she said—Mrs. Wahlsperger," said Wanda. "Nobody but a fiend would do such a thing."

"And you think they aren't out there walking around, lady?" asked Glasser sleepily.

"¡Dios!" said Mendoza. "So they are, Henry, but—"

Sergeant Lake erupted into the office. "Multiple shooting up on Virgil," he said tersely. "Two black-and-whites on it now. They say, witnesses—"

It was five-thirty-five, with twenty-five minutes of the day watch left. They all went out on it.

The sign above the door said simply, *Independent Pharmacy*. That was what it had been, a modestly successful drug-store-pharmacy owned by Mr. and Mrs. John Shaughnessy. They were both pharmacists, judging by the licenses framed on the wall behind the counter at the rear of the store.

There were witnesses: five people who had been walking past, three on the opposite side of the street, two on this; and Mr. Abraham Teitel from the kosher butcher shop two doors up, who had been on his way to the drugstore after aspirin, and Mrs. Bernice Kelly from the gift shop next door. They had identified the bodies.

"We'll have the lab out," said Mendoza, and used the phone in the Ferrari.

"But who would do such a terrible—" Mrs. Kelly, having fainted dead away, was now sitting wanly in a chair in her own shop, looking ready to faint again. "John and Sarah—and Sue!—oh, Sue—she always comes right to the store after school, to do her homework in the back room before they close up and go h— But she's only *sixteen*, she can't be—"

The bodies told a story, after a fashion. John Shaughnessy sprawled across the prescription counter at the back. Susan Shaughnessy in the open doorway behind that, which led to the back of the store. There was a stockroom back there, for pharmaceutical supplies, and another room partitioned off, with a couple of old upholstered chairs, a little desk. On the desk was Susan's homework, an English essay half finished. The last sentence she had written was, "So I think it is important to be optimistic because if you expect bad things to happen they will." Her mother, Sarah Shaughnessy, hadn't been found at first: she was lying behind the front counter where cosmetics and colognes were on display.

They had all been shot. The doctors would say definitely, but Susan had apparently taken at least two slugs, in the head and the body. To be hoped Ballistics could tell them about the gun. There seemed to be powder-burns on the man's tan cotton smock. Shot at fairly close range, then.

"But a robber," said old Mr. Teitel, shaken and shaking, "why does he shoot? Mr. Shaughnessy is not a fool! His wife and child there, a robber comes with a gun, he gives over the money like any man with sense— A good man he was, nice people, it makes not very much sense—"

What made even less sense was that the cash register hadn't been touched; it was closed and full of money. Shaughnessy's wallet was in his hip pocket with forty dollars in it. Both Susan's purse and her mother's contained billfolds with money in them.

The lab truck with Marx and Horder, Duke and Scarne, arrived, and they began their quiet, precise work, dusting for latents, taking photographs. There were statements to get; the day-watch men took names, addresses. "Would you mind staying around to answer questions, it won't take long—"

As a contrast to all the dirt and evil they saw, they were grateful to find the average citizen to be a good citizen, willing to go out of the way to help them. "Listen, Officer, if I can help you get whoever did this, I sure will, but I got to call my husband, tell him where I am—" "You want me to testify in court, I'll be glad to, we all got to cooperate with you fellows—" It hadn't come to that yet; maybe it never would.

The whole night watch came out on it. And a picture emerged, by the time the bodies had been taken away, while the lab men were still busy in the store.

"I was across the street, I heard the shots, like backfires, only so many, I don't know how many, six, seven maybe. I looked across where they come from, and I saw this fellow run out of the store—yes, I'm sure, the drugstore. He ran around the corner onto Geneva Street—well, with the rain and all, all I can say is he was a white man, and the way he ran he was young. He had on dark clothes some kind—"

"I heard the shots, gunfire I know, I was in the Army. I won't say for sure and anyway I guess your ballistics people can say, but it sounded like a light gun to me—twenty-two maybe. I saw him run out—"

"He came running out of the store just ahead of me, I was just passing the TV repair place there—a kid, white, yeah, I'd say nineteen or twenty, but I only saw his back after he turned and ran—"

"He nearly knocked me down, I was just at the door when he came running out, I'd heard the shots and it kind of paralyzed me, I stopped right there, dead, and then he came out. Oh, I couldn't see his face—his head was down—I don't remember seeing a gun—but one thing I can tell you, he had on one of these what they call berets—it was all so fast—"

The night watch took over and the rest of them went home.

The witnesses could come in tomorrow, next day, to sign the formal statements; there was always the endless paperwork.

Mrs. Kelly peered nearsightedly at Landers when he told her that, and that she was free to go home. "I'll be glad to cooperate however I can—such a terrible, terrible thing— why, I'd known John and Sarah ever since they had the store here, Susan was only a baby. It just doesn't seem possible— only sixteen, and such a pretty girl, a nice girl too, and straight A's in school— You know, young man, you don't look old enough to be a real police officer—"

And that, Landers had heard before. He had hoped that his peculiar ordeal of last year, getting identified as a pro

hood and suspended from duty, might have aged him somewhat; apparently it hadn't.

He wondered suddenly if it would help to grow a moustache.

Only Phil might not like it.

Six

When the day watch came in on Friday morning, back to strength again except for Piggott, they found that the night crew had left them a good deal more than usual—lists of witnesses on the Shaughnessys, laconic notes of what statements they'd got, addresses. One bullet had evidently been fired wild; they'd dug it out of the wall near the back counter. After they had done all there was to be done at the scene, they'd come back to base to find they had a new one—a heist at a bar on Second Street. Landers and Conway had taken that, and Landers had left notes in his sprawling hand.

"Here they are," said Mendoza, handing the notes to Grace. "Robinson and Barnard. Either the grapevine hasn't told them that Epps has been picked up, or they don't care. He said they were planning to pull another last night."

The witnesses in the bar, bartender and eleven customers, described the heisters as two big Negroes, one with a gun. They were in and out fast, and they'd taken around a hundred and forty bucks altogether.

"Yes, but the grapevine—" Grace smoothed his moustache. "We've got an A.P.B. out on them, and that they'll find out soon enough, so you know they'll never go near that other bar on Washington again. They've got a little stake to lie low—or get out of the area."

"Which reminds me we never asked Ballistics about Epps's gun," said Higgins. "I sent it down to them. Let's find out."

Sergeant Lake was off today, Sergeant Rory Farrell sitting on the board. Two minutes later Higgins was talking to Ballistics.

"Oh, that gun you sent down Wednesday? It's an old S. and W. Police Positive .38—" Higgins said he knew that. "Well, you also sent us a slug out of it—lessee, Tuesday morning. Heist at a liquor store the night before, the slug was out of the wall there. The S. and W. fired it."

"So he's still got the Colt .45," said Higgins to Grace.

"And we've got more to think about than that pair of louts," said Mendoza. "Art, you and I are on the Shaughnessys. Oh, Henry, I forgot to ask you—on that lineup yesterday—"

"The bartender identified Epps positively."

"*Bueno.* Art—"

"The parolees," said Palliser. "I suppose we go on looking."

"The rest of you," said Glasser. "I'm still cleaning up that Biltmore Hotel thing. The Cole woman. It seems she was on a vacation here before going over to Vegas for a divorce. I got her husband via the Boston police, he's flying in today to claim the body—which he can't have right away."

"Come to think," said Palliser, "I've got a date with Mrs. Sutton and Mrs. Kowaljic for a session with an artist."

"So let's get on—*¡Vamos!*" said Mendoza briskly. He led Hackett out to the elevator.

"Where are we going?"

"What the Shaughnessys look like," said Mendoza, "is simple and obvious. A nervous amateur, possibly inexperienced heister came in intending to hold Shaughnessy up, and either the gun went off—that wild bullet—or Shaughnessy put up a fight and he panicked. But ten to one, even if he killed Shaughnessy without half intending it, one like that would just run away. This one, panicked or not, made sure of all three of them, Mrs. Shaughnessy and the girl too."

"On the other hand," said Hackett, "he needn't have panicked at all. Why should any heist man, these days, hesitate to kill potential witnesses? He can't get more than life—

which he can also get for a third felony—and he's out on parole in seven years."

"All too true. But if he was a pro just coolly killing witnesses, he'd have taken what was there to take. *¿De veras?* Now, as I've said before, we know that nine times out of ten a thing is just what it looks like, but we have to proceed on the assumption that the worst might have happened and it isn't. So what you and I are going to do is have a long hard look at the Shaughnessys, to see if anybody possibly had a motive to get rid of them. I don't really think so, but it is possible—just possible—that that was a hired job."

"Well, it's possible," said Hackett cautiously.

"So, *¡siga adelante!*"

One of the first jobs they'd had to do yesterday was to track down any relatives. Mrs. Kelly had told them that Shaughnessy had a brother living in Santa Monica, and they'd found the phone number in the phone-index at the store. Mendoza had been gone before he showed up; the night men said he had got there about eight o'clock, but in such a state of shock they couldn't get much out of him. He was Walter Shaughnessy, had a small construction company down there; he'd given them his card.

Mendoza and Hackett found the modest old house on Fourteenth Street by nine-fifteen, and were greeted by a subdued good-looking man a little younger than the dead man, probably: graying hair, hard workman's hands, casual clothes.

"I didn't know what to do—to call you, or ask— But come in. This is—" he hadn't any words for it. "Things like this, they just don't happen. All of them—all at once. It just isn't— Oh, Myra. My wife. Er—"

"Lieutenant Mendoza, Sergeant Hackett."

"Please sit down," she said in a low voice. She wasn't pretty or plain; these were ordinary people, settled in ordinary routines of life.

"What—happens now?" asked Shaughnessy. "I—we sent the children to school, Pat didn't want to go, she thought the world of Sue, two years older and— But what have you found out?"

"Not much. We've got some witnesses—a description of sorts. Has your brother ever had any trouble in the store that you know of? Recently, of any kind?"

Shaughnessy shook his head. "No, of course not—it's a pretty decent neighborhood, and John was a quiet man, he didn't—have trouble with people. Arguments. I don't know what to say. No, I don't recall him saying anything about any trouble."

Mendoza went on asking questions, and a picture emerged. The Shaughnessys had owned, or been paying on, their own home on Lakeview Avenue in the Silver Lake area. They had led quiet lives, the parents in the store every day from eight to six, Sue going to high school, a good student. She wasn't allowed to date much, and she'd been a serious girl, not interested much in dating anyway. She got along with her parents, no problems, no rebellion; she was a religious girl, they all were, never missed a Sunday Mass. The Shaughnessys seldom went out; they had friends, surely, a few good friends from the church, the neighborhood, but they gave few parties. The humdrum lives—ordinary people.

"I'm afraid we'll want to have a look through the house," said Mendoza. "We won't upset it."

"Oh—sure," said Shaughnessy. "Anything you say. I suppose you've got John's keys." They'd be at the morgue, presently sent up to Mendoza's office with everything else on him. "If you have one—"

Shaughnessy said heavily, "Sure. We want to help you all we can, anything we can do." He went away and came back with a key: it bore a tag with the address on it. "When can we—I called Father Simon last night—"

"It's mandatory to have autopsies," said Mendoza. "We'll let you know when you can claim the bodies."

"Sure," said Shaughnessy. "It just seems—" he made a helpless gesture. "I know it isn't so—they're all all right somewhere—but it just seems as if all of a sudden they're—

snuffed out. Like you blow out a candle." His wife started to cry and he turned to her.

The house bore out what they'd heard from Shaughnessy. An ordinary house, bastard Spanish on a quiet street. A few pieces of good old furniture, but the newer cheaper pieces chosen with taste, the pictures inexpensive, but showing some imagination. The house was clean and mostly neat, but a lived-in house. Hackett had the ghostly feeling that its occupants might walk in any minute. A girl's blue coat discarded across the front-room couch—Sue had been going to wear it to school yesterday morning, changed her mind at the last minute and wore her raincoat instead. A small solitaire-diamond ring in yellow gold in a dish beside the soap-tray on the sink: Mrs. Shaughnessy, perhaps hurried, had forgotten to put on her engagement ring again after she'd washed the breakfast dishes.

The front bedroom—double bed made up, dresser neat—had a walk-in closet; it was filled with the elder Shaughnessys' clothes, shoes ranged tidily on a shoe-rack: a modest array of clothes, not many dress-up items. The girl's room was a little untidy, costume jewelry spread on top of the dressing table, a drawer open, a few clothes on the bed. But it was an innocent room, an innocent house. A bookcase in the girl's room: they looked at the titles. Religious books, adventure stories, a few young-adult love stories, some research material: an encyclopedia, a dictionary, a Spanish-English dictionary. She'd probably been taking a Spanish course in school. A bookcase in the living room: unexpectedly, quite a few books on archeology, well-read by the look of them: Shaughnessy's hobby?

"*Ver y creer,*" said Mendoza. "Seeing is believing."

"*Ya lo sé,*" said Hackett sarcastically. "Ordinary people, as we heard. Though it's kind of refreshing to come across as innocent and simple a sixteen-year-old as Sue seems to have been, these days."

"Isn't it the truth," said Mendoza. "Especially with Mr.

Moreno and his minions prowling around. Yes." He looked around the living room in a dissatisfied way. They'd left the front door open, and now there was a little scuffle of feet on the porch; they looked round.

Another teen-age girl, and a pretty one: sweater and a modest-length skirt, long brown hair. "Oh!" she said; she had a hesitant hand up to knock. "Who are you? I thought—oh, are you—the—the police?"

"That's right," said Hackett.

"I'm Diane Parrish, I live three doors down. I was Sue's best friend. I—I'm sorry, I saw the car here and I thought it might be Sue's uncle, I c-came to say how s-sorry everybody— But I won't bother you."

Hackett said, "Just a second, Miss Parrish. You knew Sue pretty well, did you?"

She choked back a sob. "We were best friends from the time we started school. That's why I'm not in school today—I *couldn't*. We heard about it—we saw it on the late news— and it was *just horrible* hearing it like that—just *news,* just people dead, killed, and it was Sue and her mother and father! We couldn't believe it, but they gave the address— I'm sorry. But I can't help—why, it was just the night before Sue was at our house all evening, we're both in the class play and we were studying our parts, and I c-couldn't get Don to do the prompting— But you don't want to hear all that—"

"Miss Parrish, was Sue having any trouble at school?" asked Hackett.

She stared at him. "Sue never had trouble at school—she was awfully smart."

"No, I mean with boys, or anybody offering drugs—"

"Oh, no! I know the public schools are pretty bad that way, but we go to Holy Family, the sisters are strict. Besides, neither Sue or me'd be silly enough to *take* anything. Mr. and Mrs. Shaughnessy, well, they knew about things like that, being pharmacists, and Sue'd never have— Did somebody say she *did?*" She was indignant.

"No, no," said Hackett. "We're just asking."

"Well, you can just stop thinking bad things about Sue." She turned and went down the steps, still a little offended; and then she turned back and said, "I—I surely hope you catch whoever did it."

They watched her hurry down the sidewalk. "Wasting time," said Hackett. "No, we had to look, I know. But it's the anonymous nervous heister as far as I can see, Luis. The completely impersonal thing. That makes you wonder about fate and free will."

"It may make you wonder, Arturo. Let's wait and see if the lab turns up anything."

All they had so far was from the witnesses last night: the general description. Geneva Street was residential, nobody had been out in the rain, and nobody along there had seen the gunman.

At least it wasn't raining today.

Palliser had ushered Mrs. Kowaljic and Mrs. Sutton into Garcia's little office in one section of the lab and settled them down there. He came back an hour later to see how they were doing.

"Pretty sharp eyes these ladies have," said Garcia genially. "I think we've got a good sketch for you."

"Oh, that's him," said Mrs. Kowaljic confidently. "I get a good look before I let him in. You can see, he looks like a nice young fellow, nobody would suspect he's a bad one." Mrs. Sutton was less sure, but she hadn't had as good a look at him; that hallway had been darker.

Palliser looked at the sketch with interest. It was full face, and showed a man in his twenties, round-faced, more blond than dark but not a light blond, scanty eyebrows, a small thin mouth, big ears, a pug nose. It looked like an individual, at least. He thanked them, called up a black-and-white to ferry them home, and going back to the office ran into Grace just coming in. "Where've you been?"

"I had a little idea, I went to that bar on Washington, but I should've known it wouldn't be open yet. What have you got?" He looked at the sketch interestedly. "It looks like some-body, not just a composite drawing. How about us looking at some mug shots, John? Just for starters."

"Anything's better than hunting these damned parolees. Let's. They're making up some copies of this, but if we can spot him—"

They went down to R. and I. and found Phil O'Neill. She really was a very cute blonde, thought Palliser—little and neat with a snub nose and curly hair—and he'd wish Tom luck. She looked at the sketch, asked what it was on, and gave them two thick books of mug shots: men with that general record, robbery with violence. They sat down at a table side by side with the sketch between them and started looking.

An hour later, with the ashtray overflowing and Palliser's stomach beginning to rumble, Grace said suddenly, "Hold it. What do you think about this one?" He shoved over the book, finger on the little photograph.

"If that sketch is good, bingo," said Palliser. In the photo-graph the face was a trifle less full, the mouth slightly wider; otherwise it was a damned good match. The subject was de-scribed in terse officialese: Robert Carlson, now twenty-nine, Caucasian, blond and blue, six-one, a hundred and ninety, no marks. First arrested at seventeen as a juvenile, attempted burglary; later, armed robbery, mugging, assault with intent, a few D.-and-D.'s. There was an address in Chatsworth, but out of date.

"Well, let's go see if he's still there," said Palliser, "but if it is him conning the old ladies to let him in, on Central's beat, I would doubt it."

"You never know," said Grace. "Take my car." But Pal-liser refused to squeeze his six feet into that poor man's racer, he announced firmly. Awhile ago, looking for a transportation car so Virginia could have the Chevy, Grace had fallen for that little blue Elva— "And *she goes* all right," he always added. They took the Rambler, and stopped for lunch first.

The address in Chatsworth was a fairly new apartment house on Independence Avenue. At apartment four an old lady with a Siamese cat sitting on her shoulder peered at them incuriously and said she'd never heard of Robert Carlson. She'd lived there a year. They asked about the manager, and she said, "Downstairs, apartment one. Mrs. Tyler."

Mrs. Tyler, angular and violently henna-haired, was just leaving for somewhere and impatient with them. "Carlson?" she said. "Oh, he moved away when he got married, last year. I suppose this place wasn't good enough for that little snip." She sniffed. "No, he didn't leave any new address, he never got any mail anyway, why should he? I'm sorry, I'm late for an appointment now—"

Palliser brought out the badge. "This is police business, Mrs. Tyler. We'd like to find him. Anything you remember —who his friends were, places he might have frequented here—"

"Police? You mean you *want* him for something? Well, if that doesn't beat all—nice quiet tenant, never any loud parties—I'll be damned!" she said frankly. "Well, I suppose you know your own business." She didn't look at all convinced of it.

"Do you know anything about the girl he married?" asked Grace.

She looked from him to Palliser. "I only saw her a couple of times. Looked like a little tart—dyed black hair and fake eyelashes. Her name was Margie. Well, I remember she worked at a place up on Devonshire."

"What kind of place?"

"Oh, a restaurant or bar, some place like that. George's, or was it Jordan's, some name like that."

That was all they got from her, so they cruised up Devonshire Street slowly looking for bars and restaurants. They passed Georgia's Grill and tried there; but it was a tiny lunchroom and no Margie had ever worked there. Farther on they passed a very expensive-looking tan brick restaurant with its own parking lot and a flashing neon sign: *The Georgia Peach Tree, cocktails, entertainment nightly.* They asked there, but it had only been open a few weeks and employed no Margies.

"Were you complaining about the legwork on the parolees?" asked Grace as they got back in the Rambler.

A couple of blocks up, on the other side of the street, they spotted a sign in the middle of a block of older store fronts: *Jorgenson's Palace Bar, Rex Morgan on piano every night.* Palliser made a U-turn, came back and parked, and they went in. It was a medium-sized place, old and comfortable-looking with red-checkered tablecloths, a curved bar at the back, a few booths, a little stage. At this hour there wasn't a customer in the place. There was a man sitting on a high stool behind the bar reading a copy of the *Reader's Digest.*

"Excuse me, have you got a girl named Margie working here?" asked Palliser.

The man looked at them curiously, a big bald old man. "Not now," he said. "Did have last year, till she got married and moved away."

"Do you know where she moved?"

Without getting up the old man shouted, "Helen?"

"Well, what now?" A woman came out of the door to a back room. She was young, too plump, blond by request.

"You know where Margie moved to when she got hitched? These fellows are lookin' for her."

"Oh." She stared at them. "Yeah, they went back to L.A. —Bob got a new job there, I think. Last time I seen her before she quit, she give me a phone number, new place they went."

"Have you still got it?"

"Gee, I dunno. I guess, some place. I'll look." She went away and came back with a huge red handbag, started to rummage through it. She finally came up with a scrap of paper much smudged with *Margie* and a phone number on it. Palliser thanked her; she just shrugged.

"So let's hope our excursion into the wilds of the San Fernando Valley has got us somewhere," said Grace. It was three-thirty and beginning to look like rain again.

* * *

It was too early to ask the lab what they might have picked up in Shaughnessy's pharmacy. Mendoza and Hackett went to lunch at Federico's and found Glasser and Higgins already there, occupying the big table up in front. Once in a while most of them happened to land here more or less at the same time. The tall brown waiter hurried up without being asked, with a cup of black coffee for Mendoza, and took their orders. Hackett studied the menu unhappily and ordered the small steak. "Are you up again?" asked Higgins.

"Well, damn it, I am six-three-and-a-half." Hackett looked rather annoyed, and maybe he had cause. Higgins was only that half-inch shorter and stayed comfortably at two hundred on the nose whatever he ate.

He said now, absently, "Hamburger and french fries, and I'll have a piece of apple pie later."

"You're annoying Art, George," said Mendoza. "The small steak, Adam."

Glasser ordered a hamburger. "E.M. started out on the parolees—I guess he's still at it. The dogged sleuth."

"Dogged is the word for E.M." Hackett lit a cigarette and sat back. "He disapproves of you, Luis. The way you get hunches, and make jumps from here to there. He's a great believer in the routine."

"Well, it breaks cases," said Higgins. "In fact quite often. Are you any good at electricity, Henry?"

"I don't generate it. Oh, your darkroom— Matt said something about it. What sort of installation would it be?"

"Run a line in—there's a light in the garage, and I'm going to partition off a corner at the back. We'd want about four plugs, for safelights and an enlarger later on."

"Well, that should be simple enough," said Glasser.

"You could do it? Thanks, Henry, I'll let you know how it comes along."

When they got back to the office at one o'clock they found Piggott there talking to Farrell. "You're supposed to be re-cuperating," said Higgins.

"Oh, I only came down to get my car," said Piggott. "I'm taking Prudence out to dinner." Mendoza had gone into his office and now came out again with a report in his hand.

"Here's something for you, Matt." It was the F.B.I. kickback on those latents from the coffee can. "They weren't known to the Feds."

"I never supposed they would be," said Piggott. "Well, I'll see you." He was halfway down to the elevator when Farrell called him back.

"Your fish-fancier wants you."

"Mr. Duff?"

"Say, Mr. Piggott, I told you I'd keep an eye out and I meant to, but I haven't got eyes in the back of my head. Ron Babcock came in just now and we went into the back to look at some bluefin killys he wants to buy, and I'll be damned but when we came back to the front, there's another coffee can with four of my Regal Angels in it!"

"Yes," said Piggott. "We guessed he meant to bring them back after he'd collected the eggs. But it's—" he substituted "odd" for "funny"—"all the same."

"It's damned odd," said Duff. "But I'm not complaining. How are all your little fellows doing?"

"Oh, fine. Just fine. Those cardinal tetras—they're something to watch. My wife likes the angels best now, she says. Well, I hope you get the other two back."

"So do I. Just thought I'd let you know," said Duff.

There wasn't any point, of course, in printing the new coffee can. Piggott told Higgins about that; Shogart had just come in with another of the parolees.

"That is the queerest thing we've had in a while," said Higgins as Piggott went out.

"You like to help me lean on this guy?" was all Shogart said. E. M. Shogart, that hardworking officer, vaguely disapproved of queer things. They shouldn't be there, cluttering up the plain cause and effect, the logic.

"Sure," said Higgins. He didn't think they were ever going to get the X on Reynolds-Jowett this way, by the dogged routine, because of the kind of case it was. The usual run-of-the-mill cases, the routine usually got you there; but when a wild card came along, quite often the routine was a dead end. They'd just have to hope that Luis would have an inspiration about it.

Scarne called Mendoza at three o'clock. "Knew you'd want whatever we can give you as soon as possible, on this multiple shooting. Bainbridge's office sent over the slugs out of the bodies. Two slugs in each, I understand, and the one we got out of the wall."

"Have you made the gun?"

"Right off. It's a Hi-Standard revolver made by J. C. Higgins, sold by Sears. Not a very old gun, and never used much —the marks are very clear. It's a seven-shot, so he had a full load. The slugs are .22 long ammo."

"So, every little bit helps. Thanks so much."

And then Carey called him again and insisted that he come down to the Missing Persons office to meet Charles Borchers. "*¡Qué va!* Don't bother me, Carey—"

"This is going to be a case for you sooner or later," said Carey grimly. "You'd better be kept up to date on it."

Mendoza swore, and went downstairs. Among other things that annoyed him, even as he had predicted, the *Times* and the *Herald* had both run the funny human-interest stories about sweet-faced Grandmother, and what repercussions that might have he didn't like to think.

In Carey's office he found thin dark Mrs. Donahue, still looking anxious, and a large redfaced man in rather sloppy sports clothes who turned out to be her husband. A thin-faced gray-haired fellow was introduced as Charles Borchers.

"Now, you know the background on Mrs. Borchers, Mendoza. How she's disappeared completely, and the money, and so on—"

"We just can't get over it," said Jack Donahue. He looked rather stupid but honest; of course not every male would be attracted to the little dark woman beside him. "We asked the police to look then, that same night when she didn't come home. It was when I was out of work, I'm a construction worker, I got a job with Stevens Company now. I took her to the doctor that day, Mrs. Borchers I mean, and—"

"She asked you to drop her at The Broadway, yes," said Mendoza, bored. Jack Donahue was the type who always told you a story three times over. As he thought that, logically the line from Lewis Carroll slid across his mind: *What I tell you three times is true.*

Borchers leaned forward, looking grave. "Naturally I'm concerned that Lieutenant Carey is so sure Mother must be dead. But the evidence—and anyone who knew her— Well, I've never been easy about it in my mind, but there wasn't a damned thing I could do. Nobody could claim she was incompetent, in spite of her age. And—I expect they've told you that she was a very difficult, obstinate old lady."

"Her oldest friend put it a little more bluntly," said Mendoza.

Borchers laughed unhappily. "Lizzie Eldon. Well, her own worst enemy, don't they say? Yes, well, Lieutenant Carey was interested in her source of income, and what I had to tell him—I'm bound to say it makes it all the more probable that he's right. As I say, I had suspected, but I don't know for certain. All I can do is tell you what I do know."

"Which is?" Mendoza lit a cigarette.

Borchers leaned back. "I was pretty close to my father. You could say, especially as I grew up, we—got together for safety." He smiled. "He was a land speculator, and often very shrewd. You've heard that Mother tends to be a miser, and disapproved of what she called gambling." He got out a cigarette, tapped it on Carey's desk. "Well, I happen to prefer a more regular income—I'm with International Harvester, in the purchasing department. But that's neither here nor there. This goes back, my God, thirty years. I was in the Army—it was during the war—on embarkation leave, and I came out here to see Dad. He was on top of the world, told me he'd just made the hell of a deal. It was some land over in Nevada, quite a parcel he'd bought on spec a few years back, and he'd just sold it. To the government, he said. Since then, I've thought—uranium? It was about then there were all those hush-hush experiments going on."

"Mmh. Any figure mentioned?" asked Mendoza.

"There was. He told me he'd taken a clear profit of half a million bucks. But he also said something else. He said there was a piece of land in Colorado he'd had his eye on for some time, he had a hunch about it, but the old fellow who owned it was asking seventy-five thousand and he wanted cash. Queer old fellow, Dad said. And now he was going to buy it."

"Oh, indeed?" said Mendoza.

"Well, I shipped out to England," said Borchers, "and it was two months before the cable caught up to me—you know how it was—that Dad had dropped dead of a heart attack the day after I left. It was a year and a half before I got back home, and another couple of months before I got out here to see Mother. I didn't know how Dad might have left his investments, what he had or where—" Borchers finally lit the cigarette. "And do you think I could get anything out of her? 'Your father left me well provided for, Charles,' and that was that. I—"

"Did he leave a will?" asked Mendoza.

"No. I expect he intended to, but he was only fifty-six. I never could get anything out of her. I asked her if she needed anything, wanted anything—I offered her an allowance, and it would have meant some sacrifice, Martha and I were just married and as the children came along— But she wouldn't tell me anything. And no matter what he'd left her, she wouldn't have lived any better than she did—a little cheap room, scrimping and saving—oh, hell, you see how it was. But I've wondered, since, if Dad had got together that wad of cash, and that's what she'd been living on."

The Donahues had listened to all this in apparent bewilderment. Now Mrs. Donahue said, "She always paid me in cash. But I thought she had a bank account, because she'd go out just that day, go uptown, and when she came back she'd give me the money, like she'd just cashed a check—"

"Such a very canny old lady, Mother," said Borchers.

"But what about the rest of the half million?" asked Mendoza.

"That's what we're looking for now," said Carey. "Bank records—stockbrokers' records—but it's thirty years back, and not so easy."

"But if she had that pile of cash," said Borchers, "and if I know Mother, even after thirty years there'd have been some left. And if somebody found out—just disappearing without trace, from this department store—"

"What do you think, Mendoza?" asked Carey.

"I think," said Mendoza, "that this thing is just as much up in the air as several things in my own office. At the moment, you still haven't got any evidence of homicide."

"Well, I know that, but probabilities—"

Mendoza went back to his own office. "Look," said Higgins, "we're getting nowhere just questioning all these men on P.A. It's all too vague—and the type we're after, likely he can't remember what he did from one day to the next. We're wasting time going at it like this."

"You have any suggestions about another way?" asked Mendoza.

"Yes. You have a hunch about it," said Higgins.

"¡Maravilloso! My subconscious doesn't produce on demand." He sat down at his desk and called the lab. "Is it too early to ask, did you pick up any latents at that pharmacy? Possibly on the counter?"

"Yes. Quite a few. Whether they have anything to do with the homicide is something else," said Duke. "We'll let you know."

Mendoza fidgeted around the office another half hour and went home. It had started to rain again.

The twins swarmed over him as he kissed Alison. "Daddy, Daddy, come read!" "Mamacita says about ice and we don't know ice or skates, you tell about ice, Daddy!"

"Ice?" said Mendoza, nonplussed.

"Oh, heavens," said Alison, "it's a picture in the primer, Luis— *¡Bastante,* you two—"

Sheba leaped at him from behind and he staggered. The twins erupted in mirth. "Little monster!" said Alison, plucking her off. "For heaven's sake, *mi amor,* take the offspring away and try to explain ice to them, Máiri and I are concentrating on a special recipe, and between Cedric and the cats and the twins—" Cedric was insistently offering Mendoza a paw.

"How we came by all this livestock—" But, obediently he took the twins down to the nursery and settled them in his lap. "Now, ice. You see, in some places—"

"Mama makes in trays in the 'frigerator," said Johnny. "Too little pieces, you can't stand on." The picture showed some bundled-up boys on ice-skates. Mendoza regarded it, wondering how to explain latitude and longitude to a three-year-old.

"I don't care about ice," said Terry firmly. "Silly! I want to know about the old man." She seized the primer and flicked over pages. "There! Daddy, tell about the old man— he's got a broke leg—*¿de veras?*—all the bandage—"

Mendoza looked at the picture, feeling curiously helpless, and said, "He's got the gout, Terry. It's—"

"What's gout? What's the stick the *muchacho* runs away with?"

"It's the old man's crutch—"

"I can read it all," said Johnny. " 'A man and a lad.' Don't I read good, Daddy? But what's ice?"

The hostages to fortune, reflected Mendoza, posed a few problems not faced by the LAPD on its regular routine.

Higgins went home and conferred seriously with Steve about the construction of the darkroom, to be interrupted by Laura who had a new piece she wanted him to hear. "It's the hardest piece Miss Betts ever gave me, and I want you to hear it, George—I've been practicing *hard*—"

He never could resist her mother's big gray eyes, and he listened solemnly. Doing his best by Bert's good kids. He wasn't any master carpenter, but he guessed he could get those partitions up all right—two-by-fours for the corners, and half-inch planking. If Henry could run the electricity in, damned nice of him, but of course he'd been a friend of Bert's too.

The Piggotts got home at ten-thirty, having gone out to dinner at the Brown Derby in honor of Prudence's birthday and then visited her mother, whom Piggott liked very much. His arm was feeling better; and they had taken the book along, to show Mrs. Russell about all the pretty little fish. "But you really have to see them," said Piggott. "The way they go chasing around, and stop all of a sudden and wave their fins—"

"And the colors," said Prudence. "You've got to come and see them, Mother."

Now, as Piggott hung up his raincoat, Prudence called him. "Matt, look! One of those cardinal tetras—there's a sort of dark spot on the red part—wait a minute, you'll see—*that* one. And he isn't swimming as fast as the rest. The book said about a fungus—"

Piggott watched the cardinal tetra as it turned lazily and moved in and out of the planting. There was certainly a dark spot on its red bottom. "Well, see what it looks like in the morning," he said. "I can ask Duff."

Seven

When the Shaughnessy case had erupted on Thursday afternoon, the latest hit-run had gone out of Mendoza's mind, largely because he thought that was exactly what it was, a hit-run they'd never have any evidence on. It wasn't until Sandra Wahlsperger called in on Saturday morning to ask if she should come to make a formal statement as the officers had asked, that he remembered it. He was slightly annoyed: a waste of time. But they had to go by the book. He went out to see who was in.

Wanda was off today; they'd miss their secretary. Palliser, Hackett, Higgins, Glasser and Sergeant Lake were clustered around Grace who had a handful of snapshots. "I understand you and John did us some good yesterday," said Mendoza. Piggott was bent over the phone on his desk.

"I'm inclined to agree with you about this camera," Grace was saying. "Kind of foolproof. Here she is in her bath—" He looked up at Mendoza. "Oh, that."

Inevitably Mendoza looked at snapshots of fat brown Celia Ann and admired them. "Dead end? Did you get an address?"

"Oh, sure. The phone company gave it to us right away, it's an apartment on Fountain Avenue. We tried it then, and the name's on the door so I guess they're still living there. So I didn't bother to ask the night watch to go out on it. We'll see if he's home this morning."

"Just you," said Mendoza. "That hit-run on Thursday

—nobody's seen the boy yet. I suppose we ought to talk to him, if he's in a condition to tell us anything. John, you chase over to the hospital and see."

"Right. I'd better call first."

The hospital said that Timmy Jordan was getting on nicely: he'd lost some blood from a severed artery, but they'd got him in time. He had a broken leg, some fractured ribs and numerous lacerations, but the nurse in charge of the floor added, "Seeing that he's just had a breakfast big enough for a grown man, I'd say he's doing as well as could be expected."

"I can see him now?"

"I suppose so, if it's about the accident."

Palliser went over to Central Receiving and was sent up to the fourth floor, a tiny cubicle at the end of one wing. "It's not really a room at all," said the nurse, "there isn't usually a bed in it, but his mother wanted to stay with him the first night, and so we— Hi, Timmy! This is Sergeant Palliser from Police Headquarters, he wants to talk to you."

"Hello, Timmy," said Palliser. He thought that if the baby turned out to be a boy, maybe ten years from now he'd have one like this at home. To be hoped he and Robin could do a good job as parents.

Timmy was a little small for his age, defiantly freckled and redhaired and snub-nosed. He'd been reading a sports magazine; he put it down and looked at Palliser with a mixture of scorn and interest. "Say, it's about time the police came to see me, Sergeant," he said. "Two days ago it happened, you sure take your time, don't you? I suppose nobody got the plate-number."

"Well, no," said Palliser, sitting down in the chair beside the high bed. "Do you remember exactly what happened, Timmy?"

"You don't think I'm stupid, do you?" Timmy looked offended. "My life was attempted, was what happened. I suppose there weren't any witnesses either."

"Yes, there were. Mrs. Wahlsperger and a Mrs. Mularvey."

"Hah!" said Timmy darkly. "I don't suppose Mrs. Wahlsperger got it straight. So what'd they tell you?"

"Let's hear from you first," said Palliser, straight-faced.

"So O.K.," said Timmy. "Only I don't know why anybody'd want to kill me, for gosh sakes. I mean, Joe Hunter might be mad at me because—well, that doesn't matter—but he can't *drive,* and anyway— So I tell you how it was. I came out of school about five minutes after the bell, I stayed to talk to Miss Clancy, and the rear tire on my bike was flat. I guess I need a new one. Anyway, I had to go hunt up Mr. Ragsdale, he's the head janitor, and the only pump he had was way at the other end of the grounds in the basement under the auditorium, and it took a while to get it. I guess it was maybe three-thirty when I started home—I'd called Mom and told her why I'd be late, see. I came out the school gate to the street, and I looked for cars—I know you grown-ups think kids are dumb sometimes, but after all I'm not *that* dumb. I don't want to get killed, I look for cars, don't I? There was one car about a block up, good long ways off, and not another car any place—except for parked ones, I mean. I *looked,* I know what I saw! It was raining hard but you could see, not like fog or anything. So I coast out into the street, turn right, and I'd just almost got to the corner when I hear it coming. This car that'd been way a block up. It'd speeded up like a—like anything, it was coming right *at* me about seventy per, I just didn't have time to get out of the way or yell or anything! Boy, was that ever an experience, Sergeant! I didn't even have time to wonder why the heck anybody wanted to kill me. I just saw it coming, and then, zowie!— next thing I know I'm here, feeling like I been in an elephant stampede, and Mom and Dad here and about ten nurses. Boy!"

"You were lucky," said Palliser.

"You better believe I was! When I looked round and saw that heap about to hit me— And I tried to tell Mom and Dad and everybody, that guy really tried to kill me, the car came at me on purpose, and they said I imagined it! I tried to tell 'em, but grown-ups— How dumb can you get? I was there, wasn't I? I saw it, didn't I? I suppose you're gonna say I imagined that too."

"Well, no," said Palliser. "Because Mrs. Wahlsperger and Mrs. Mularvey said so too."

"They *did?*" Timmy was gratified. "I wish you'd tell my mom that."

"Listen, could you have any kind of guess as to what kind of car it was? Sedan, convertible, what color or—"

"Oh, well," said Timmy condescendingly, "I suppose Mrs. Wahlsperger wouldn't have noticed. Women and cars—you know. Sure I could. Couldn't help it, the heap headed right at me. That year they put a V-shaped chrome thing on top of the hood, all their models, you couldn't miss it. It was a 1955 Dodge sedan, dark brown. I never had a chance to see the driver, but that's what it was."

Palliser looked at him appreciatively. He certainly hoped, if the baby turned out to be a boy, that he'd grow into one like Timmy. He shook hands with him seriously. "Thanks a lot, Timmy. I don't suppose we'll ever find out who it was, but I'm glad you're going to be O.K."

"What I'd like to know," said Timmy, "is why the heck anybody wants to kill me."

Piggott called Prudence ten minutes after he got to the office. "Duff says to try that salt cure, it's in the book. You've got to catch him and put him in a dishpan or something."

"For heaven's sake, Matt, we haven't got a dishpan," said Prudence.

"Well, anything that'll take about a gallon of water. And the proportions are in the book, under Diseases. I wish you luck in catching him, they're fast as greased lightning."

"Well, I'll try," said Prudence doubtfully. Piggott hung up to find Grace at his elbow. "I suppose you've got some more snapshots." He took them. "She is a cute one, Jase."

"What was all that about?"

"I don't know that it was such a smart thing to do," said

Piggott, "but I got Prudence all these beautiful little fish for her birthday. Prettiest things you ever saw—but after looking into that book, I think I've let us in for a lot of work. What with seasoning the water—I don't really understand that yet—and cleaning the filter, and all it said about common diseases—"

"How's the arm?"

"Oh, getting on fine." Piggott handed back the snapshots.

"So how'd you like to come pick up somebody? If he's there now. He ought to be sometime." Grace told him about Carlson as they went out. And Piggott had no objection to the little Elva, but they took his Nova to transport the prisoner, if they picked him up.

At the apartment house on Fountain Avenue, they climbed stairs to the front apartment on the right, where the name-slot bore a handwritten slip, *Carlson*. Grace pushed the bell. In a moment the door was opened. "Morning, Mr. Carlson." They pulled out the badges simultaneously, and Carlson stepped back. He'd taken on a little weight since the mug shot was taken, and lost a little hair, but he was still a nice-looking, honest-looking fellow.

"What the hell do you want with me? I haven't done anything—"

"A couple of old ladies and an Identikit sketch say you have," said Grace. "I expect the ladies'll have no trouble identifying you in a line-up. You're under arrest, Mr. Carlson, and before we go any farther I have to read you your rights." He recited that little rigmarole and Carlson started to bluster.

"You haven't got a thing on—you can't do this—bunch of Gestapo cops think they can walk in here—"

"Wrong again," said Piggott. "We seem to have some pretty concrete evidence. Do you want to ride in peacefully or shall we use the cuffs?"

"My wife—my wife won't know where— What the hell you think you've got—"

"You're allowed a phone call," said Grace. "Let's not do it the hard way, Mr. Carlson."

But in the end they put the cuffs on him, brought him back and stashed him in an interrogation room. Palliser was back, talking to Mendoza and Hackett, and they heard about Timmy Jordan.

"So now we can't drag our heels on it, Luis," said Hackett. "When even the boy says it was deliberate—but that is the damnedest thing, John, his making the car for us! Of course, he's right, that's a distinctive model, with that V of chrome on the hood—an oldie but you still see them around. In fact, quite a few of them. We'll get nothing from the D.M.V. on just the car."

"Adding insult to injury," said Mendoza. "Boys on bicycles! No rhyme or reason!"

"And I'll say it again," said Grace. "The McLeod boy was the first one. And obviously it's a nut. Just like this other thing. A nut with some obsession about boys on bicycles."

"But what the hell could it be—even a lunatic, why boys on bicycles?" said Hackett.

"That may emerge when, as and if we locate the lunatic," said Mendoza. "And there can't be all that many 1955 Dodges around, Art. We can ask the D.M.V. for a list—"

"My God," said Palliser, "not a job like that again!" He vividly remembered that, the case where all they'd had was the make, and the hunt for that damned green Anglia.

"In this area," said Mendoza. "They've got computers too."

"All right, all right," said Palliser. "Meanwhile, did you pick up Carlson?"

"Third time lucky. He's waiting down the hall."

"Wait till I send this teletype, I'll help you lean on him." Palliser started for Communications to send that request to the D.M.V. in Sacramento. Higgins, protesting that it was a damned waste of time, had gone off hunting the parolees; Shogart, unprotesting, had gone with him, and Glasser was typing a report on Mrs. Cole. They'd have the husband here sometime today, probably. Wanda was off today; they missed their secretary. There wasn't much they could do on the Shaughnessy case until they got a lab report. The thorough Scarne had had an afterthought, and there were a couple of men at the pharmacy now checking the actual stock against Shaughnessy's books. It was just possible that drugs and not money had triggered that shooting.

Grace sat down at his desk and lit a cigarette, waiting for Palliser to come back. Piggott, with a list of parolees, had plodded out. Waiting, Grace looked at the new snapshots again. A cute one she was, all right. It would be funny, he thought, if his father was right: as chief gynecologist at General Hospital he might be—saying it happened so often, couple adopted a child and right off the wife got pregnant where she never could before. Well, that would be all right with both of them.

He was dimly conscious of Sergeant Lake at the switchboard, plugging in. "Robbery-Homicide, Sergeant Lake." He jumped up when Lake started to laugh, and got up to look into the hall curiously. Lake's round face was convulsed with mirth; he made two attempts to speak before he said, "J-just a moment, sir, I'll let you speak to the Lieutenant." He plugged in. "Lieutenant, you've got to"— he exploded into giggles again—"hear about this."

"¿Que ocurre, Jimmy?" said Mendoza from his office.

"It's the groundskeeper or whatever they—from the Evergreen—he's on the l-line," said Lake, and went on laughing. For a while he and Hackett had compared diets, but a couple of weeks ago Lake had temporarily given up, and had gained a few pounds since. He shook all over, and his face was red. Palliser, coming back, stared at him in alarm.

"You having a fit?"

"Oh, my God," said Lake. He sat up and mopped his eyes. "The Evergreen Cemetery out on Brooklyn—the custodian or whatever they— Somebody's stolen one of their tombstones!" Grace and Palliser started to laugh. Mendoza came out of his office with Hackett; they were grinning.

"*Oro esta, oro estotro*," said Mendoza. "Now this queer little thing will occupy us while we wait for the damned lab to finish all the scientific work on the Shaughnessys."

"It may be queer but it's not little, *compadre*," said Hackett. "He said it's seven feet high and weighs half a ton."

"My God!" said Palliser. "Now there's a thief who thinks big."

It was tiresome work, leaning on one like Carlson. It was one of the jobs they had to do, and it was another job that wasted time, but it had to be done.

"Come on, Carlson. You know they'll be able to identify you. The sketch we got from the Identikit matches your mug shot, and your record matches the jobs."

"I don't know anything about it," said Carlson sullenly. "I want a cigarette."

"We've applied for a search warrant on your apartment, you know," said Grace. "Maybe we'll find some more evidence there. Did your wife know what you were up to?"

"I didn't do anything. I don't know what you're talking about." He'd insisted on the privilege of his phone call, and called his wife. She worked at a dress-shop downtown.

"We're going to arrange a lineup," said Palliser patiently. "Those are two pretty sharp-eyed old ladies, Carlson. They'll know you. It was a damn stupid thing to do, really calling attention to yourself like that."

"I had the same thought," said Grace. "A neat enough little trick to get let in—say he's from the gas company, the phone company—but naturally they had a good look at you before letting you in. Didn't that occur to you?"

"You go to hell," said Carlson.

"With the rise in crime these days," Palliser pursued that, "anybody is going to look hard at a caller before letting them in. A stranger. But you didn't think that far ahead, did you? Just saw the nice gimmick to get inside, and tidied yourself up to look like the respectable citizen. Which is why we picked you up so easy."

"You go to hell too," said Carlson.

Grace sighed. "It really doesn't matter whether you admit it or not, you know. You're going to be booked on armed robbery, and it's your third time round for that. You could get life." And be out on parole in seven years. Possibly, the way the legislature had been acting lately, less. "Do we waste more time on him, John?"

"Not much. We've got other things to do. Why not make it easy on yourself, Carlson? Tell us what we know."

Carlson said, "You just pick on anybody ever been in trouble. Don't bother to look for the real guy did it, just pick any ex-con. I didn't do anything."

At this point there was a knock on the door and Palliser opened it. "Listen, for God's sake come out and deal with this girl," said Sergeant Lake. "Nobody else is here and I've got the switchboard—" He looked harassed.

Palliser raised his brows at Grace, who followed him out. In the entrance hall by the switchboard a small, fierce, dark female pounced at them. "Are you the *officers* who arrested Bob? I'm Mona Carlson, and he hasn't done a thing! He wouldn't! He promised me! You just pick on people who've been in trouble, he's told me that! You tell me where he is right now! Is he in jail?" She faced up to them, a diminutive mother tiger, all but arching her back; in another minute she'd spit. She was barely five feet tall, slender, with a mop of curly black hair, milk-white complexion, flashing blue eyes.

"Not yet, Mrs. Carlson. We've applied for a warrant," said Grace politely.

"Well, you can just unapply for it! What do you claim he's done?"

"We've got good evidence that he pulled two robberies," said Palliser. "He gained entrance by saying he was from the gas company, the phone company, and beat two old women and ransacked their apartments."

"Oh! *Oh!*" She looked ready to burst into flames. "I never heard such a terrible wicked *lie!* Bob! You just like to make trouble for anybody's been in jail—go out of your *way* to—"

"Now we really don't, Mrs. Carlson," said Palliser. "Why should we? But naturally a man with a record of crime is more apt to commit another, and—"

"You just never think anybody who's been in trouble can reform and get himself straightened out and live a decent life! Oh, no! A crime gets committed, you just go for anybody like Bob and beat them up into confessing—"

"Calm down now," said Palliser. "Come on, sit down, Mrs. Carlson. Nobody's beating your husband, we really don't operate that way. We've got an identification on him from the victims, you know."

"Then they're wrong, is all!" she said furiously. "He promised me, he swore on the Bible, he'd never do the slightest thing wrong again! He loves me, he wouldn't break his promise. We've been so happy—" There were tears in her eyes, but tears of anger more than grief. "He was the first person I met in California, I didn't know a soul here, he worked in that gas station I went to—" She was calming down a little. "I couldn't get any job but in that awful bar, I liked Helen all right but some of the people who came in— And Bob *told* me about the trouble he'd been in when he asked me to marry him, he was absolutely straight with me, and he gave me his solemn promise he'd never do anything wrong again, and he *wouldn't*—"

"You know, Mrs. Carlson," said Palliser gently, "we're going to get a search warrant for your apartment, in case there's any more evidence—" And she fired up again.

"All right, all *right!* You don't need a search warrant, you can look anywhere you want to in our apartment, we haven't got anything to hide! You come right *now* and search our apartment, I *demand* that you come and search!" She was on her feet, yanking at Palliser's arm.

"You give us free permission to search your place, ma'am?" He looked past her at Sergeant Lake, who rummaged in a drawer for that little form.

"Yes—yes, I will! I want you to come *now* and look everywhere, so you'll see we haven't anything to hide! Bob hasn't done anything, I want you to—"

In the end, all three of them went back to Fountain Avenue in Palliser's Rambler. They didn't have a car, she said; they were saving to buy one.

It was a humble small apartment, but interestingly, a home had been made there. Sparse, new furniture, but well-chosen and cozily arranged, and everything neat and clean. Homemade curtains in the kitchen, and chair-pads. A few dime-store pictures, but pretty scenes and gay colors. The bedroom had only a small rug, but the dressing table was tidy, the wardrobe sparsely filled with their clothes. "It's hard for Bob to get a job, the way you *police* follow ex-cons around, but he *tries*—we get along. We're saving—we want a family. Now you just look anywhere and everywhere you want to! Go on and look! I know Bob, he hasn't done anything!"

They looked. In the likely and unlikely places. She watched them triumphantly, following them around with her arms folded and a little smile on her mouth. They didn't find anything useful to them in the living room, kitchen, or bathroom, and her smile turned scornful.

In the bedroom, they looked inside the wardrobe thoroughly, checked the pockets of his two suits and three sports jackets and slacks. They didn't find anything. There were two rather scuffed airweight suitcases at the back of the wardrobe; they were both empty.

"Those are mine," she said.

"Does your husband have any luggage?" asked Grace.

"Oh, there wasn't room for it in there. It's under the bed."

Palliser lifted the spread, reached under and brought it out. It was an old brown leather suitcase, and it was locked. "You know where the key is?" asked Grace.

"Oh—I don't know. But you *open* it! Break the lock and *open* it right *now!*"

"If you say," said Palliser sadly. He had felt the weight as he pulled it out, and he had a good idea what they were going to find. He felt sorry for Mona Carlson. He opened his knife

[123]

and after a few probings felt the lock snap. He lifted the lid of the suitcase.

"The nice evidence," said Grace; but his voice was sad too.

In the suitcase was a length of iron pipe about eighteen inches long: on one end, stains and a few hairs. The lab would do a lot with that. There was also a hundred and fifty-two dollars. "About what he'd get for the loot he's taken," said Grace.

They looked at her, standing up. She was staring down at the suitcase, hands gripped together before her, as if she were hypnotized. Slowly she looked up at them; her milky skin took on a green tinge, and Palliser said, "You'd better sit down, Mrs. Carlson." He guided her to the bed.

"You—mean—" she whispered, "you mean—he *did? That* —what you said—beating old women—with that? Bob? After he promised—promised on the Bible—he was all reformed and wouldn't ever—"

"It happens sometimes," said Palliser quietly, "but not really very often, Mrs. Carlson. We know. I'm sorry, but there it is."

"I thought—I'd helped him—get all reformed and straight," she said dully. "It wasn't *much* he'd done wrong, just stealing a little when he was in high school, and getting drunk and hitting that man—"

"That what he told you? I'm afraid a little more," said Palliser. "He's got a record of armed robbery and mugging."

"Bob?" She stared at them wildly, and then she said, "You can't—you can't trust anybody—I'll never trust another soul in my life—oh, God, I'm going to be sick—" She stumbled into the bathroom.

"You think she's all right to be left alone?" asked Grace.

Palliser hesitated, but remembering her at the office he said, "I think that one's got quite a lot of spunk, Jase. She won't think of suicide. But I hope Carlson doesn't expect her to take him back when he gets out on P.A."

"There I'll have to agree with you."

They took the suitcase back to headquarters and dropped

[124]

it off at the lab. "Have you picked up anything useful to us on the Shaughnessys?" Grace asked Duke.

"Wait for the report. Any public place like that, a million prints, mostly bad. They're still checking the stock."

Palliser and Grace went back upstairs. "He asked for a sandwich," said Sergeant Lake. "I sent out for one. Shogart and Higgins have got another parolee."

They found Carlson sitting crosslegged on the little chair smoking nervously. He looked around as they came in. "What happened to you guys? Where'd you go? Just leave me sitting here—"

"Your wife came in," said Palliser. "She gave us permission to search your apartment. We found the suitcase, Carlson, and the pipe, and the money."

There was a little silence. Carlson looked up blindly. "Mona—knows."

"That's right."

"Oh, my God," he said dully. He looked as if he were going to cry. "I meant to do it. I meant to try—what I promised her. But the damn cruddy jobs, all I could get, a real drag—and I wanted to buy her things—and a guy's got a right to have a few drinks sometimes, and it costs—" He was silent, and then he said, "I'm just so damn sorry about Mona."

"She's not the first woman who thought she could reform a crook—or a drunk—or a gambler," said Grace. "Just the latest one. You'll have time to think about what you did to her, Carlson."

"It's sacrilegious desecration and I'll sue the cemetery— I'll sue the city!" said James Power excitedly. "I never heard of such a thing and if that McGrath harridan thinks she can get away with it— At the very least it's grand theft and I want her arrested!" It wasn't the first time he'd said it.

"If you ask me she's a lunatic and ought to be put away!" said his wife Marion. Both the Powers had red hair and tempers to match.

"Now, please, please, calm down and let me explain to

these officers. You made me call the police and the regular officers wouldn't do, you had to have detectives, so let me explain everything in order," said the stocky little man who had met them at the gate. "I'm John Horelica, gentlemen, I'm the caretaker here—head caretaker. It's this matter of the tombstone Mr. Power has recently had erected on his family's plot. This plot here."

They were standing in the middle of Evergreen Cemetery. It wasn't raining today, but a cold wind was blowing and the sky looked gray.

"I promised Grandma on her deathbed!" said Power. "I promised I'd put up a stone for her and Grand-dad and great-grandfather—we never could afford—they're expensive, and it wasn't till I got the better job I could start to save—"

"Five hundred dollars!" said his wife.

"*And* the carving. The angel with the trumpet. And all the names—and a truck to bring it in and set it up—"

"Please, please," said Horelica. "The Power family plot, it's the one right beside the McGrath plot, they're old graves, they're all old graves—"

"Nineteen hundred and two Great-grandma died, and Grandma nineteen forty, but I promised her—"

"And Mrs. McGrath, first time she happened to come in here afterward, she said the tombstone was over on part of her family plot, she wanted it moved—"

"It was *not* on her plot. Not an inch!" said Marion Power.

"The woman's a lunatic," said Power. "She shouldn't be at large."

"Like to never stopped arguing at me," said Horelica. "I don't see the point in it myself, the McGrath plot is full, no room for her, so what does she care? Last body put in that plot nineteen fifty, her husband, and earliest one goes back to nineteen hundred. I mean, gentlemen, dead people are supposed to be at rest, and besides they're not *here*. Argue, argue, argue, move the tombstone, it's part on the McGrath plot."

"It was *not*," said Marion Power. "And furthermore it was

in *perfect* taste—that woman saying the angel looked pregnant and it was indecent—"

"*¡Porvida!*" said Mendoza. Hackett exploded and coughed. "Now this Mrs. McGrath, did she—"

"I was very careful to direct the men setting it up—I'd never have done it if I hadn't promised Grandma, this is an old cemetery, a run-down part of town—it was all different when my great-grandparents lived here, quite a respectable section—and as for the angel, all I can say is that Tompkins and Company are supposed to be the finest stonecutters in—"

"The best butter," said Hackett *sotto voce*.

"—And I told her she had an indecent mind to *imagine* such a thing as a pregnant angel, and furthermore I said—"

"So *I* said, finally," blared Power, "we measure the damn plot and prove it to her, and so we came out this morning to—"

"As if we wanted anything to do with the McGrath plot!" said Marion Power. "Probably a bunch of riffraff, and why your great-grandfather had to buy a plot right next to them in the first place—"

"*¡Qué mono!*" said Mendoza.

"And it's gone! Vanished! Stolen! And my God, it must weigh half a ton, how anybody—"

"Not quite, Mr. Power. Possibly five hundred pounds. And they came to find me—I was mowing the grass at the other end of the grounds. Excuse me, I don't know your names."

"Lieutenant Mendoza, Sergeant Hackett."

He ducked a little bow at them. "I had just got here, you see we don't have perpetual care like Forest Lawn, but people with plots here pay a small sum yearly for maintaining the grounds. I was *astounded*. A tombstone! But I went to look, and it is certainly gone. And Mr. and Mrs. Power insisted I call the police—"

"What about the gates?" asked Hackett. "Locked at night?"

Horelica looked flustered. "I can't say we bother about it

—such an old cemetery, we don't have many people coming. Really I'm sorry I ever took this job, I'm retired from a city job, I was with the pound, and I thought a quiet part-time job—"

"A dogcatcher!" said Hackett, and coughed tremendously.

"This Mrs. McGrath," said Mendoza gently. "Mrs. What McGrath and do you know where she lives?"

"Obnoxious!" said Marion Power. "Pushing! She always says, *I'm Mrs. Bathsheba McGrath* like she was the Queen of England—"

"Bathsheba—*¡Es hermoso sin pero!*" said Mendoza ecstatically.

"I suppose," said Hackett, shaking, "we do something about it, Luis?"

She lived on Pebblehurst Street in Monterey Park. She was in her sixties, angular and steel-spectacled, tall and erect, with gray hair as short as a man's. The little frame house was old, but painted, and the lawn was green.

She looked at the badge in Mendoza's hand and said belligerently, "Well?"

"Now it really wasn't very nice of you, Mrs. McGrath," said Mendoza gently, "to steal Mr. Power's tombstone. Was it?"

"Them," she said with a sniff. "Make a little money, have to show off. That great big monstrosity of a thing, over on Mike's family plot a good six inches—he'd have had a fit. I told 'em, but they wouldn't move it. So I did. Maybe now, if they want to put up any stone, they put it where it belongs."

"But where is it?" asked Hackett. "How in—well, how did you move it?"

She was surprised. "Didn't nobody see it? With the truck, o' course—Mike's half-ton, bought new in nineteen thirty-nine, Ford, and I've kept her runnin' good. I hooked a chain round that monstrosity and dragged her right out to the street, outside the gates. I guess I let it down kind of sudden, it busted in a few pieces, but—"

It emerged, on inquiry, that Saturday was the day when the city's refuse trucks passed along Brooklyn Avenue.

They finally caught up with the right refuse truck, its crew now industriously picking up rubbish along Velasco Avenue. The two men, questioned, said they'd already filled the truck once: the big truck with the grinding machine inside, chewing up anything and everything. "The cemetery?" said the pickup man. "Well, I noticed, sure, pieces of a tombstone, but it's an old cemetery—maybe they're throwing some out, how do I know? There was a can of cut grass, too— What? We already dumped one load, it'll all be out there—they're filling up this canyon up by Burbank—"

The pregnant angel had gone to serve ecology.

Piggott called Prudence before he went to help Higgins lean on the latest parolee brought in. "How'd you do?" he asked.

"Well, I couldn't find a dishpan, but I got an asparagus steamer. It looked about the right size. And I did just what the book said, two teaspoons of salt to the gallon at seventy-six degrees. I had a perfectly awful time catching the tetra, it's so little, and it kept going into the plants—and I caught a cardinal tetra seven times but it was always the wrong one, one of the other three." She sounded harassed. "But finally I got it, and it's been in the salt solution ever since, and it looks fine. Just swimming away."

"Well, good," said Piggott.

Grace, at one o'clock, was pursuing his little idea in that bar out on Washington Boulevard. He had introduced himself to the owner, a Mr. Seymour Watson, who was much concerned about his reputation and that of his business. Mr. Watson was the color of milk-chocolate, a deacon in his church, and anxious to cooperate with the police. Which Grace had figured any businessman with a liquor license would be.

"I'll tell you, Mr. Grace," he said, "I don't like the ones

like them to come in. These you're asking about, Robinson and Epps and Barnard. The ex-cons, men with police records. Most of the people come in here, they're decent quiet people. They don't like to find that kind in here either. But if Lonnie Epps drops in here, buys a beer, he don't do nothing or say nothing I can object to, I can't order him out." He looked troubled.

"I see that," said Grace easily. "But you don't know where either Robinson or Barnard lives?"

"I wouldn't know that. Just, I heard they're ex-cons and I don't like 'em in here. Give us all a bad name. I told that Barnard once, don't come in here, he just badmouthed me and says he didn't do nothing wrong. I can't claim he did."

"And you never heard anything about where they—" Grace's voice was drowned by Watson's sudden laugh. "Something funny?"

"It's just, that Robinson—you know the way some people think, Mr. Grace, but we're all different, isn't it the truth."

"It is. What about Robinson?"

"Well, he's from Lou'siana, seems like, and he likes his snuff. He said to me once, no place he can get it up here, and this old fellow has a little grocery on Seventy-first, he sends for it special for him. Old-fashioned! This day and age," said Mr. Watson.

Grace called in at one-thirty and got Palliser. "We'd better set up a stakeout," he said. "You and me." He told Palliser about the snuff. "I found the obliging grocer—Watson remembered the name. His daughter sends it up from St. Louis, the snuff. He tells me Robinson usually drops around Saturday afternoon to pick up a new supply. I just thought— Robinson doesn't know we've tagged him, and possibly—"

"Very possibly," agreed Palliser. "That's smart work, Jase."

"Just following my nose," said Grace.

Eight

When they got back from Monterey Park, Mendoza left Hackett telling Sergeant Lake about the tombstone, and went into his office. There were new reports on his desk; as he picked up the top one the phone rang and he reached for it automatically.

"Well, Luis, I thought you had a murder to solve," said Goldberg. "First you went to meddling in Narco business and then you forgot all about us. We thought—"

Mendoza uttered a sharp yelp. "¡Caray!—and likewise mea culpa! We ought to be better organized." Delgado had gone out of his mind entirely. "Not that we haven't had reason to —but I meant to get back to you on that, Saul."

"We've got Moreno up here now if you'd like to question him."

"I would not. Moreno's not our boy, as I told Pat. He didn't know Delgado was dead, and if he knew the name at all it was one of his boys' customers. Don't interrupt. We had a little about Delgado from you on Wednesday, next of kin—" They hadn't found his mother yet; all Narco knew was that she lived in San Diego and had remarried. Mendoza had passed that on to the San Diego force; let them look. "—But anything else you know about him I'd like. Wait a minute, I've got the autopsy report here, his effects were probably sent up from the lab. O.K., where was he living? Oh, Hartford Street, sure—"

"He wanted to help us out with this bunch, but it wasn't a thing he planned to go on doing," Goldberg said, sneezed, excused himself and blew his nose. "He'd kicked the habit, and he was going back to San Diego and get a job. But while he was undercover for us he had to look right, as if he was still part of the cult as it were, or nobody'd have talked to him. We were paying him—not much—and he had this cheap little room on Hartford Street."

"Mmh." As he listened, Mendoza dumped the contents of a manila envelope on his desk. Effects of deceased: from his one rented room. A cheap wristwatch: a dollar and ninety-two cents: a ballpoint pen: a dime-store wallet feeling thin: a handkerchief, crumpled and stained: an unopened pack of Pall Malls. He opened the wallet: two tens and a five in it, and only one of the little plastic slots for cards and snapshots was filled, with an I.D. form. *"¡Mil rayos!"* said Mendoza eyeing it. "Well, better late than never, at least here it is." The form was filled out a little carelessly: Frank Delgado, a scribbled address on Hartford Street, and under "Who to Notify in Case of Emergency," *Mrs. Anthony Tumminello,* an address in San Diego. "Yes, go on."

"To what? What've you got?"

"The mother's address. When was the last time anybody up there saw him?"

"I was wondering when you'd remember to ask. That's one reason we thought of Moreno right off. Delgado met Steve Benedittino the night he was killed, at a bar over on Broadway, uptown."

"Oh, indeed?" said Mendoza. "And Steve gave him a quarter century to go on with."

"That's right."

"Mmh. What time?" He was rapidly reading the autopsy report now. Time of death, between nine and midnight that night.

"About ten o'clock."

"Indeed, isn't that pretty? Would you know any of the people he hung around with, and where?"

"Not much. I suppose he was still keeping up with some of his old pals, to look right—a pack of the freaked-out punks, and I don't mean kids—twenty on up. Punks who got hooked as kids and are just waiting around to die—which they don't know. We've had some of that crowd in here from time to time. Frank's closest pal used to be Arty Lopez, and there was Fritz Nye, Chester Larsen, some girls—" Goldberg was shuffling papers—"Shirley Neely, Ann Parker— Hell, Luis, just names for the carbon copies. You know the type. Just punks. Freaked-out punks. Well, that particular bunch used to have a hangout—the Parker girl's uncle owns a half block on South Vermont that's condemned, only nobody's got round to tearing it down yet. The punks took over one of the stores, have their own pad—"

"*Asi, asi*. Rock and the new morality."

"No, they go in for Yoga, I think," said Goldberg. "The meditation and chanting."

"I'd like to see Steve sometime if he's got five minutes. How Delgado was acting when he saw him."

"I'll pass it on," said Goldberg.

"That'll do for the moment, thanks, Saul. Art!" Hackett looked in. "I know we've got excuses, but we haven't done a damned thing on Delgado. What did you do on Wednesday?"

"Damnation," said Hackett, startled. "So we haven't. I got sidetracked on something—"

"Well, we'd better do some poking around now." Mendoza told him what Goldberg had said. "Have a look at his room, not that I expect there'll be any clues there. Possibly the pad on south Vermont."

"We had. I suppose you know where Hartford Street is?"

"Somewhere over past the Stack, north."

"Oh," said Hackett. "Delgado was on his way home. From meeting Benedittino in a quiet bar where the freaked-out punks weren't likely to see."

"I think so," said Mendoza; he swiveled around and looked out across the city. "It rather looks that way, doesn't it? On the other hand, he'd been making up to this Lamb's sister as an excuse to linger around there. If one of them had any little suspicion—*Pues no*. It wasn't anything to do with that."

"A hunch."

"A feeling," said Mendoza. "The slit throat—nothing to do with ill-gotten profits or even treason, from their viewpoint. Something more emotional. I wonder if he was mixed up with a girl—Narco wouldn't know that, I suppose."

"It's time for lunch," Hackett pointed out.

"Have a look at his room. You're on a diet anyway," said Mendoza.

It was a dreary and anonymous room. Delgado had just been camping out here. There wasn't even a landlady to notice whether roomers were in or out: the building had a row of dingy storefronts at street level, and the tenant in the drugstore on the corner collected rents for the owner. Upstairs, there were two floors of cubicles partitioned off, masquerading as the *Rooms by the Week* advertised downstairs. Probably all of them much the same as this one: a narrow bed, no rug, no chair, a three-drawer unpainted chest, an ancient speckled mirror on the wall, a window with a broken pane. The bathroom was down the hall. There were a few clothes in the drawers, a suit hung up on the back of the door. There wasn't a scrap of writing in the place.

They went back to Federico's for lunch. Glasser was there; he said that Mrs. Cole's husband had come and gone, the body had been released today. That was the autopsy report Mendoza hadn't read.

"These former pals," said Hackett, "you know we'll get nothing, whether they knew what he was doing or not. The blank stares. The jingle of love beads. *¿Para qué es esto?*"

"Your accent doesn't improve. I'd just like to have a look at them, Arturo. Now we've got back to him. What's going on at the office, Henry?"

"These damn men on P.A.," said Glasser. "George is fed

to the teeth, he says it's a complete waste of time and we'll never make him this way. We're getting nothing out of them, how could we?"

Mendoza looked thoughtful but said nothing to that. Finishing his coffee, he said, "Come on, Art—let's waste a little time ourselves."

When they found it—Goldberg had supplied the address —it looked to be just another empty store; the whole block of empty stores was ramshackle, looking ready to fall down. This one had been a florist's shop once, the remnants of the sign over the door told them. The door was open, at least unlocked, and they stepped inside. All that remained of the florist was a half-partition in the middle of the place, and a stained sink at the back. There was a thin carpet in here, and all the appurtenances expectable. Floor cushions, beads hung in the archway, untidy stacks of books and pamphlets looking untouched; the place was artificially dimmed by the usual huge posters, some of them black-lighted, covering the front window and all the walls. One dim electric bulb burned at the back of the place. There were five people in the front room, when they looked close.

As they came in, the door letting in a shaft of cold March light, there was a little stir, and a voice said, slurred, "Hey, who's it? Fritzie?"

Mendoza found a light switch and pushed it: a rank of ceiling lights came on. "Hey! Who did that? Who the hell are you?"

Of the five people, two—probably—were female. They all bore the familiar marks, sad and frustrating to any lawman, who knew the odds against them. The dirty, sloppy clothes, the long greasy hair uncared-for, the bare feet, the general lassitude. They seemed to draw together against the men at the door, the men conventionally dressed, shaven and clean, the men on a schedule in life, with a purpose.

"They're fuzz," said one of the males, looking at Hackett.

"What the hell they want?" One of the girls got up to her

knees uncertainly, peering through a thicket of hair.

"Did any of you here know Frank Delgado?" asked Mendoza. Shrugs and mutters. "Do you know he's dead?"

"I heard somebody say—I thought he went back to Dago. He said he was."

"Name, please?"

"Why the hell—you got no business here, this is a private pad—my name's Lopez, and suppose you get the hell out."

"Arty Lopez. You're expecting Fritz. Is Chester Larsen here?" No answers. He surveyed them with annoyance, and brushed his moustache back and forth. "All of you sitting here practicing meditation?"

"Thass right, man—meditate, meditate, thass our thing." The first slurred voice. The girls giggled a little foolishly.

Probably all of them had had something—the Mary Jane, the bennies, the speed. The sad thing was, Mendoza could take them in now—they were all of age, on looks; and by tomorrow they'd all be out again. Court appearance ordered: probation. And the day after that they'd be right back here. Most of them would have little records: shoplifting, petty theft, purse-snatching; it was how they lived, without routine or direction. Of course, they were taking a quick route to an early death, but meanwhile they cluttered up other people's lives.

Mendoza turned and went out, Hackett after him, and breathed the fresh air, cold after the rain. "And what did that get us?" asked Hackett.

"I had a look at them." Mendoza rocked a little, heel to toe. "Drugs do things to people. Inhibitions get lost. And rationalities."

"Indubitably," said Hackett.

"Well, let's get back to base and see what's going on."

When they got there, they found the office in a state of quiet excitement. Shogart was sitting at his desk saying, "I told you sooner or later we'd drop on him. It's the routine that breaks cases."

"I don't believe it," said Higgins, his heavy jaw looking stubborn. "Luis, thank God you're back—we've got this thing, but to me it says nothing at all—we're waiting for his P.A. officer, see what he can tell us."

Businesslike, Shogart handed Mendoza a file from Records. "Here he is, our boy on Reynolds and Jowett. I never did think we should have put Reynolds in Pending. Teamwork and the old routine legwork always gets you there."

"Five words!" said Higgins.

Mendoza opened the file without sitting down. "Who've we got? Giorgio Zapada. On P.A. from Susanville. That's minimum security, E.M. What was he in for? Oh, latest time, horse-theft. *¿Cómo no?*" There were earlier charges: Zapada was now fifty-two. When he was nineteen he'd been charged with rape, found guilty, sentenced to ten-to-twenty. Paroled. The second charge, and all the rest, was theft: mostly horses and cattle, a few dogs. Mendoza's brows shot up. "*¡Caray!* What the hell is this?" Then, money: two hundred bucks, from one Floyd Buckmaster. Trespassing—little charges. At the age of forty-five he had been brought up on an obscure count of "being an incorrigible and uncontrollable person," and sent to Susanville on indefinite sentence. "Now what is this character doing here?" asked Mendoza.

"Look, for God's sake," said Higgins. "He got on this list because of that old rape, and he was paroled last New Year's Day. So E.M. on his dogged routine comes across him selling newspapers at Broadway and Third, and fetches him in. And while we're questioning him, if you can call it that, he comes out with this—"

"He said it, he said it!" said Shogart. "He said, 'God bless the parole board.' Just like the note. He's our boy. You can see he's illiterate, a dumb lout."

"Just exactly what did you say to him before he came out with that?" asked Mendoza interestedly.

"Well, we'd been asking him where he was on Monday night. On account of Jowett. And he couldn't remember where he was. And then he said something funny about night being the best time to walk, but not in the city. And then—"

"I remember exactly what he said," said Shogart. "He said there weren't any pretty sounds in the city at night, but God bless the parole board to let him out free, even if it had to be here."

"My God, it's nothing," said Higgins. "He's a queer bird, but it doesn't say he's the X on Reynolds and Jowett."

"He fits the description of the kind we're looking for," said Shogart. "I see we want to talk to his P.A. officer, but otherwise I'd say we've got as much evidence as we're going to get."

"I called Welfare and Rehab," said Higgins. "Ballard's chasing him down. His name's Knight. If they can find him, he'll come right over."

Glasser was smoking quietly, contributing nothing, but his glance was a little sarcastic on Shogart.

"So, we wait to see what Knight says about him. Where is he?"

"First interrogation room."

Mendoza went down there and looked in, curious about this character. Zapada was a powerful man, tall and broad. He had a flat, almost Slavic face, dark-skinned, with bushy eyebrows and rather wild gray hair. He was dressed in non-descript old clothes, unmatching, casual. He sat quietly, and looked up at Mendoza without curiosity or fear, only patience. "We're sorry to keep you waiting here, Mr. Zapada. We're trying to find Mr. Knight."

Zapada nodded once. "Mr. Knight, he is good man. He will tell about me."

Palliser and Grace had been waiting, in the Rambler parked across the street from the little grocery, for nearly three hours. At intervals one of them got out and put another nickel in the parking meter. Grace told him about the new camera, and Palliser said thoughtfully he might get one, they'd want pictures of the baby.

At three-thirty a black-and-white cruised by and stopped, and the two uniformed men got out. "Excuse me, sir, but we noticed you've been parked here quite awhile, and wondered if you're having any trouble." The polite overture to investigating suspicious behavior. Palliser hauled out the badge.

"We're on a stake-out," he said. "And I hope to God he shows pretty soon, we're both bored as hell." The uniformed men laughed and went back on their route.

At four o'clock Grace was saying sleepily that he'd bet when they got back to the office they'd find that D.M.V. list waiting. "That is the damndest thing—the boys on bicycles. Three of them. And I can't imagine what kind of reason even a lunatic—"

"There he comes," said Palliser, sitting up. "Isn't that him?" Across the street a tall man was crossing the intersection toward the little grocery.

"That's just who," said Grace. They had seen his mug shot by now, of course. Robinson was one of the other two heisters minus the Afro; he was big, very black, and by his confident air, had no reason to suspect that he'd been fingered. "Let him go in."

They waited until he was in the store, got out of the car and went across the street. The store had a creaky screen door and an old-fashioned smell inside. Robinson was at the rear, back turned, in front of the counter. That Colt .45 was still around somewhere: either Robinson or Clarence Barnard had it. Without consultation, both Grace and Palliser drew their guns.

But they took him completely by surprise. The aged grocer had his head bent too, didn't see them approaching, to alarm Robinson by his own alarm. They each took Robinson by an arm, and Palliser said, "You're under arrest, Robinson."

He whirled and tried to pull away, but they were too close. He swore and swung at Palliser, but Grace already had the cuffs out; they caught him between them, and before he could try anything else got the cuffs on him.

"Oh, Lordy, oh, Lordy," said the grocer, agitated. "You get him outta here—I dint know he was no bad man! I just do him a little favor—I don't know nothin'—"

"That's all right," said Grace, "we know that." He went over Robinson then, and came up with the Colt from an outside jacket pocket; he looked at it pleasedly. "Two down, one to go. Let's take him in."

Robinson swore monotonously all the way in. The only other thing he said was, "How you drop on me, man?"

"Brother Epps mentioned your name," said Grace. "You and Clarence. Has Clarence got a gun too?" But that just set Robinson swearing harder.

At the office, they found Mendoza, Hackett, Higgins, Shogart and Glasser all sitting around talking about Zapada and still waiting for Knight. Neither Palliser nor Grace thought there was anything to Zapada, but of course he'd have to be looked at harder. At the moment, they had unfinished business of their own. They took Robinson into an interrogation room and started questioning him.

.The only thing they hoped to get out of him was the whereabouts of Barnard, but he only growled at Palliser's tough brusqueness and Grace's soft persuasion. He didn't know where Barnard was, he wasn't saying nothing to no pigs, and that was that. At five o'clock they took him over to the jail on Alameda and booked him in.

"I hope they don't put him in the same cell as Epps," said Grace. "We might have another homicide on our hands."

When they came into Robbery-Homicide again, everybody was in Mendoza's office. "Knight finally got here," said Sergeant Lake. "And your list arrived from the D.M.V."

Palliser took it and uttered a dismal groan. The computer up in Sacramento had come up with two hundred and fifty-three 1955 Dodges registered in L.A. County. "I don't understand it," he complained. "The damn car's nearly twenty years old! There can't be that many—the computer's got a screw loose."

"I don't know," said Grace. "That was a pretty good model, I've heard. Kind of a medium-sized reliable car goes perking along, owner to owner—or kept by an original owner, good transportation. But this is going to be one hell of a job, John."

"Are you telling me? When I think of all the legwork—"

"On the other hand," said Grace, "there are a lot of boys on bicycles around. Like Timmy Jordan."

Thinking of Timmy, Palliser smiled. "And let's hope this lead turns up the lunatic before he gets the urge again."

"Amen," said Grace. "I wonder what the Lieutenant's decided about that Zapada."

"I just don't see old Giorgio doing anything like that," said Knight dubiously when he'd heard all about it. "He's a queer old fellow, you can see that, but he's really a gentle man."

"That rape," said Shogart.

Knight laughed. "In his distant youth. He told me all about that. The girl had a grudge on him, she'd been making up to him and he wanted no part of her, she was a bad girl, he said. She claimed rape, and because he is a queer one—and evidently was even then—he got convicted. It's the only count of violence on him."

"We noticed," said Mendoza. "What about all these other charges?"

Knight laughed again. "Look, the old guy's what they call an anachronism. He belongs to some other time or place. He hails from a wide place in the road called Lookout, up in Modoc County, all he knows is farm work and the great outdoors. Nature. I know about all those charges, he told me all about it. That first one—the horse. The man who owned the horse was a bad man, he said, worked the horse too hard, whipped it. So he took the horse up into the mountains to a herd of wild ones where it'd be safe."

"Well, good for him," said Hackett. "The rest of these—"

"That's right. He's fond of animals, got a touch with them, I'd say. He'd see a dog not treated right, or some other animal

—most farmers, I'd guess, take good care of their livestock, it's property after all, but you get good and bad anywhere. He just couldn't stand to see cruelty. He'd take the animal, do what he could for it, see it got a decent home. Where he got into trouble was trying to give stolen cattle to nice kind farmers. Look, he's simple—I don't think he understands the basics of personal ownership. I really don't."

"How do you mean?" asked Shogart. "Is he mentally retarded? He sounded a little that way to me."

"No, no. He's just—well, about these animals. I tried to get him to admit they'd belonged to other people. Personal possessions. But he couldn't grasp the idea at all. He just said, 'We all belong to God, Mr. Knight, but we belong to ourselves too. The animals—little dog or cat, big horse or cow, the wild things, they are creatures of God and if we do wrong to them we do wrong to God. The animal is free to belong to itself.' And that's what I get every time I try to explain it." He looked frustrated. "Oh, and that two hundred bucks. It was money this Buckmaster owed him, he says. For labor. I don't know the ins and outs, but I gather that Buckmaster lost his farm later, and I could guess that Buckmaster thought because the old man's a little simple, he could get by not paying him."

"But he said the same thing as the note," said Shogart stubbornly. Piggott had come in just after Knight arrived, and was still reading the package on Zapada interestedly.

"Oh, hell," said Knight. " 'God bless the parole board!' He talks about God a lot. He doesn't go to church, but he talks about God. He's not a city man, he can't abide the city, but he's got to stay here while he's on P.A., it was a condition of the board. Sometimes I don't think those men have the sense God gave geese. But from what I know of him, I can see why in a way. Let him go out in the wilds some place, any P.A. officer'd have to drive half a day to see him, and likely he'd go off in the woods by himself six months at a time, think nothing of it—that's the way he'd rather live. What I'm telling you is, he's absolutely harmless. A gentle old fellow."

Shogart looked dubious. "Quite a character," said Piggott.

"These two cases—my God, a woman beaten to death and raped, and now this young fellow knifed for what he had on him— No," said Knight. "Not Giorgio. Did he say anything else besides these famous five words?"

Mendoza was brooding over steepled hands. "He added to that, 'even if it had to be here.' "

"Sure," said Knight. "He can't abide a town, but at least he's free to walk around, go to the parks or wherever. I got him this little job, enough to pay for a room, food. He'll be off P.A. in another six months, and he'll make for the wilds *pronto*. I've tried to do what I could for him, I could see him just getting into more of the same trouble wherever he goes —see a kitten being mistreated or something—you know. But he says he's going somewhere all by himself. Up in the mountains, he says, where everything is nice and quiet because there aren't any people. I can see him doing that. Build himself a little shelter, dig a well, and stay there the rest of his life. Look—you aren't thinking of *charging* him with this? It's ridiculous!"

"Mmh—hardly," said Mendoza. "*Uno no puede complacer a todo el mundo*—you can't please everybody. Thanks very much, Mr. Knight. You can take Mr. Zapada away and give him back his newspapers."

Knight looked relieved. "I like the old fellow, you know. Queer as he is. Thanks."

"Well, it sounded suspicious as hell," said Shogart. He was scowling a little.

Mendoza went home and told Alison and Mrs. MacTaggart about the tombstone, which was duly appreciated. "Honestly, the things you run into!" said Alison. The cats were crouched over dinner, but El Señor abandoned liver instantly when he heard the bottle of rye taken down, and nearly landed in Máiri's shepherd's-pie on the counter.

"Och, you villainous creature," she scolded, fending him off.

"The offspring," said Alison, "have actually progressed to Lesson Twelve. I mean really progressed, picking out letters and words, not just making up stories about the pictures. That's a wonderful book."

And presently Mendoza was read to by the twins, who pointed out to him how they knew it was F, "Because the top line is bended over," said Johnny, and how the double G's "Look just like little eggs," said Terry, "so you know it's eggs with the eh part in front. *Mamacita* says easy. Only, Daddy, how do the little letters say *huevo?*"

"Now that we'd better go into later," said Mendoza diplomatically, "after you've got the English firmly in mind." And of course naturally their offspring would be smart; but he had to admit that the book was a wonderful help.

Over dinner he told Alison about Zapada. "The funny gentle old man," said Alison. "I hope they let him wander off by himself—people never understand that kind."

"I can think of one who might," said Mendoza. "Off that list too. That Arnold Hahn, who likes animals better than people."

Alison laughed. "And quite often so do I." At this point Cedric came ambling in, refreshed by a long, long drink of milk, and before even once licking his hairy chops he came to lay his head lovingly in Alison's lap. *"¡Qué molesto!* You awful *animal,* this dress has to be dry-cleaned!" She sprang up and wiped off milk vigorously. Cedric looked aggrieved.

Piggott went home and asked about the cardinal tetra. "I believe it's done the trick," said Prudence. "That spot's practically gone, whether it was fungus or not." The little tetra was swimming jauntily about in the porcelain asparagus steamer, a flash of red and blue. "But when I was feeding them awhile ago, I noticed something else. One of those head-and-taillight tetras, it looks queer. As if it's getting bloated or something. How's your arm?"

"Fine," said Piggott. "I think we can put this one back in the tank."

"Well, you can catch it," said Prudence firmly. "I never had such a job—they're like forked lightning. And I've got a beef and noodle casserole and would you like some of those breaded Italian squash sticks? They only take fifteen min-utes—"

"Yes, please."

"And you haven't studied the Sunday School lesson and you've got two classes tomorrow, at both services."

"Yes," said Piggott absently. "God knows in this job we see sufficient of the devil's work to get—motivated, you might say. It's the last two chapters of Luke, I don't have to study that. Easter's early this year. Say, that one does look a little different, doesn't it? Fatter. Better keep an eye on it."

And over dinner he told her about Zapada. "What a queer old man! But—"

"Yes," said Piggott. "I've got no doubt at all, Prue, that a lot of people thought Saint Francis was awfully queer too."

Higgins and Steve, with the little Scottie at their heels, spent the evening measuring for partitions out in the garage. In the middle of writing down figures, Steve suddenly stopped and said, "I just had a funny thought, George. Gosh, we were lucky you were *there*."

"What?" said Higgins.

"I mean, when—when Dad got killed. That you were there, a friend of his, and not married or anything. So you could take care of us. And now we've got Margaret Emily and— It was kind of lonesome, when Mother was working and not there when Laura and I got home from school. I was just thinking—"

Higgins looked at him, nearly-thirteen Steve Dwyer who was going to look so much like Bert, and he said noncommittally, "Well, I guess I was lucky too, Steve. It kind of works both ways. Was that a hundred and four or a hundred and six?"

The day watch hadn't left any jobs for the night men. Usually it was the other way round. In the old days, before the merger, bodies got found anywhere at any time, but a little oftener when there was light to see them. But robbery and robbery with violence got committed oftener at night.

They drifted in, one by one, and Rich Conway said, sitting down at Higgins' desk, "How's about setting up another double date on Tuesday?" He was dating another LAPD officer, Margot Swain up at Wilcox Street, and she and Phil liked each other.

"O.K. with me," said Landers. "I'll ask Phil. Say, I just had a thought. We're both off, we could make it early. That '1776' is on at the Pantages, why not take the girls?"

"How much are the tickets?" asked Conway cautiously.

"We can ask, anyway." Landers got out the phone book.

"Damn it," said Galeano, "I could hardly button these pants, I must have picked up a few pounds."

"Told you so," said Landers, dialing.

"I never gain weight. One-eighty ever since I got out of high school."

Schenke was reading the note Lake had left for them. "They picked up that Robinson. Two down, one to go. He had the Colt, and we haven't heard about any other gun, on that trio."

"Which isn't to say Barnard hasn't got one," said Galeano, unwrapping a chocolate mint.

Landers put the phone down and said to Conway, "First row balcony, five bucks."

"Hell," said Conway, "figure in dinner, that's the best part of forty bucks ruined, Tom. Can you afford it?"

"Let's live dangerously. It's supposed to be a damned good show."

"I know, I'd like to see it too. It's only money, after all."
The phone shrilled and Galeano picked it up. "Ugh?" he said through a chocolate mint. "O.K. A two-eleven in progress, liquor store Third and Alvarado."

"We'll take it." Landers got up. They went downstairs in a hurry, the unspoken thought in both their minds. Conway loped, keeping up with Landers' longer stride; they took Landers' Corvair. It wasn't far, and the traffic fairly thin at this hour.

At the scene, the black-and-white was in front, doors open. The liquor store was deserted except for an excited fellow in a bloodstained white shirt, who at sight of their drawn guns shouted, "The alley outside—he took a shot at me but I'm O.K.—suspected when he came in, and I told Harry call the police—the officers chased—"

They ran out to the narrow alley bisecting business fronts here, for deliveries, for refuse pickup. Two uniformed men were halfway down from the street. They glanced round at Conway and Landers. "There's a nine-foot chain-link fence up there," said one. "He won't clear that, and we know he's up there. *Come out with your hands up!*" he bellowed. *"You're covered! Drop your gun and come out!"*

Four shots spat at them from the end of the alley, and all four of them returned the fire.

"Is anybody hit?" asked Landers.

"Nope. *Come out, you're covered!*" But this time they got only silence. "Unless it's him. Fred, move the unit up, let's get some light—"

The other Traffic man, holstering his gun, went back to the car. A minute later the car's headlights shot twin streaks of light up the alley, to show the long limp body up there by the chain-link fence, unmoving.

They went to look at it. "Barnard," said Landers to Conway. "By the mug shot. So he had a gun too." It was an old Ivor-Johnson .32. Barnard was dead.

One of the Traffic men said heavily, "I wonder which one

of us got him." Ballistics would be looking at all their guns, to find out; and there'd be a hearing up in I.A., and the official report rendered: justifiable homicide.

Landers said, "Three down. At least one thing cleared away."

One thing less on the day watch's list. But doubtless other things would be coming up.

Nine

Mendoza's subconscious was working at half speed at least, and when he came in at eight-thirty on Sunday morning he asked Sergeant Lake to see if Carey was in. That wasn't as perennially busy an office as this: Carey probably took Sunday off. Hackett came in as he waited, with the reports the night watch had left.

"They got Barnard. He tried to pull a heist alone, and Tom and Rich and the Traffic men had a little shoot-out. Barnard's dead, Ballistics'll say which gun did it."

"Three down," said Mendoza. "Carey? I wasn't sure you'd be in."

"I am today. Some statements to get. Don't tell me you're finally taking an interest."

"Only as adviser. It suddenly occurred to me, if we're right and the Borchers woman had that wad of cash dating from thirty years back, the Donahues and a lot of other people are very unobservant and incurious, but then most people are. If—"

"Why?"

"My good imbecile, they'd all be silver-certificate notes. Worth this or that to collectors now, more than face value." Carey reacted belatedly with a little gasp. "A lot of people wouldn't notice, of course. Anybody who did probably wouldn't call it to her attention. And I'd say it was very typical of the penny-pincher miser like Mrs. Borchers not to be aware of that herself. But if you can possibly track down any of the actual money she paid out—maybe Mrs. Donahue squirrels dollars away in a teapot—and they're silver-certificate notes, there you are, you'll know she had that hoard."

"My God," said Carey, "that never crossed my mind. Of course you're right. But we found the rest, Mendoza. At a Security bank in Hollywood. Borchers had incorporated himself, and there it was in an ordinary savings account, inactive for thirty years. But, my God, seventy-five G.'s in the old bills—unless the Donahues still have some of the cash she paid them, there'd be no way to trace—she didn't spend much money, you know. Any more than she had to. Of course there's the doctor—she kicked like a bay steer at his charges, but evidently he'd convinced her she had to take the medicine to prevent a stroke."

"Well, it was just a little idea," said Mendoza. He started to put the phone down when Hackett took it from him.

"Carey—don't go away for a minute. Have you got on your books a girl described as Negro, about twenty, a hundred and ten, five-five? She—"

"Why, have you got one?"

"Central Receiving's got her. The Traffic men shot it up to our night watch because it looked like assault with intent. She was found about midnight up against the curb along Vernon just down from Santa Barbara. Beaten up and probably raped."

"My God, that could be this Eileen House. I didn't see the mother, she called in—wait a minute, here's the report —at eight-fifteen to report her missing. Nineteen, that's right. She goes to L.A.C.C., said to be home every day by four o'clock, and she wasn't. That's all I've got on it. I'll call Mrs. House, see if this is the girl."

"Right." Hackett put the phone down. Mendoza was reading the notes on Barnard. "We've got some of the witnesses on the Shaughnessys coming in today to sign the formal statements. That cleans up the paperwork. Now if we ever get anything from the lab—"

"And I want to read over what they had to say again, see if anything rings any bells. Where'd Wanda put—" Mendoza found the little pile of transcribed notes, neatly typed up by their secretary, but he didn't immediately start reading them. He said to himself, "The rest of that half million. *Dios,* just sitting in a bank account for thirty years—but what the hell did happen to that woman? Oh, well, Carey's problem."

Hackett shrugged at him and went out, but came back almost at once with Higgins and Glasser. They never saw Piggott on Sundays until after church. "At long last," said Hackett, "S.I.D. is ready to give forth." Scarne came in behind them and nodded at Mendoza.

"You know we like to be thorough. But we haven't done you much good." He laid a rough diagram on Mendoza's desk, and they went to look over his shoulder. "That's not to scale. The pharmacy, with bodies marked. The smock Shaughnessy was wearing had powder burns on it, so he was shot at close range—up to three feet, probably closer."

"By somebody right on the opposite side of the counter," said Mendoza, "just where a customer would stand."

"I suppose. There was a mess of latents all over the counter, which is covered with Formica and takes prints just fine. Not very many whole ones, of course. Some of Shaughnessy's. Of the whole bunch, there are ten prints good enough to classify, and none of them are in our records or known to the Feds. On the outside of the cash register there were some more of Shaughnessy's, and a couple of Mrs. Shaughnessy's. There weren't any powder burns on the girl's clothes—she was about three feet behind her father. Or on Mrs. Shaughnessy's, and she was farther away toward the front of the store. Which could indicate that all the bullets were fired from roughly one position, in front of this rear counter."

"Why didn't Mrs. Shaughnessy scream, or run out?"

asked Higgins suddenly. "That struck me at the time, you know. All right, say he went past her up the store like a regular customer going to the counter at the back. Say even she didn't see the gun or hear what he said, if he said anything. I'd have a guess that Shaughnessy was shot first, then the girl, and while that could happen fast, still it'd be six, seven, eight seconds or more. She'd have had time, after the first shot, to run out and scream."

"Would she?" said Scarne. "Look at this." He tapped the diagram. "That was an old store, not that I think many newer ones are built much different. Look at these front counters, one up each side of the store. They curve round in front so there's a counter facing the door on each side too. Joined to the wall. That store is forty-eight feet long from the front door to the rear counter—the counters along the side walls are twenty feet, from about five feet inside the door, and the only opening where you can get behind them is at the other end, where they just stop four feet out from the wall. There's continuous glass-fronted cupboards built in the wall behind them. The counters are twenty inches deep and there's just two feet two inches of standing space behind the counters."

"You were thorough," said Mendoza. "I see what you mean. Say the first she knew of anything happening was the first shot. She looked up, and of course sudden shock has the effect on some people of paralyzing them—mmh, yes, like Ada Gibbon—but in any case, to get out from behind the counter she'd have had to run toward the gunman. Not surprising she didn't."

Higgins nodded slowly over the diagram. "And while the girl was being shot, she realized that, stood there either paralyzed or whatever, and then the gun was pointing at her."

"Was it?" said Scarne. "Look at some photographs." He opened a manila folder. The first photograph, glossy eight by ten, showed Sarah Shaughnessy's body sprawled behind the counter. She'd been a little plump; but even in this photograph, not taken to flatter, you could see she'd had shapely legs, regular features. She lay face up with her head propped up slightly by something underneath, behind the glass counter. Scarne took it away and substituted another: the same scene minus the body. There was a rank of drawers built into the wall below the counter level, beneath the cupboards above, and one of them was open all the way; it contained a neat array of boxed lipsticks, upended in rows. There was a shipping carton on the floor beside the drawer, half full of more lipsticks.

"*¡Alla va!*" said Mendoza softly. "A nice point, Bill. She never had a chance to run. She was probably on her knees behind the counter, putting the lipsticks away in the drawer, she may never have seen him come in. And when she heard the first shot, it'd take her a minute to get to her feet, in that awkward narrow space behind the counter. *Interesante.* He might never have seen her till he turned from shooting the first two and saw her just standing up. And that's another point—maybe on his way out already, so he was close enough to make sure of her. There was that wild bullet—I don't think he's a marksman."

"The stock is intact," said Scarne. "Nothing missing, by his books. Just three people dead. We told you about the gun. Have you had the autopsy reports yet?"

"We should have them sometime today. And the devil of all this is," said Mendoza, lighting a new cigarette, "he really needn't have been a marksman. He could be or he couldn't be. One bullet went wild, yes. But in the relatively close confines of that store—I want to look at what all the witnesses said again. Art, you and George might get over to Central Receiving and look at that assault. Whoever she is, she's our business."

But twenty minutes later Hackett was still out in the communal office, talking to Lake, who was resigned to getting back on a diet. They were comparing the merits of those they'd tried when Mendoza looked out of his office with a report in his hand and said, "Jimmy—oh, Art, you said some of these witnesses are coming in today. This John Salter one of them?"

"I think so," said Lake, looking at a list.

"I haven't sorted them out yet," said Hackett. "The night men took most of those."

"Yes, and I hadn't seen this one before—Wanda probably still had Tom's notes. I want to see him when he comes in."

"I'll keep an eye out," said Lake.

"George went to the hospital," said Hackett. "What was all that about silver certificates? They're all called in."

"Which is precisely the point," said Mendoza absently, still looking at the report in his hand. "With this sea of paper floating around, and basic economics—which is a very simple subject—not getting taught any more, how many of these brainwashed citizens have any grasp of the fact that the pretty engraved paper is just a damned worthless I.O.U.? It's money to them, and the bit about the silver—" He stopped. He said suddenly, "*¡Vaya por Dios—de mal en peor!* If I was an honest man I ought to resign right now. My God. Talk about basic—and they say money talks—"

"What's hit you?"

"And damn it, you should have seen it too! Of all the witless wonders—I said it, and we sat there nodding at each other like idiots, which we were."

"What the hell are you talking about?" asked Hackett, following him back into the office.

"Delgado!" said Mendoza as if it were a swear-word. He flung himself into his chair. "It just hit me when I said *money*. Words of one syllable. You went and looked at the body. What was on him?"

"Hardly a thing. A few odds and ends, the key to his room."

"*Pues sí.* Prints identified him, and when we heard where he lived, from Narco, we asked the lab to go look—we were a little busy with Jowett, and besides Delgado was killed right where he was found. And eventually the lab sent up his personal effects. And then we heard that he'd met Steve Benedittino that night and been handed a quarter century. So I said to you, and you agreed, he was on his way home. *Mea culpa!*" said Mendoza. "I'm going senile. He'd already been home, because he'd left his wallet there with all his money in it."

"Oh, for God's—of all the basic— We both ought to re-sign," said Hackett. "But where the hell could he have been going without any money? At that time of night?"

"I am damned if I know. But let's keep the eye on the ball, Art, and not go goofing off like that again. *¡Dios!* Going senile!"

Sergeant Lake looked in. "Say, there's a cycle man here asking if he can see you. It's something to do with Jowett's funeral yesterday."

"*¿Qué?*" Mendoza was interested. "So, shove him in."

When the uniformed man came in he looked hesitantly between Hackett and Mendoza, who got up. "I'm Mendoza. Sergeant Hackett. You've got something to tell us?"

"I'm Cliff Flavian, sir." Like most cycle men, volunteering for the somewhat more dangerous job of patrolling on a motorcycle, he was very big and broad, and his high boots and wide belt made him look bigger; but he was a young man, about twenty-eight, and in the presence of top brass here he looked a little uncertain. He was a good-looking man, dark, with straight features. "I don't want to waste your time, Lieutenant. Ordinarily I wouldn't have thought much about it. But I knew it was a murder. I know Bill Moss, sir, we were at the Academy together, and he and his partner answered the first call on it, he told me about it. This Jowett who got knifed. Murder one."

"So?" said Mendoza.

"It's probably nothing at all," said Flavian uncomfortably, "but I just thought in case it did mean anything, you ought to hear about it. You know we get sent out to handle the traffic at funerals. If they expect a good many cars, escort 'em to the cemetery. Well, I got chased over to the Everett Funeral Home yesterday, and it's a big one, there was another funeral about the same time so they had the names posted, and I saw it was this Jowett's funeral. I wasn't inside, I was posted outside to direct people to the right entrance into the parking lot and so on. And the first thing that struck me a little funny was that the widow was all alone. Usually there's somebody—family, or close friends. There were people there already, they could see she was alone, getting out of the limousine, but nobody made a move to go up to her."

"Nothing much in that," said Mendoza. "She probably hasn't any family here. Big funeral?"

"There must have been sixty, seventy people there. Mostly young people, that is in the thirties, but I understand he was, they'd have friends that age."

"And people who knew him at work," said Hackett.

"I suppose so. He was buried up in the Hollywood Hills section of Forest Lawn. Nearly everybody went to the grave-side service, maybe twenty-five cars. It wasn't far off the road, I was just hanging around to point them in the right direction to get out." Flavian hesitated. "It doesn't sound like much now I'm telling you. I don't know, maybe they were all just respecting her privacy. But after that service was over, there wasn't but one woman went up to Mrs. Jowett. The rest of them never went near her—just trooped back to their cars and left."

Mendoza stopped with the lighter in his hand. "*¿Qué es esto?* That is just a little queer, isn't it, Art? Or is it?"

"Well, people do generally hang around and utter all the clichés," said Hackett. "But, Luis—"

"And another thing," said Flavian. "At the funeral home, before, I saw her come in—in the big limousine, you know —that's how I knew who she was. And on the front steps going in she looked at this other woman there—for a second I thought there was going to be a fight. I tell you, those two looked daggers at each other. It was funny, at a funeral."

Mendoza sat up. *"¿Cómo dice?* Or again, is it? Had Jowett had something on the side, and she knew it? What did the woman look like?"

Flavian considered. "Pretty. Cute. About twenty-five, brown hair, call it five-five, good figure."

"Así, así," said Mendoza. "The other woman."

"But, Luis—"

"That's about it," said Flavian. 'It just struck me as a little odd, and seeing that Jowett was murdered, I thought—"

"Yes, thanks very much, very interesting," said Mendoza. "Thanks for coming in."

"But, Luis," said Hackett when Flavian had gone out, "whatever that rigmarole says—some ex-friend of hers, or the other woman—it's nothing to do with the murder. On account of the note."

"Yes, we don't get past that, do we? The note that had to be left by the same X that killed Ellen Reynolds." Mendoza swiveled around in his chair.

Sergeant Lake looked in. "Mr. Salter's here."

"Bueno." Mendoza swiveled back.

Hackett went out, and John Salter came in.

Last Thursday there had eventually been quite a crowd up there outside the Shaughnessys' pharmacy. The day men had left about seven o'clock, leaving it to the night crew to sort out those who had any real help to offer, and it had been after Mendoza left that Tom Landers had talked to Salter, taken down what he had to say, asked him to come in when it was convenient to sign the formal statement. All of the people from all of the shops there had come out, there had been the usual number of people on the street, and the night men had taken a number of notes. When Mendoza had read through them on Friday, Wanda hadn't copied Mr. Salter's offering; coming across it just now, neatly typed, Mendoza thought it took them a step farther on.

"Come in, Mr. Salter, sit down. I'm Lieutenant Mendoza. I've just been reading what you told my men about that shooting on Thursday, and I'd like to hear it from you, if you don't mind."

"Any way I can help you." Salter was about fifty, looking as unshakable and stolid as Shogart. He'd told Landers he was a teacher; he looked more like a bricklayer. "Where should I begin?"

"What were you doing there? Usually buy at that drugstore?"

"Never been in the place before. I teach at a junior high just down from there on Virgil. I'd stayed late to supervise a club meeting and then go over some papers. I was on my way home when," said Salter, a small glint of humor in his eyes, "I suddenly remembered it was my wife's birthday." Mendoza grinned. "It was pouring rain, and when I spotted that drugstore I thought I'd try there for her favorite perfume. I found a place to park, for a wonder, about half a block down, and I was on my way up there when I heard the shots."

"Guess how many?"

"Six or seven. I'd say seven." He seemed to be a careful witness.

"Did you hear anything else? Any screams, shouts?"

"No—but I thought later, the sound of the rain could have muffled anything like that, from inside the place. I was almost in front of the shop next door. I stopped—surprised, you know, at the suddenness of it—and a woman came belting out of there and passed me—" Mrs. Kelly— "and then I woke up and went after her, and it was at that exact moment that I saw this fellow come running out of the door of the drugstore. I didn't see his face—only to see he was white. The rain was like a sheet of fog. All I can say is, he was big, six feet at least—I wouldn't guess at his build, all bundled up in dark clothes. I didn't see a gun. But he ran around the corner onto what I found out later was Geneva Street, and that's the last I saw of him. In the meantime, several people had come out of doors, running to see what was up, and one man barged into this old fellow who was about even with me, and I stopped to catch him from falling, steady him on his feet." Mr. Teitel. "He's one of your witnesses too. And that delayed us just enough that when we got to the door together I'd say it was about a minute, a minute and a half, since I saw the fellow come out."

"Yes," said Mendoza.

"Now there's nothing certain about it, as you'll have seen," said Salter. "But just as I was going up the three steps to that door, I caught a little flash of red just going past—over to the left. And I was a lot more concerned with what might be inside that store, which we didn't know yet— but I turned my head just enough to see a red car turn onto Virgil from Geneva."

"Yes," said Mendoza. "It could have been him. Just nice time to get back to it, if it was parked, say, within a quarter block. On Geneva, headed toward Virgil. That's a narrow street—making a quick getaway, he wouldn't try to turn around, just take the chance that nobody would notice one more car."

"It's just a possibility, which is why I thought I ought to pass it on. And I couldn't give you any idea about the car. It was just a blur, in the rain, and I wasn't interested at the time."

But it was, or might be, suggestive. Mendoza sat thinking about it, when Salter had gone to read over Wanda's neat typing and sign his statement. And then his mind switched back to Flavian's nebulous little tale. Art was quite right, of course, but one of the things that made Luis Rodolfo Vicente Mendoza an efficient detective was his 'satiable curiosity, and he was wondering about that little scene at the funeral home. It could be, and probably was, nothing more than some former friend Rose Jowett had had a quarrel with. Even if it was the other woman, that was nothing to do with the homicide.

On the other hand, all these damned parolees—

Piggott came in at one o'clock thinking about the sermon. Of course, the smartest thing the devil had ever done was to convince people he didn't exist. The trouble was, reflected Piggott, not so much the devil himself, but all the minions he had recruited into his service here. Any cop realized a good deal more clearly than the average citizen just how many of those there were, and sometimes he felt a little harried, coping with them.

He'd stopped at First Aid to have his arm rebandaged; it was healing fast. As he came into the office, Lake said, "Here he is now," and nodded at Piggott, who picked up the phone on his desk.

"Mr. Piggott?" It was Duff; he sounded oddly shaken and abrupt. "Could you come out here right now? It's kind of—important. I'd be obliged."

"Well, I suppose so," said Piggott, surprised. He went back to the elevator, and as he rode downstairs he wondered if Duff had lost some more of his expensive exotics. It came home to him suddenly, out of recent experience, just what a tricky little job it must have been, too—getting hold of those angels. These exotic little fish, swimming serenely around in their tanks, might look merely graceful, but aim a net at them, or try, they were unexpectedly elusive.

When he got out to Scales 'n' Fins, he noticed that Duff had wired a loud bell to the top of the inside door. Duff came up the aisle to meet him rather slowly, looking grave. "Something else up?" asked Piggott.

"Well, I would say so. Just come back here," said Duff. At the back of the shop there was a little rear room partitioned off, with a back door leading out to another small building behind this. Duff had said something about more tanks there, for breeding.

In the back room, on an old desk burdened with many odds and ends, sat another large coffee can. The remaining two Regal Angels were sailing around in it calmly; they looked to be in good health. Sitting in the chair behind the desk was Ron Babcock, looking ready to cry.

"You see, Ron didn't know about that bell," said Duff. "I'd just put it up. He figured he'd do it the same way he brought back the second ones. Wait till I was back here, slip in quick and leave 'em, and a bit later walk in and make an excuse to get me out back, so it'd look like they were put there while we were gone." Ron's head sagged lower. "Only he didn't expect the bell. Soon's I heard it, I come down to the front, and there he was with my Regal Angels."

"What about it, Ron?" asked Piggott.

He didn't look up at either of them. "I know it was an awful thing to do, Mr. Duff—awful wrong. But I—I wanted some of those Regals so bad! And they cost so much—but the more get bred, the price'll come down. But it wasn't just that, Mr. Duff—honest it wasn't. It was *because* they're so expensive. You know how Dad got killed in that accident last year. And things getting so high—Mom makes a good salary at the market, but she's got to have new glasses, it'll cost nearly ninety dollars, and she was worried. She doesn't mind about the fish mostly, except for sayin͜ I spend too much time on them, but I thought if I could raise some Regals, sell them, maybe enough for her glasses, so she'd see—"

"And that's a favorite trick of the devil's too," said Piggott. "Thievery in a good cause. Stealing's stealing, Ron. There's a Commandment about it."

"I *know*," he said wretchedly. "I—but the fish are all I *have*. Mom's gone all day at work and tired when she gets home, and all my sister's interested in is dates, and—the fish are all I've got, of my own at all. I know it was wrong. I'm sorry. Tell the truth, Mr. Duff, I been feeling so bad about it, I'm glad you found out. I was real careful about the spawn, it's all coming along great, the first ones are hatched already. But—if I'm arrested, who's going to take care of them all? It'd be burglary—I did break in here—and I don't know how long in jail—I'm sorry, Mr. Duff, I'm sorry I ever even thought about it! You've been awful kind to me, I hadn't any business to—"

"Well," said Duff. He looked uncomfortable. He said to Piggott, "See you a minute?" and led him down to the middle of the shop, where they were surrounded by aquariums where the bright-patterned little fish darted in and out of the waving plants, and the silent bubbles rose ghost-like. "Hum!" said Duff. "It's true enough the boy hasn't got much, Mr. Piggott. He's only seventeen. I guess his mother's a good enough woman, but it's hard for her, having to work. He's always been crazy about the exotics, and he knows as much as a lot of professionals. He's a bright boy. I wouldn't like to see him collect a police record at his age."

"You don't want to charge him? You know, Mr. Duff, whether he's sorry or not, he ought to get some punishment for it. I see what you mean, but—"

"I figured, maybe he can work it out. Hell, what's it amount to? The new lock and a little worry and fuss. Your time. I've got my Regals back, and I'll have the spawn—" Duff looked suddenly rueful. "Devil of it is I'll have to leave that with him till the fry's big enough to move. But I figure he can come, clean up the store, do the feeding, clean out the tanks. He'll work it out, I promise you. And another thing, it'll stop him taking the extra jobs, cutting people's lawns and so on, earning money for himself. I'll see he doesn't forget this little affair."

Piggott nodded. "If that's the way you want to do it, we can write it off. Charges dropped."

"That's the way," said Duff. "I wasn't sure I could do that, once I'd called you in. Thanks, Mr. Piggott." He insisted on shaking hands. "How are all your little fellows? Now, you have any questions about 'em, any problem comes up, you just call and I'll do my best for you. Any time, any time at all."

At Central Receiving Hospital, Higgins was listening to some more evidence of the devil's existence—in fact he had thought of what Matt would likely say about it.

Mrs. Rowena House, taken to the hospital by Carey, had identified her daughter at once. She was semiconscious when Higgins got there, and now, slightly sedated by pain-killer, she was getting the story out slowly, mostly to her mother, hardly aware of Higgins.

"That Ringo Dillon," she was saying, eyes closed. "Always at me—nothing but trash—" She'd be a pretty girl again when the bruises and cuts healed: her skin the color of creamed coffee, small straight features. Mrs. House was a nice-looking woman too, tall and slim and well-dressed. She'd said her husband was a lab technician at General Hospital. These were the kind of people who kept their lawns green and houses painted, had standards and principles.

She said now, "Oh, my God," and turned to Higgins. "It's one of those terrible motorcycle gangs—that Dillon, he wasn't going to school, but his crowd used to hang around there, and he'd been after Eileen then—I thanked God when she was out of school. She's going to L.A.C.C. now, she hadn't seen him again till just last week, he was waiting for her at the gate and tried to— And swearing at her, she said, calling her such names, she thought she was too good for him. I should hope so!" She was patting her daughter's shoulder mechanically. "It's all right now, darling."

"Oh, Mama, it was so terrible—I wanted to die!—this girl —she seemed nice, I met her in the cafeteria—thought she was—student too, acted like—" She was moving her head back and forth restlessly. "Dorrie May Smith. Dorrie May Smith, said—her name—I thought she was—all right."

"Yes, darling, it's all over now."

"She said—give me ride home—her car. I thought— all

right, I'd seen her—on campus—we talked—in the cafeteria. But she took me—that place, that awful—garage. They were just like animals, Mama—just animals—I was so frightened, they hurt me so—"

"It's all right, Eileen, you're safe now." Mrs. House looked at Higgins. "Animals! Even animals don't do things like this! Please, Sergeant, you'll go after them, and—and do something to them."

"We surely will," said Higgins. "We surely will, Mrs. House." The girl could probably identify her attackers.

The doctor said she'd been severely beaten and repeatedly raped, by a number of males. She would probably lose the sight of one eye. She had a broken arm and kneecap, several broken ribs, and a number of knife-cuts and contusions. He also said that up to the forcible rape she'd been a virgin.

The motorcycle gangs—Higgins thought he'd go down to Juvenile and see what they could say. They saw the punks in the street when they began to go wrong.

Mendoza was just thinking of going out to lunch when Sergeant Lake brought him Mrs. Anthony Tumminello.

Coming across her address, if belatedly, he had had Farrell call the San Diego police yesterday. He hadn't seen Delgado's corpse; he wondered if he had looked like his mother. She had once been a beautiful woman, was still pretty in middle age.

"Can I have the body?" she was asking. Direct, grieving, but in control.

"Any time," said Mendoza.

"He came to see me, you know," she said, looking out the window. She had very black hair with a white streak over one temple, and big dark eyes like an Italian madonna. If she wasn't dressed in the height of fashion, her simple black suit was becoming. "At least I can remember that. Oh, I had it all, Lieutenant!" Her eyes were rueful. "The rebellion, the scorn, the arguments—until he left home. His father was dead then, and there was nothing I could do. Knew how to do—to try to reach Frank. But he did—come back. He came to see me just after New Year's, and we had a good talk. He told me all about it, how it had been for him—what do they say—kicking the habit. He—he told me he was sorry he'd caused me so much trouble and worry, my Frank." She tried to smile. "He said he was luckier than most, he'd always been too chicken to try the heroin—just the marijuana, the pills."

"He was a little smarter than most," said Mendoza.

"He told me about helping the police here. He felt he was doing some good—but he said it made him feel so dirty. Oh, not because he was—like betraying these people, giving them away—it wasn't that! But because he had to keep associating with them, these—friends of his, or the ones had been friends. So that nobody would know he wasn't still like them. So he could help the police. He said he hated it, he wanted to quit and come home and start to—build some sort of life. He was going to church again—I was so happy about that."

"Mmh," said Mendoza the renegade from organized religion. "You hadn't seen him since." He thought of that bare room. "Did he write you?"

"One letter, just last week. I didn't know if you'd like to see it, I brought it." She opened her bag.

She wore an Italian name but she was of another people. *"Con su permisión,"* said Mendoza absently.

"Felizmente, señor." She gave it to him.

He scanned it rapidly, a loose scrawl. It was written in Spanish, dated February twenty-sixth. "The worst thing is having to pretend I'm still on the stuff, still using the speed, still part of that useless, mindless existence. I'm no missionary, maybe, but when I see them killing themselves with that stuff I want to scream at them, where are your brains? I used to think Art Lopez was my best friend, but when he came here tonight begging me for money, he needs a fix so bad—a couple of times I've nearly yelled at him, idiot, fool, you can get off it if you try and act like a man! And

[165]

I can't do that, because these people musn't know. If I can help the police get this one bunch, then I'm through with the undercover job. But meanwhile—"

Mendoza dropped his cigarette and exclaimed loudly, "*¿Con qué esas tenenaz—puede ser?*"

"*¿Qué?*" she said, startled.

"Clichés," said Mendoza. "Clichés—yes. I should have expected that. The reformed sinners. Alcoholics Anonymous. I really should have seen that—"

Ten

Mendoza snatched up the phone. "Get me Callaghan's office, Jimmy! . . . Saul? The punks we were talking about— erstwhile pals of Frank Delgado's. I know they're drifters but most of them have some sort of address they call home, if only temporarily. Yes, well, what about Art Lopez? . . . Oh. Oh, isn't that interesting. Very pretty indeed, *gracias.*" He put the phone down, reached for his hat, and said to the woman, "You'll excuse me. I think we've got there."

As he came into the hallway, Hackett was just coming in. He had in tow a dispirited-looking man with a cold, who was blowing his nose and coughing. "Who's that?" asked Mendoza.

"Burglar on P.A.," said Hackett briefly. "Where are you off to?"

Mendoza regarded the burglar with disfavor and said, "Leave him. Come on. I really should have thought of that before. Art Lopez's father kicked him out long ago, we're told, but he has an aunt who'll always take him in when he's down and out. She lives on St. Vincent Court, and isn't that very suggestive indeed."

"Of what?" asked Hackett, following him out. "And where the hell is that?"

"We will, however, try the pad on South Vermont first," said Mendoza. "And you haven't, of course, seen Frank Delgado's last letter." He told Hackett about that on the way downstairs. "The clichés," he said. "And with an addict off the habit, I'd think it might be an even more urgent urge, so to speak, than with the reformed drunk."

"I follow you just so far."

"I think there's a County Guide in the glove compartment," said Mendoza. "You might look up the aunt's address for yourself."

On Sunday, there were parking slots along even this main drag; he parked in front of the mass of the dingy condemned building and marched up to that door. It opened on the same ill-lit, poster-hung, dreary room. There was a stir and grumbles about the light; Mendoza pushed the switch and the ceiling lights sprang up.

"I want Art Lopez," said Mendoza, "is he here?" His smile turned a little wolfish as he spotted him, the one who'd back-talked him before. Lopez was lying half propped against the wall on a couple of cushions. He was thin and dark and looked unwell, with the reddened eyelids of the chronic drug-user, skin pitted with old acne scars. He was barefooted, his stained jeans torn, his sweat shirt grimy. "Up!" said Mendoza. "Are you on a trip?"

Lopez eyed him sneeringly. "What's it to you, pig?"

"It might complicate the trial later on," said Mendoza. He reached down and took him by both arms, hauled him up to his feet. But as of right now, Lopez wasn't acting as if he'd had anything recently; his pupils were normal, his speech unslurred. "So I'm taking you in, Lopez. I want to ask you some questions, about Frank Delgado's murder."

Lopez tried to jerk away. "You're crazy, man. Leggo of me—Frankie went back to Dago."

"A little farther. I know about how it happened, of course," said Mendoza conversationally. "You went to see him that night about eleven-thirty. You wanted some money—for speed or bennies or maybe horse. He wouldn't give it to you. And then all of a sudden he started to lecture you on what an idiot you are, to get on the stuff at all—and you realized what the truth must be about Frankie—because he was still play-acting the part—and that's when you decided to kill him, wasn't it?"

Lopez stared at him, going white around the mouth. "How'd you—know all that?" he muttered. "Nobody else was there—nobody—"

"I've got a little imagination," said Mendoza. Of the several others in the place, two were motionless on the floor, evidently passed out, and only one glaze-eyed girl was watching them, listening. "Come on, let's take a little ride downtown."

Lopez was still eyeing him superstitiously as they put him in the back seat. "As I've said before," said Hackett, "another time and place you'd have burned as a warlock, Luis."

After that it wasn't any trouble to get him to talk. "I thought he was my best friend," he started out dully, and he sounded very sorry for himself. "I thought we were pals. He usually had a little bread—just lately his ma'd send him money from Dago. Sometimes before he'd bailed me out, I needed a fix, and I needed one that night. I don't remember which night—how long back—awhile ago. I went to his pad, but he wasn't there. I went back a couple times, good old Frank, he'll let me have some bread, I thought—but he wasn't there till late, very late. He let me in, he said he didn't have any bread—but he'd take me—home. I mean, where I was—"

"You were staying at your aunt's," said Mendoza. "St. Vincent's Court, a funny little cul-de-sac just the other side of Pershing Square."

"Yeah. Yeah. Just a couple weeks ago Frank got a old heap, to get round. It's a mess, but it runs, sort of. Old Chevy." That, Narco hadn't known. "I was still askin' him, didn't he know where I could get some bread, but he wouldn't say nothing to me—he was real quiet, just driving—and then all of a sudden he started yellin' at me, callin' me names and sayin' what a fool I am—I don't get it at first, but then I ast him, he's off it, he's kicked it, and he says a lot more—I don't remember all of it, but it come to me—nobody knows he's gone square, out of it—and it come into my mind, couldn't be no other way—he'd been smellin' around Al's sister—it had to be, he was finking to the Man—Frankie! *Frankie* was— And I needed a fix so bad, and Al was the only seller I knew right then, if he got took out of the market—I started to hit Frankie in the car, I guess, we got out of the car some way, and I got away and ran but he chased me—it was all dark and nobody around—and I fell over a chain sort of thing, and next I know, I don't remember so good, Frankie helped me up and I knew I hadda kill him, I hadda kill him or him and the damn fuzz would take away my supply—"

"What about the car?" asked Hackett.

His head sagged lower. "I been drivin' it around. It's parked some place—where you picked me up."

Mendoza let Hackett take him to jail. "The dirt at the bottom," said Hackett, "as per usual. They'll try to give him treatment inside, but you want to bet it'll get called murder two, and he's out in three years? And back on the hard stuff?"

"I may be a gambler, Art," said Mendoza, "but odds that long I won't take." When Hackett had taken him out, he asked Sergeant Lake, "Where is everybody?"

"There was a new body," said Lake. "John and Jase went out on it. George is still on that messy assault, I guess. Everybody else is out hunting parolees."

"Jowett," said Mendoza. "I don't like Jowett, Jimmy. There is something the wrong shape to it. But there's another thing I don't like either. Having just had one hunch, I think I'll meditate on it and see if I have another."

In his office, he sat down at the desk and got out the set of photographs Scarne had brought in. The stark black-and-white glossies showing where death had hit, in a very ordinary place, the three innocent honest citizens. He studied the ones of the woman's body raptly, and he said to himself, *"¿Por qué—a son de qué?"* Just why had he shot all of them?

It was very likely indeed that he hadn't even seen the woman, on her knees behind the counter, when he came in. John Shaughnessy had probably been behind the rear counter, visible; he'd walked up there—with the gun showing or not. And then what? What had gone wrong with the intended heist?—for 90 percent sure, that's what it had been. A nervous, inexperienced heist man who panicked? In that case the odds were that he'd simply have run out, away. Did the gun go off by accident?—there was that wild bullet. But not by accident seven times.

Mendoza muttered, called Sergeant Lake and asked if the Shaughnessy autopsy reports were in. "In your current file," said Lake. "They came in while you were gone." Mendoza pulled the desk box toward him; they were on top.

He went over them interestedly. He said, looking at the report on Sarah Shaughnessy, *"Lo creo*—so that could say something indeed. But—"* Shaughnessy had taken a bullet in the stomach and one in a lung. Susan had been shot in the chest twice. Powder burns on his clothes, none on hers. But, said the third autopsy report, powder burns on Mrs. Shaughnessy's forearms and face. And that was interesting. He had shot the first two at the rear of the store; she had got to her feet, alarmed, just as he came running past, down that aisle close to the counter, and he'd fired the last two shots at her, getting her in the chest too. And why?

It was a senseless killing, beyond the mere panic of the moment. The Shaughnessys ordinary people, no enemies, no money troubles. Nothing showed to make any motive. Why had they ended up getting killed?

When Palliser had left that morning, Roberta had been feeling better. She'd finally got the doctor to give her something for the pseudo-indigestion. "But I'll be very relieved to have this project over," she told him. "I feel like the fat lady in the circus."

"Not much longer now, Robin."

But his mind was mostly on that incredible D.M.V. list, and he looked at it again in the office and said to Grace, "I still don't believe it. That many. My God, Jase, with everybody in the office on it, it'd take a month of Sundays to cover it!"

"Now leave us not lose our heads here," said Grace. "I know that. Which is why I say, we give it to Wanda and ask her to weed out all the addresses on the Central beat, to look at first. If we don't strike oil anywhere there, expand it some and look some more."

"I don't see why—oh," said Palliser.

"Because," said Grace, "when we have a lunatic with the urge to run down boys on bicycles, and he's done it three times on our beat, I'd have an educated guess he doesn't live far off. If he lived in Pasadena or Beverly Hills, that's where he'd be running down boys on bicycles."

"That is a fact," agreed Palliser. "We give it to Wanda." Wanda looked a little daunted by the job, but good secretary that she was, took the list without protest.

"I'll get to it as soon as I can," she said. "I've got a report of Henry's to type up and then one for Piggott."

And just then the new call came in, so they went out on that.

The body was in a little alley behind Wilshire Place, a side-street down from the boulevard. It was the body of a man about fifty, a little too fat; he'd been fairly well-dressed before somebody beat him up and stuck a knife in him several times. He was cold. He'd been spotted by some children, reported to parents who called in.

Palliser went through his pockets; he'd been stripped of everything but a ring of keys, a couple of handkerchiefs. They went hunting up and down the alley and near the street were rewarded by finding an empty wallet. The I.D. in it was for a Richard Bliss.

The Traffic men were still there, and looked at each other. "Did you say Bliss, sir? Yeah, I thought that's who it was when we first saw him. I wasn't sure—dead people look different sometimes. But if that's Bliss, we can tell you something about him, Sergeant. He was a fag."

"You know him? You'd picked him up?"

"Well, not exactly. But there's a fag joint up on Wilshire a little way, the Blue Pony. Where that kind, and that kind exclusively, hang out. Once in a while there's a little trouble there—you know, a fight or something. We keep an eye on it, and we know some of the regulars there. He's one. Reason we knew his name, just awhile ago Vice pulled a raid on the place, there was gambling going on in the back, and he was one of those there that night, got picked up."

Palliser exchanged a glance with Grace. "Thanks very much, that's helpful." There wasn't much reason for photographs; they let the ambulance take the body and went back to Parker Center, and up to the Vice bureau.

Lieutenant Perce Andrews was still there, a little grayer, and at the moment unoccupied. They told him about Bliss and he said, "In an alley just off Wilshire. Half a block from that fag joint. So you former glamor-boy cops are learning some of the sordid facts of life about robbery these days. That's just one more."

"Spell that one out," said Grace.

Andrews sighed. "The little gangs of j.d.'s. The city-wise, smart kids—damn the color—from the amoral homes in quotes. We've picked 'em up young as ten, eleven. They found out long ago that that's a very ready source of income. Hang around the fag joint, wait for one to come out alone, jump him, strip him. He'll never yell cop. This time—as sometimes happens—they mauled him a little too much."

"Sordid you can say," said Grace with a grimace. "So even if the lab gets any prints off the wallet, we'll never know who." They couldn't print the juveniles.

"I wouldn't think so. They melt into the jungle."

"Know if he had any relatives? There wasn't anything but the address in his wallet." But Andrews couldn't say.

They found his car parked down there, about a block from where the body had been. They went up to the home address listed in his I.D., an address on Cahuenga Boulevard in Hollywood, and discovered that Bliss had lived with a muddle-headed spinster sister who had probably never suspected he was a homo. She wept and carried on, but when they left she was talking to herself about moving into the bigger bedroom, so evidently she wouldn't be missing him much. It was getting on for lunch time then—they usually came in a little late on Sundays; but at Federico's, they were the only men from the office there.

"I wonder what George is getting on that assault," said Palliser.

What Higgins was getting was enough, but he was feeling just a little incredulous—which he shouldn't have. He'd been a cop long enough to know that, especially of late with the courts so anxious to oblige the criminals, the wild ones who lived by no laws were more arrogant than ever.

He'd gone down to Juvenile to see what they could tell him about Ringo Dillon and his gang. Ten to one Juvenile knew them, even if they'd legally turned into adults.

"Oh, yes," said a Sergeant Donlevy sadly. "That kind get their start with us, all right. He's a bad one. That gang calls itself Satan's Angels. It's not a settled bunch, there's juvies in and out of it, and the older ones too, but there's a nucleus of about ten. Dillon's the boss and the next boss is Jo-Jo Jackson. He's still a j.d., seventeen. Dorrie May's his girl."

"What about Dillon? He was after this girl before—"

"Sure," said Donlevy. He was a big, broad, sandy man. "The girls are common property—except for Dillon's and Jo-Jo's. Dillon's chick, they called her Jitsy—I've got her real name in the files somewhere—came down with a galloping case of V.D. last January, she's still in the hospital."

"My God," said Higgins; but probably the doctors had considered that possibility. "But, my God, are they all idiots? This girl using her own name to lure the House girl like that —they might know she could identify—"

"Sure," said Donlevy. "They just don't care, Higgins. They're the wild ones—anything comes into their heads to do, bingo. If it'd occurred to them to go on and kill her just to see what it felt like—"

"They damn near did," said Higgins.

"Yeah. They don't give a damn. For anything or anybody. Oh, some of them think they do. Jo-Jo'd claim his Dorrie May'd always stick by him. Sure, as long as that suits her—and him. Sell each other out to the Man when they needed a fix, any day. I tell you, what you've told me I can see how it went. Ringo all of a sudden took it into his head that this snotty girl thinks she's too good for him, he'll show her, no-body's gonna treat Ringo that way—so they set it up."

"My God," said Higgins. "Well, we've all seen some cold-blooded things, but—"

"You get tired," said Donlevy. "And you wonder what kind of world it is going to be tomorrow, with these animals running around. Damn the color—there are white gangs just as bad and worse, and a few that Ringo lets hang around are Mex. And then you go home from the office, and you read about kids earning scholarships and working for the church and you get a little perspective. But it's frustrating. Annoying, not being able to do something—" he paused— "either to or for them, these louts who think rules are made for other people."

Higgins sighed and lit a cigarette and said, frowning at it, "Four thousand dollars. Or, we heard about it too when it went through, and we all did some cussing."

"We can pick up a j.d. for murder," said Donlevy, "and he's back on the street tomorrow." And some rather unrealistic rules had got made up recently, but that was the most monstrously unrealistic of all. In effect, if a juvenile was put on probation instead of taken into custody, the county was promptly entitled to payment of four thousand bucks per juvenile of Federal money—ostensibly for purposes of rehabilitation. Nobody seemed to know where the money went; but the net effect was that, whatever the charge, where at all possible the courts put juveniles on probation, greedy for the long green.

"Well, I'll have to find these louts and make the gesture of picking them up," said Higgins. "Where?"

"You'll find them, or some of them," said Donlevy, "at their permanent hangout, a garage on Forty-first. Did the girl say how many of them raped her?"

"I don't think she knew," said Higgins.

"Not surprising. Some of us had better go with you."

Donlevy and two of his men, Peters and Gault, went along, and they took a black-and-white wagon to transport them. At the garage on Forty-first, they found ten motorcycles, Dillon, Jackson, the Smith girl, two other girls and five boys, four of them juveniles. They even, this type, looked like the wild ones they were: Dillon and Jackson with oversize Afros, the one Mex kid that was over eighteen sporting hair to his shoulders and a bandit's moustache. The bare feet, the outlandish clothes, the dirty bodies, all marks of this breed. And it wasn't, thought Higgins, that some of them lacked a certain intelligence. Eileen House had said that Dorrie May "seemed all right"—so on a couple of occasions at least Dorrie hadn't smelled of sweat and wine, had been reasonably well dressed. Setting up the girl for Ringo and the other boys. The snotty girl who had turned up her nose at Ringo, the big man.

They were all charged with assault with intent. Higgins phoned the Robbery-Homicide office with the names, told Lake to apply for the warrants. He hoped a judge would at least look at the charge and not turn them loose, but of that you couldn't be sure.

At the jail on Alameda, as they were processed in, he wanted to say to Ringo, "Do you know what you've done to that girl's life?" But of course it would be wasted breath. Either to or for, he knew what Donlevy meant. Either try honestly to rehabilitate them, get them straightened out if possible: or see that they got punished swift and sure, for the mindless malicious trouble they made. As it was, it was possible that they'd be back on the street before Eileen House was out of the hospital.

"I'm due to retire in four years," said Donlevy. "I'm going

to move to the country—as rural as I can get—and keep a cow and some chickens. Go fishing every day." He sounded wistful.

Palliser and Grace came back to the office at one-thirty, to find Sergeant Lake on the phone and Glasser just in with another parolee. "The boss had an inspiration or something," said Lake, "and he and Art went tearing out somewhere. That was a new body."

"Oh, hell," said Palliser.

"Look, I want somebody to team up to question this guy," said Glasser.

"It doesn't sound like much," said Lake.

"All right, I'll go look at it and you can help Henry," said Palliser.

The new body was on East Kensington Road; he had to use the County Guide to find it, and it must have been one of the oldest streets in the city, just north of the old Plaza. It was a narrow, short street, mostly empty lots where houses had been torn down, but a few still stood. He spotted the one he wanted by the black-and-white in front.

It was a three-story frame house which must be nearly a hundred years old, Gothic Victorian. The front door was open so he went in. The uniformed men were talking to a fat old woman in a bright pink-flowered dress. Palliser introduced himself.

"This is Mrs. Galloway, Sergeant. She owns the house, rents out rooms. She called us."

"I thought it was funny," she said in a flat voice. "He's up later on Sundays, but usually he goes out about noon. And he's not a young man—not old either, but not young—could have had a stroke or something. So I finally went up and knocked, case he was took sick."

"And called us," said one of the uniformed men. "We had to break the door in."

"So let's go see it," said Palliser. It was on the second floor. She panted up behind the men.

"Everybody else lives here is out, to the park or some place. He usually went out too, nice days. And when I couldn't make him answer me, I knew something was wrong, so I—"

"Queerest thing I ever saw," said the other uniformed man. "Makes you think about fate."

"You see," panted Mrs. Galloway, "he was deathly afraid of vampires. His name's Polachek, I guess they got a lot of vampires where he comes from, and he thought they were all around everywhere. He was always what he called taking precautions against vampires."

"What?" said Palliser.

"He took precautions all right," said one of the men.

Palliser looked into the room, and was momentarily speechless. It was a large square room, not uncomfortably furnished. In his anxious precautions against vampires, Mr. Polachek had hung large crucifixes on every wall, and a careful trail of salt surrounded the bed; there were cloves of garlic hung from the bedposts, another clove wedged into the keyhole of the door, more on each windowsill, and crosses traced in salt all over the carpet.

Mr. Polachek's precautions, thought Palliser, had resulted in again proving the truth of the old adage that the things you worry about never happen.

The large iron crucifix over the head of the bed had fallen down in the night and brained Mr. Polachek. He was forever safe from vampires.

The night watch drifted in. There was a note on Higgins' desk for Conway, and when he read it he uttered some very rude words. "My God in heaven," he said. "Of all the God-damned things! Of all the Goddamned nuisances! It would have to be me!"

"What's up?" asked Landers.

"It had to be my gun," said Conway. "Goddamn it! It was my gun accounted for Barnard, and the I.A. hearing's set up for Tuesday afternoon! Of all the—"

"For God's sake. But of course they didn't know, Rich,

That it's your day off, and you've got a date, and tickets—"

"I would really take no bets," said Conway bitterly. "Those bastards up there hounding us—after what they tried to do to you, I wouldn't think—"

"Just hope it's a short hearing, you can get away by six."

"And I'll take no bets on that either!" said Conway.

A few minutes later Schenke, going down the hall to the drinking fountain, noticed with surprise that in the slot of the first interrogation room the little card read *In Use*. He opened the door.

Everybody had forgotten the burglar with the cold, and he was sound asleep across the little table, making snuffling noises.

They shook him awake and told him he could go.

"Reflex action," said Alison. She was wearing a favorite amber robe, and her hair was burnished copper in the lamplight. She had Sheba and Nefertite in her lap.

"Reflex action be damned," said Mendoza. He took back the series of photographs of the pharmacy and the bodies and studied them again. "He knew what he was doing. That wild shot—why? Not that he had to be much of a marksman. Shaughnessy wasn't a foot away, the girl about three, Mrs. Shaughnessy less, right behind that counter. Why the hell did he shoot them?"

"He knew the shots would have been heard, *obvio*. So he ran without taking anything. An amateur heist man who panicked."

"Posible," said Mendoza. "I still say—" He brushed his moustache back and forth. Cedric ambled in, presumably having played watchdog until the twins were safely asleep, and lay down with a thump at Alison's feet. El Señor came over and began to chew one of Cedric's ears. Cedric slurped at him affectionately.

"That wild shot," said Mendoza, "was the first one."

"¿De veras? Not one single thing tells you that. It could have been any one of the seven."

"Theoretically, yes. But I think it was the first one. I think—" Mendoza was standing in the middle of the living room staring into space.

"You had another inspiration."

"Pues no. But I think that shot got snapped off because he was—mmh—caught off balance. Some way. By something. . . . I need a drink."

El Señor abandoned Cedric and pursued him to the kitchen. He poured half an ounce of rye into a saucer and filled a shot-glass for himself. When he came back to the living room he put the photographs away in the manila folder and stood staring at Alison absently, sipping rye.

"There is also Jowett. The parolees, *Dios.* And I may have a constitutional distrust of coincidences, but they do happen. Rarely, they do. The crimes are so completely different— but as Art says, the violence of any kind, with a man given to violence—but, just possibly, my love, just at the outside edge of possibility, could that note be a fantastic coincidence? There must be, when you come to think of it, quite a lot of men who have at one time or another thought or said, God bless the parole board."

"Not," said Alison, "when it was a note. Deliberately written."

Mendoza sighed. "It couldn't possibly be. About nine million to one. *Estoy apuradillo*—Jowett makes me feel uneasy, *cara.* That little scene at the funeral—it says nothing. Everybody dislikes somebody—even nonentities like Rose Jowett."

There was a silence while he finished the rye. El Señor came back, licking his chops, made for Cedric and batted him on the nose. Liquor affected El Señor as it did Mendoza, arousing his belligerent spirit. Cedric looked offended and Alison laughed.

"But," she said, "I can see you're getting nowhere on it, all those men on parole. Just because a man can't prove exactly where he was at any given moment—"

"Up in the air," said Mendoza. "Like that Borchers thing.

But on that, what with the very possible wad of cash—and that is a very queer thing in itself—I'm now inclined to agree with Carey. The woman was very likely murdered. Somebody found out about the cash— But just how she was spirited away from The Broadway—"

"You haven't told me about that one." Alison rumpled Cedric's ears. "You know, I really do wonder what's happened to that mockingbird. How long do they live, Luis, do you know? He could have just died, I suppose—"

"I'm not worried about the mockingbird. Let the damned thing annoy somebody else."

When Piggott came in Prudence returned his kiss enthusiastically and said, "You'll never guess what, Matt! That tetra —the head-and-taillight one—I'm positive, I looked at the book, and I'm sure it's a female and full of eggs wanting to spawn! It looks just like the description—"

"Well, what about that?" Piggott was interested and went to look at the tank.

"And, Matt, wouldn't it be fun to see the little ones? The book says it's very easy with that kind. We'd have to have another aquarium, a five-gallon one—and you put in one of those green nylon mops to catch the eggs. And after they're free-swimming you feed them hardboiled egg yolk—"

"Hey," said Piggot. "Just a minute, my girl. Fact of life. You've got to have a he tetra to fertilize the eggs."

"Well, we have! I looked very carefully," said Prudence, "and the book says, 'The males are identified by a small white spot on the anal fin.' And we've got four head-and-taillight tetras and the other three are all males. I'm sure. You look —you'll see."

Piggott looked, trying to pick out those particular tetras of all the tiny fish sailing about, and said, "Well, I'll be. They sure seem to be. I wonder if I could rent an aquarium from Duff."

"It says, raise the temperature to eighty degrees, and take

the parents out when all the eggs are deposited. And you almost need a microscope to see the babies at first, but they grow fast—oh, Matt, let's try it!"

Piggott bent again to look at the gay little fish as they swam round and round. That was a pretty tetra, its fore-and-aft luminous color shining. The fourth one was definitely fattened all out of shape. He looked at the book, and she was quite right. "Might be kind of interesting at that. I'll ask Duff if we can maybe rent an extra tank."

Prudence was bending over the tank. "Just like us really, or anything God made. She *looks* maternal."

"Only," said Piggott, "as I said to Duff, and it's a funny thought, Prue—He made so many things more beautiful." The pretty little fish—lower form of life, he thought, but a nicer form of life than some he could think of.

Eleven

Just as Mendoza reached to switch off the bedside lamp, the phone rang in the hall. He went out to answer it. "Mendoza."

"I didn't think we'd wake you up," said Landers. "We thought you'd like to hear about it—there was a patrolman shot in Century City about an hour ago. It's not our beat but there's an eight-county A.P.B. out. Patrolman William Steiner. He stopped this car for an illegal left, and by what they got from him—"

"He's not dead?"

"No, he'll live, they think, but he's not in too good shape —slugs in the stomach and thigh. He's in surgery now. But he got the plate-number, and he was still holding the driver's license. We ran it through, and it's Estéban Guttierez, pedigree from age eleven, mostly mugging and theft. He's just out on P.A. from Folsom."

"Nice," said Mendoza.

"He's driving a sixty-nine Ford sedan, white. There's a want on it, we're waiting to hear about that. I just thought I'd fill you in on it."

"Thanks so much. We'll hold the good thoughts on it."

"And you'll also be interested to hear that somebody has been experimenting with L.A.'s new method of homicide."

"The rocks thrown off freeways."

"That's just what. Convertible out of control when a rock came through the windshield out on the Harbor freeway, slammed into a car in the next lane. Chain reaction, and four dead."

"*¡Santa María!*" said Mendoza. "I'm going to bed, Tom."

On Monday morning, with Palliser off, Mendoza sat at his desk and thought over the last week and the coming one. Sometime this week Lorna Easely would be arraigned, and Epps and Robinson, and Carlson. They still had the Shaughnessys and Reynolds-Jowett—he frowned over that—and he'd take a bet they'd hear from Grandmother again. Those damned would-be funny stories in the *Times* and the *Herald* —that could have repercussions.

He went out to the communal office, where Higgins was just putting down the phone. "That is the damnedest thing," said Higgins. "That poor damned House girl—I wanted to know how soon she might be able to make a formal identification. The doctor says she'll be in at least six weeks. I wonder, Luis—arrange a lineup there? It has been done. You know if she doesn't identify before then the defense can claim—"

"It might not be a bad idea, George, just to tie it up tight."

"At least Ringo is adult, legally speaking. And Dorrie May." Higgins went out looking thoughtful, to start all the machinery on a parade at the hospital.

"Nothing on Guttierez yet," said Hackett. "But at least Steiner's still hanging on. Now what about these parolees, Luis? We're working through them, and it's a handful of nothing. E.M. says the routine always gets results sooner or later, but here I don't see it."

Suddenly Wanda began to laugh. "Oh, dear," she said, "I'm sorry, I just came to Sergeant Palliser's notes about that Polachek man. Did he tell you—"

"The man who was afraid of vampires," said Grace. "He did indeed. Look, lady, we'd kind of like priority on that D.M.V. list."

"Oh, I know, I'd already made a start, I'll get back to it."

"Luis—" But before Mendoza could make any pronouncement on the parolees, Sergeant Lake brought them a communication from NCIC. It seemed that the New Jersey State Police had belatedly found some bodies in the mountain mansion: a retired multi-millionaire and his third wife. From information received, the killer was identified as his son by a second wife, incensed because his father wouldn't let him have control of a million-dollar trust fund. The son was described as Harold Burger, description appended, and was believed to have set out for California in a brand-new bright red Ferrari, plate-number thus and such.

"How the other half lives," said Grace. "Did some bleeding heart say that violence is triggered by poverty?"

"I don't know that we'd ever get anywhere with the P.A. thing either, Art," said Mendoza. "But having begun it that way, let's carry on to the bitter end. But that case is"—he frowned and brushed his moustache—"the wrong shape. And yet, damn it, there's nothing else it can be but what it looks like—" He went back to his office to brood.

A new call came in: man attacked and robbed in the street outside a public school, by a pack of boys. He wasn't seriously hurt, but he was mad. The Traffic man said he'd handle it, if it wasn't for the time it would take. Piggott and Glasser went out on that.

Every cruising car in the county was looking for that white Ford sedan, the plate-number memorized. In the hospital, Patrolman Steiner was reported to be holding his own.

Mendoza was staring at the Shaughnessy photographs and trying to force a hunch on that, at nine-fifteen, when Sergeant Lake came in looking purposeful.

"They've got Grandmother—Federal Savings and Loan on San Vicente—teller spotted her and yelled, and the manager's holding her—I alerted the Feds. You're not interested?"

"I'm interested," said Mendoza, getting up, "but if it is, they've got her, there's no hurry. I've been trying to have a hunch, but this one I had awhile ago. Come on, Art."

He didn't use the siren on the Ferrari. When they got to the Federal Savings and Loan, the men from the black-and-white were unobtrusively guarding the door to the manager's office, and the Feds were just coming in. "Well, we've got her this time," said Valenti cheerfully.

"There's a saying about eggs," said Mendoza. In the manager's office, a woman who certainly fitted Grandmother's description was sitting in a chair by the desk, and the manager, a distraught little man with a naked bald head, welcomed them in with relief.

"I'm glad to see you, gentlemen—she's been trying to claim she's not the thief, but you can see—"

The woman was smoking a cigarette, which somehow detracted from her resemblance to Grandmother. She looked at them calmly, a trim and pretty woman even well into her sixties, and she said, "Good heavens, I hope there's some way I can prove I'm not. The funny thing is, Bob and I laughed when we saw those stories in the paper, and he said the description fit me just fine. But really I am just a new depositor here, rather we are, and I just came in to deposit my husband's pay check. I'm Mrs. Robert Vandercook and I really didn't plan to rob the bank."

"Yes, and I was afraid those damned human-interest stories might have just such a result," said Mendoza, annoyed. "Where were you last Wednesday afternoon, Mrs. Vandercook, and can you prove it? Say from one to six."

"Well, I had my hair done at one, and went out to a matinee at the Ebell Club with some friends—"

"Yes," said Mendoza. He shrugged his shoulders at Valenti. "False alarm."

"You mean she *isn't?*" gasped the manager. "You mean she's a real depositor—one of our customers?" He looked at them in horror, and turned to her agitatedly. "Really, my dear lady, I do apologize most sincerely—I'll see that girl's fired at once—we try to treat our customers with every consid—"

"You'll do no such thing," said Mrs. Vandercook calmly. "She was only doing her duty, and you must admit I do look like the description. Good heavens, I'll never hear the last of it from Bob! But what I would like to do is deposit this check."

"Of course, of course—I'll see to it personally—" When they left he was escorting her to the head teller, still talking.

"And I wonder how many other women in the county there are who match that description," said Hackett.

"You have such cheerful thoughts," said Mendoza.

Just as they got back to the office, a call came through from Carey. "I've got a little further with this, via your ideas about the silver certificates. I just thought you'd like to—"

"I would. I'm inclined to agree with you now that the Borchers woman is dead. What have you got?"

"Well, you hit the nail on the head. She didn't spend much money period, the only place I could think of that we know she did was the doctor's office. Like most of 'em now he's got one nurse who does nothing but make appointments, keep the books, take in the money. Her name's Helen Pitt, divorcée about thirty-five. I tackled her about it, how did Mrs. Borchers pay, in cash or what. And right away she looked a little—you know—shy of me, so I kept at her, did the cash look different from any other, anything special about it, and of course technically there's nothing illegal about it, and I finally got it out of her."

"Silver certificates, and she'd noticed them."

"Yep. Her father's a numismatist. She says Mrs. Borchers always paid in ten- or twenty-dollar bills. She noticed it right away, about it being old money, and she said something interesting, Mendoza. She said that anybody else, she'd have called it to their attention, because the bills are worth over face value, but that Mrs. Borchers was such a horrid quarrelsome old woman, she didn't. She just quietly took the bills, substituted others of her own, and took the silver certificates to her father."

"Interesting, yes. So now we know. Was she interested in where it came from, suspect that wad the woman had?"

"She was curious, yes. She said so. But," said Carey doubtfully, "I don't think she—pursued it any farther. Took it for
granted the woman was a miser with a little hoard. She seems
to be straight, good reputation."

"Mmh. At least now we know, about the money. And I
think she is dead, Carey, and that the money is behind it—
whatever happened. I think somebody found out about that
money, and made a plan to get it away from her. I've got a
couple of ideas I might pass on—"

"Anything welcome."

"Where else might she have spent money, where somebody
else would possibly notice? Drugstores for sundries— And almost anybody might have noticed those bills. Quite a lot of
people taking an interest these days in the numismatics, not
per se but because of buying silver and gold. Clerk at a drugstore, clerk in a— You might ask Mrs. Donahue if she remembers whether Mrs. Borchers bought anything new about
that time. The woman must have bought a new dress occasionally. But somebody noticed, Carey. And furthermore,
somebody must have got her confidence somehow, unlikely
as that sounds. Just building a little tale on what we've heard,
I'd say most likely a woman. Who made up to her subtly,
and gained her confidence. Mrs. Borchers wouldn't have con-
fided in anyone about the money, but while she seems to have
been rudimentally the cunning miser, she wasn't really very
shrewd—she didn't know enough about money to be aware
of the significance of the silver certificates. She might have
let out enough that somebody thought it was worth a gamble.
Mmh. Had anyone been asking questions about her, around
that neighborhood?"

"I'll ask," said Carey.

"Anyway, this woman may have persuaded her that she'd
be happier elsewhere—maybe offered her cheaper accommo-
dations," said Mendoza vaguely. "Because she had her belongings packed, all ready. It could be that there was an
appointment at The Broadway that day—some mix-up so her

[188]

things weren't sent for till the next day— But I think that could be the general outline."

"And when she, they, whoever, came across this windfall, they killed her?"

"Well, stop and think what we know about her," said Mendoza. "Do you see anybody hanging on to it any other way? She'd have raised an outcry you could hear in Washington."

Carey laughed. "You've got something there all right. The son's gone back to Chicago. I told him I'd keep working at it. I'm interested in this, you might say, because nobody's missing the old biddy much. She doesn't sound like a very nice woman, but she had the right not to get murdered, after all."

"*Pues sí.* Let me know if anything turns up." As he put the phone down, a stray half-thought slid across Mendoza's mind; he pounced after it, but too late: it was gone. What? He could only pin down that it had something to do with Mrs. Eldon—Mrs. Eldon not expected to live, back in November. No, it was nothing—it was gone.

He picked up the Shaughnessy photographs again.

It really was a tedious little job, going down that D.M.V. list, picking out the addresses on Central's beat. Half the time Wanda had to use the County Guide to check; and Grace finally took pity on her and went to help. He took the second half of the pages from her, sat down at his desk, and began to run addresses down. It was the kind of finicky job that used up time, and he was surprised to see, glancing at his watch awhile later, that it had got to be nearly eleven forty-five. He was only about three-quarters of the way through the pages he'd taken, and Wanda was looking tired. He took time out to light a cigarette, yawned, and bent to the job again. San Marino Street, the twenty-six-hundred block—that was well within Central's beat—

"Robbery-Homicide, Sergeant Lake . . . oh, my God!"

"Oh, my God!" said Grace suddenly. "But that's—my God, it's not possible—"

Wanda looked up. "You've got another hit-run," said Lake. "The Traffic man says the boy's dead."

"Oh, my good God!" said Grace. "And here it is, isn't it? I want the Lieutenant's—"

"What?" asked Wanda.

"Kevin McLeod, Senior," said Grace. "San Marino Street. He's got a 1955 Dodge sedan."

"Oh, no—"

"John told me his reaction at the inquest. I think this is it," said Grace. He looked shaken.

Glasser had just come in, to hear that. "My God, Jase— we'd better do something about it, anyway. I'll come. Matt went to see some parents."

They went to the accident scene first and heard the witnesses. It was an intersection a block from an elementary school, and the boy had been deliberately run down, by what four witnesses said, as he stopped for the light there. The ambulance was gone; he'd been tagged D.O.A. at the scene. But the uniformed men had an I.D. on him from his wallet, Gilbert Helpern, an address on Quintero Street. He'd just left the same school where Timmy Jordan went, to ride home for lunch.

First things came first; they went to find the parents. No cop ever enjoys that part of the job, and they didn't complicate it by telling them it had been deliberate homicide. The father was at work, of course, and they had to call him home. The boy had been an only child.

They hadn't any chance for lunch at all. From there they went to the address on San Marino where the McLeods lived, and Mrs. McLeod let them in. He wasn't there. "Do you expect him in soon?" asked Grace, and felt a first pang of doubt about this. If the man had a job—

"I expect so," she said faintly. She looked alarmed. "Why? What do you want to see my husband for?"

"We'd like to ask him some questions," said Glasser.

"A-about what?"

"Well, I think we'll wait and see if he comes home soon. Where is he, Mrs. McLeod? Does he have a regular job?" She shook her head. "He can't—he's been sick. I didn't like to do it, but we had to take the welfare. When he wasn't home, I worked—at a store up on Third—but since he's been home, I mean better, I stay with him. I don't like being on welfare. But he's much better now," she added hastily, "much, much better. I knew he would be. I said to the doctor, he misses all the good home cooking and fussing over him, he'll be much better at home." She was talking rapidly, emphatically, repeating herself. "He just went out a little while ago to get some things for me at the market, I'm sure he'll be back soon, but whatever the police want of him I'm sure I don't—"

They heard the car turn into the drive. And Grace said quietly, "Home from where, Mrs. McLeod? Which hospital?"

She looked at them a little wildly and shook her head, wet her lips, and then whispered, "Camarillo. He's been there—off and on. But he's been much better really and—" She stared at them. The back door slammed. "He's—he's—done something again, hasn't he?" she whispered.

"Well, I'm back," he said abruptly from the door to the kitchen. "I couldn't get— Who are you?" The sudden savage suspicion in his eyes was startling. "What do you want?"

They were both on their feet, wary. Grace said, "We'd like to look at your car, Mr. McLeod. To see if it's been involved in an accident a little while ago."

McLeod stepped back. "You're going to say I'm crazy again," he said in something like a growl. "Well, I'm not! I thought the whole matter through reasonably and thoroughly and *it was not fair* that my boy should be killed and other people's boys be left alive! There was nothing fair or just about it, and I was given a special commission to remedy the matter. To remedy the matter. A very *special* commission, and I will not be deterred from carrying it out—" As they came toward him, he grabbed up a kitchen chair and lifted it high, poised to bring down.

"Now, Mr. McLeod. We'd just like to talk it over with you." Grace's voice was softer than ever. "Just talk it over—and hear all about how it happened—"

"Just—talk?" He looked uncertain.

"That's right," said Grace, and aimed a swift judo chop at his left wrist. The chair toppled, Glasser got tangled up in it and rose swearing to help Grace hold him down. They got the cuffs on him. Mrs. McLeod was sitting on the couch crying in a helpless kind of way, and McLeod was roaring at the top of his voice.

They finally got her to give them the name of the doctor at Camarillo. The ambulance came and took him away, down to the General. Since he'd been committed to Camarillo before, it wouldn't be necessary to hold him twenty-four hours before recommitting him. They called Camarillo and talked to the doctor. McLeod was manic-depressive, but had never exhibited any violence before. There'd be red tape on it, but presently now he'd be transferred to Atascadero, to the asylum for the criminally insane. They didn't get out of there so easily.

It was three-thirty by the time they got clear of that, and could sit somewhere over a sandwich and coffee. Grace called Palliser to tell him about it, gave him all the details.

"You know something, Jase?" said Palliser. "I think I'll go and tell Timmy about it."

He wasn't doing anything special on his day off, and he put on a tie and drove down to that hospital. Mr. and Mrs. Jordan were with snubnosed Timmy, and Timmy introduced him with aplomb.

"You found out anything, Sergeant?"

"Oh, really, Tim," said his father, "if you think you can make us believe somebody tried to kill you, bringing it up—you didn't try to tell the police that, I hope—"

"Well, I'm afraid somebody did," said Palliser. "We've just got him."

"Tried to kill *Tim?*—but my God—thought he was just dramatizing—" Jordan looked completely astounded.

"You did?" Timmy was pleased. "Why was he after me, Sergeant?"

"He wasn't after you specially, Tim. Just any boy about ten on a bike. You see, he's a man who isn't quite sane, but they'd let him come home from the hospital for a while because nobody ever suspected he was dangerous. And he had a boy about your age who was killed by a hit-run driver about ten days ago. He got the idea that it wasn't fair for other parents to have their boys alive when his was dead. He'd run down another one before you, and I'm sorry to say that he did it again today and killed the boy."

"Gosh, what a story!" exclaimed Timmy. "Boy, am I ever going to have a story to tell!"

The parents were exclaiming and asking questions; Palliser turned to them. "There's something else," he said. "Nobody could tell us anything about the car, but Tim remembered —he told us it was a 1955 Dodge. And that's how we traced him and got him. If you hadn't spotted that car, Tim, he might have killed or hurt some other boys before we found out who he was."

"Timmy!" His mother hugged him. "You're a hero!"

Timmy wriggled out of her embrace. "Well, for gosh sakes," he said, "I just hope from now on you won't go thinking I'm so dumb!"

Piggott, that mild-mannered man, was feeling annoyed and frustrated and wondering how the devil managed to get hold of so many people. The man who had been knocked down and robbed was George Santo, and he was an upright respectable citizen, a retired carpenter, and he wanted those little punks found and punished. Three boys, he said, and they couldn't be over fifteen—all this juvenile delinquency was an outrage. It was the principle of the thing, he said, and Piggott agreed with him; they'd only got about four dollars, but he wanted them apprehended. He could identify them, he said definitely, by their clothes and faces—one white boy, two Negroes.

They had seen the principal, who just looked resigned. Some of the public schools were no more than jungles these days. He let Piggott and Glasser and Santo look into class-rooms, and just how any of the decent kids were going to get educated with so many of the other kind also there was a puzzle too—and eventually Santo picked out all three. They got them in an empty classroom and confronted them, and the boys were brazen, arrogant. Nobody couldn't prove it wasn't their money. Nobody couldn't do anything to them—

In the end, Mr. Santo lost his temper. He was a man of common sense, and he knew, even as Piggott and Glasser knew, that the main reason for this kind being what they were at fifteen was that nobody had tanned their hides the first time they did something wrong; and that swift and sure punishment for wrongdoing was the best deterrent for not doing it again. Mr. Santo, seventy and retired, was still bigger than they were.

He interrupted Piggott richly. "You three louts," he said contemptuously, "are worthless little bastards and bound for hell, if you've got souls for the devil to claim," and before they could stop him he had punched one boy in the jaw, slapped another hard enough to fell him, and kicked the third hard in the seat of the pants. The boys, of course, started howling. Mr. Santo marched out, and Piggott and Glasser had all the explaining to do. And of course it was too late to cure them that way now; it just made them mad.

Glasser went back to the office, and Piggott went to see the parents. It used to be, with most parents, if you did something wrong at school you got whomped when you got home, but that day was long gone, long gone. From the first set of parents he met with such complete indifference—not active partisanship, but entire apathy—that he didn't bother to look up the others.

While he had lunch he ruminated as to just how much the indifference to evil aided the devil in doing evil. People—

"Did you hear it was Conway's gun accounted for Barnard?" said Hackett. It was four o'clock, and they'd heard the tale on McLeod from Grace and Glasser, sitting around the office; a little silence had fallen. "He's mad as hell, he and Tom have a double date set up for tomorrow and I.A.'s called the hearing for one P.M."

"Well, that kind of thing doesn't take long," said Glasser.

Shogart came in prodding a man ahead of him, a heavy-set, angry-looking man. "Somebody like to join me on this?" he asked.

"No," said Hackett. Shogart and his faith in the routine. "Waste of time, E.M."

Shogart looked annoyed. "Stash him away," said Mendoza, and Shogart led his captive down to an interrogation room and came back. "Who is he?"

"Edward Huber, pedigree of burglary, fraud. He's on P.A. from Chino."

"No," said Mendoza gently. "He really doesn't sound likely for Reynolds-Jowett, does he?"

"He's been on P.A. the right period. All I'm saying is, on the routine you've got to follow through," said Shogart stubbornly.

Hackett sighed and got up. "So, let's talk to him, make it short. He's about as likely as—"

Sergeant Lake called urgently, "Lieutenant! Guttierez' car's just been spotted in a public lot on Hoover! I've got the patrolman—"

Mendoza shot out to the switchboard and seized the phone. "Mendoza—who's this? Moss—¡no tocar! O.K., now listen. Where is it exactly?" Higgins came in; they'd hear the results of the lineup in the hospital later. "What's around there

[195]

where he might be? . . . Four bars, *sé*. All right, get the black-and-white out of sight, and yourselves, but stay around. We'd better not let him see any uniforms, if he is somewhere around and hasn't just abandoned the car. But I don't think he's bright enough to realize that Steiner got his plate-number, that he's been spotted." They had all seen Guttierez' record and mug shot by then: the low I.Q., the illiteracy, the tendency to simple violence. "There's a good chance he's around there somewhere. What else is on that block? . . . drugstore, tailor's, dress-shop, secondhand furniture," he repeated for the benefit of the others. "He's in one of the bars. Call up a couple of backup units, but stay out of sight! We're on our way." They knew the gun Guttierez had, an S. and W. 357-magnum.

Hackett said, "Not without the gun you're not, *amigo*. Go get it."

"Por Dios—" But Mendoza didn't argue, opened the top drawer of his desk and got out the .38, dropped it with extra ammo into his pocket. They were all there—Hackett, Higgins, Piggott just in, Grace and Glasser. "Let's take two cars —George's and Matt's—and have a nice easy ride down there."

They cruised down that block once, and spotted the white Ford sedan innocently parked in the metered lot. "All right," said Mendoza. "We'll have a look into these bars one by one. In order. Art, you and I'll do that." There were three on this side of the street, one across: holes-in-the-wall of bars, shabby, with tired-looking neon flashing. "If we spot him, one of us will come out and give you the sign—you can all come in and we try surrounding him. No telling how many people are sitting over drinks in there, and it would be nice, boys, to take him in without any vulgar shooting, *¿cómo no?* Art—*¡vamos!*"

The Pontiac and the Nova waited quietly and illegally in the driveway of that parking lot. The black-and-whites were waiting round on the side streets.

Mendoza and Hackett sauntered into the first bar. The only trouble with trying to spot anybody there was that it was, like most bars, dimly lit. Alison said it was a thoughtless holdover from Prohibition, and she could be right. It wasn't a very big place, but it was dark, and the few men huddled at the bar just vague shapes. Mendoza muttered to himself, and Hackett peered.

As Hackett said afterward, Mendoza sometimes did his jumping too precipitately. "What would have happened if the bastard had been there, Luis? Sure, it'd have spooked him, and he'd have run straight out, with the rest of the boys unprepared, and all hell been up. If you'd just think when you get these brainstorms—"

The fact remained, Mendoza hadn't. He said suddenly and rather loudly to Hackett, "What you suppose those cops are after outside?" Hackett jumped, the bartender looked nervous, and nothing else happened at all.

"What'll it be, gents?"

"Never mind," said Mendoza. They went out, and Hackett lectured him. "I just thought it might flush him if he was— *pues sí.* I'll be good. Second try."

In the second bar, there was more light, from two TV screens, and not as many customers. He wasn't there. They came out and started for the third. The Pontiac and the Nova nosed slowly up the street behind them.

The third bar was the smallest, and as soon as they went in they spotted Guttierez. And he was in an excellent position from their viewpoint, sitting in a booth alone. Mendoza said to Hackett happily, *"¡Siga adelante!"* and sat down at the bar and ordered rye.

Hackett slipped back to the door, stepped out to the street and gave the high sign. Higgins, Piggott, Grace and Glasser piled out of the two cars.

At this unfortunate moment, the driver of the car parked at the curb where the Pontiac was double-parked stepped off the curb directly in front of Higgins. "Hey," he said, "you can't double-park here—I wanna get out of here, for God's sake—move the heap, will ya?" He was nearly as big as Higgins and he was a little tight.

"Get out of the way!" snarled Higgins. Piggott, Grace and Glasser were nearly up to the door.

"You can't leave that here—I wanna get out—"

In desperation Higgins backhanded him and the man fell against his own car. Higgins loped after the others. He was the last into the bar.

Mendoza slid off the bar-stool, drink in hand, and walked over to the booth. "Anybody sitting here?" He bent over Guttierez, and let him see the badge. The five men crowded behind in a little bunch. "Now let's just take it quiet and easy, Guttierez. There are five men behind me and we'd like you to come along without any fuss—"

Guttierez rose up with a wordless shout, tilting the table and shoving Mendoza back to impede the little crowd of men, Hackett and Higgins looming over the others. Somehow he stumbled back away from the booth, and he had the gun out—it wasn't going so nice and easy at all. They all brought out guns, fast, but Guttierez fired first, blind. Mendoza dropped like a shot bird. Hackett and Higgins lunged forward together, heedless of that 357-magnum, and fell on Guttierez like avenging furies. In a wild tangle they got the gun, got the cuffs on him. The place was in an uproar, men shouting and running, Guttierez swearing, and uniformed men pouring in, summoned by the single shot.

Mendoza lay flat on his back on the filthy floor, a small spot of red on one temple.

"My God, he got Luis in the head—get an ambulance—" Hackett flung himself down over the corpse, which was in the act of sitting up, and their heads cracked together smartly.

"*¡Válgame Dios!*" said Mendoza. "Must you turn this into low comedy, Arturo? Ow!" He put a hand to his head. "He must have just creased me—knocked me out for ten seconds. *¡Santa María—qué demonio!* I just got this suit back from the cleaner—" He got up and began brushing himself down fastidiously. Guttierez had knocked the glass of rye out of his hand to spill all over his Italian silk suit jacket; he got out a handkerchief and tried to repair the damage.

"My God!" said Hackett crossly. "You'll be complaining to Saint Peter about the fit of your halo, I swear! You scared me, boy."

"At least we've got him," said Mendoza.

"And you'd better have a doctor look at that—"

"¡Tonteria! I'm O.K."

The uniformed men had hauled Guttierez away. There'd be a little paperwork on it. It was five o'clock, and as they came out of the bar something indefinable in the late-afternoon air said things about early spring: a vague warmth in the air even as darkness was coming on.

All the signs pointed to it: they'd be getting the usual short-lived March heat wave.

It had been, on the whole, quite a day. Piggott drove out to Scales 'n' Fins, and found Ron Babcock industriously sweeping the floor. He told Duff about that tetra, and Duff said in surprise, "Now, I could've sworn I gave you all males. Just fancy that, now!"

"My wife wants to try to breed some. You think we could? If I could rent a tank from you? The book says it isn't hard with those, and we're pretty sure the other three are males."

"Sure you can," said Duff. "The characins, they'll spawn any time o' year. You'd find it interesting, Mr. Piggott. I'll let you have a tank, sure, and some good seasoned water. You want to put in something for the eggs to land on, like the book says. And put her in half a day before you put him—"

"It's all in the book," said Piggott. "Might be interesting at that. How many will she have, probably?"

"Oh," said Duff casually, "she'll drop two, three hundred eggs altogether."

Piggott stared at him, aghast. "But what would we do with three hundred tetras?" The ten-gallon tank was just big enough to accommodate about thirty of the pretty little fish—

"Oh, you won't raise 'em all," said Duff. "And I'll give you twenty cents apiece for all you can raise to three months, say. There's always a good market for those little fellows. I sell 'em for forty, and everybody's happy."

Piggott did some rapid figuring and wondered just how long this had been going on. What with inflation, they could always use some extra money. "You would?" Sublimely unaware that most breeders of everything from guppies to prize-winning poodles had started out with the rosy vision of easy profits from letting nature take its course, he beamed at Duff. "It's a deal."

Twelve

When Mendoza came out to the back yard at eight o'clock Tuesday morning his entire household was there, everybody except the cats staring up into the alder tree.

"Don't tell me—" said Mendoza.

There was a subdued flash of gray and white and a bird soared into the distance. "It's not him," said Alison. "Not big enough." Cedric barked.

"Och, I'm afraid something's happened to the puir thing," said Máiri MacTaggart.

"Nothin' bad happen to *el pajaro, Mamacita?*" asked Terry.

"*El pajaro* comes back pretty soon," said Johnny confidently.

"And as for you," said Alison to Mendoza, "I trust you'll spend the day in the office deducing or something instead of getting mixed up in another gunfight."

"Remains to be seen," said Mendoza, with a baleful look at the alder tree, and made for the garage.

He landed at the rank of elevators at the same time as Hackett, who asked, "And what did Alison say about your getting knocked out?"

"Reminded me that only the good die young," grunted Mendoza. It was Grace's day off; he was probably doing some more practicing with the new camera. Upstairs, they found Lake, Higgins, Palliser, Piggott and Glasser grinning over the notes the night watch had left. Two things had shown up to enliven the night watch, leaving the day men one to do a little work on. A couple of patrolmen had brought in the young sailor, wrapped in a blanket, about midnight; he'd been enticed into a dark alley by a prostitute, who had made off with his pants, containing three months' pay. Landers' note went on to say that the other one was even funnier: a middle-aged couple, Mr. and Mrs. Warren Baker, held up on the way back to their car from a movie. It seemed that Baker had been accumulating a secret little hoard by holding out on lunch money, cigars, claiming haircuts had gone up, and he'd had it on him, nearly a hundred bucks his wife didn't know he had. She'd been madder about that than the heist. However, they had given a good description of the man, enough to try for a list of possibles from Records. Piggott and Glasser went down to R. and I. with it.

A new call came in just then, as Lake, looking glum, was saying he'd got back on that low-protein diet. Somebody had found a corpse over on Westlake Avenue. Hackett and Higgins went out to look at it. Notice came in from the D.A.'s office that Lorna Easely would be arraigned tomorrow, Epps and Robinson together on Thursday. Mendoza took Palliser into his office and thrust the Shaughnessy photographs at him.

"You can listen to me deduce, John." He marshaled his first reasoning on the series of photographs, and Palliser nodded.

"The powder burns on Mrs. Shaugnessy bear that out—she was shot as he came by, on his way out. But no leads on it at all, just the description."

"And what Mr. Salter saw, the glimpse of the red car turning from Geneva onto Virgil—it just could have been our boy. *No sé*," said Mendoza, "but I think maybe we might develop a lead if we stop and think. Why did he shoot them? All of them? And run out minus any loot?"

"He panicked," said Palliser.

"Why? All right, say he's an amateur, still Mr. Teitel was right, Shaugnessy wouldn't have resisted him, with his wife and the girl there. Now, I'm saying that wild shot was the first one."

"Why?" asked Palliser. "Nothing says so."

"I say so. It got fired because he was—startled. Spooked. And I've done some thinking on this, and I see a possibility —just a possibility—that might give us a lead." Palliser sat back and lit a cigarette, listening interestedly. "The description we got, young, possibly a teen-ager but big. All right. Suppose he walked in there, intending to pull a heist, and just as he gets up to the rear counter Sue comes out of the back room and he recognizes her as a girl he knows at school, who knows him. Could tell it was him. He's startled, surprised, the gun goes off—"

"Just one little thing," said Palliser. "Somebody said she went to a parochial school. They're not co-ed, are they?"

"I have the impression the high schools are— Hell," said Mendoza, "I don't know. But all right, try this. That Diane girl said Sue didn't date much. How much is much? She probably had had dates, in little crowds of teen-agers anyway —beach parties and so on. And the Shaughnessys being very upright people, they'd have known any boy she'd gone with —have met him when he picked her up at the house, all proper. So try it the other way round. X came in and found himself facing Sue's father—somebody who knew him."

Palliser nodded. "It would explain the general setup. But there's no evidence on it at all."

"I can see it going like that," said Mendoza. "He was all set to pull that job, and then he had the hell of a shock— a surprise. And what else could it have been, John? I want to find out about that school—it'd be a place to start looking —and about any boys, from the school or elsewhere, Sue had dated." He looked at his watch. "I wonder if the brother and his wife would know."

"Who would know," said Palliser, "is that other girl—her best friend. Lives on the same block, you said."

"So she would. And damn it, she'll be in school now, and I don't even know which one. *Mil rayos.*" But he told Lake to try Walter Shaughnessy's house in Santa Monica; after three rings a boy's voice answered and he asked for Shaughnessy.

"Oh, he's not here, can I—"

"Do you know where he is? This is the police—"

"Oh, yes, sir, he said if anybody called tell them, he'll be at my Uncle John's house in Hollywood by ten. To—"

"O.K., thanks very much."

The new body looked like the usual sordid and simple thing. The old apartment house on Westlake was ready to fall apart, and wouldn't attract the most desirable citizens, but one of the tenants, leaving for work, had seen the body past an open door across the hall, and reported it to the manageress downstairs.

"It's Mis' Cutter," she told Hackett and Higgins. "Leastways, I dunno if she's married to him or not, but that's who it is—Thelma Cutter." The body was that of a woman about fifty, dressed in a sleazy chiffon robe; she'd been strangled. "They musta had a fight," said the manageress incuriously. "No, I don't know if he's got a job or where. They was behind on the rent some."

They called up a lab truck and while they waited asked her if she knew of any relatives. She shook her head and then said, "Well, she had a daughter. She was allus talkin' about her daughter Norma, ungrateful child turnin' against her."

Among the miscellany in the old, cluttered, dirty rooms was an address book, and in it they found an address for a Norma Woodin in West Hollywood. They left the lab men busy in the apartment and started out there.

"I'm going to get a start on that darkroom on Thursday," said Higgins as they got into the car; they were using Hackett's scarlet Barracuda. "Get the partitions up anyway. It'll be good practice for Steve. He thinks now—you know he always wanted to join the force—he might go in for the lab end of it. God knows I suppose it might be more interesting than the run-of-the-mill stuff we see."

"Except when the funny things come along," said Hackett, thinking about the stolen tombstone and the man who was afraid of vampires.

At the address in West Hollywood, they interrupted a pretty dark girl vacuuming the living room of a modern, middle-priced apartment. They told her who they were and why they were there, and she sat down looking pale and finally produced a few tears.

"It's terrible," she said. "Just terrible—to feel so—*not* to feel anything—for your own mother. I'd better call Dad. And Ken—my husband. Oh, how awful. *Murdered*. But—she left Dad when I was twelve, he'd only stayed with her on my account. And I got away as soon as I could and went back to him. It's just terrible to have to say it, tell you, but she was always p-picking up men, and—"

"Do you know anything about this Cutter?"

She shook her head. "The latest one, I suppose. Oh, it's terrible, isn't it? When—when she was a little drunk she used to phone me, beg me to come and see her. Ken didn't like it. I'd better call Dad. I don't suppose she had any money, and I know he'll feel he ought to pay for the funeral."

At ten-thirty Mendoza was systematically stacking the deck for a complicated crooked deal when Sergeant Lake ran in. "Bank job again—any bets it's her? Corner of Hill and Fourth—"

Mendoza dropped the cards and ran out. Palliser was the only one in. "Come on, John. I doubt if this is another false alarm, two days running." Downstairs, he switched on engine and siren; it was only a few blocks away.

That was normally a busy, congested intersection. As the Ferrari braked, heading in for the red curb on Fourth just outside the bank, Palliser said, "Look there—the Feds couldn't have beaten us—"

A scant quarter-block ahead, two well-dressed men were herding a woman between them, a woman who certainly looked like Grandmother; each had her by an arm, and they were walking her quickly back toward the bank. Just ahead of the Ferrari here, stopped to disgorge and take on passengers, was a big yellow bus. As Mendoza and Palliser got out of the car, the woman suddenly jerked free of her captors and started at a little trot for the bus. The men shouted and waved, but she made it; and Mendoza and Palliser flung themselves at the front door just as it sighed and began to close with a whoosh.

"Police—hold it!" snapped Mendoza. The driver, startled, stamped on the brake and threw everybody off balance. Grandmother was still in the aisle, and Mendoza took her by the arm.

"Oh, dear," she said pathetically. "Oh, you won't hurt me, will you?"

"Listen, Mac," said the driver. "If you're a cop, I wanna see your badge! I don't let you take this poor little old lady nowhere unless you can prove you're a real cop!"

"How very kind of you," she said, looking at him sweetly.

"Listen—"

"Here's the badge, for God's sake!" Palliser thrust it at him. He examined it minutely, grudgingly decided it was real, and reluctantly opened the door for them. They got Grandmother out and into the manager's office at the bank. The Feds were there by then.

Mendoza and Palliser listened to the bank personnel while the Feds had a first look at Grandmother. She'd got a haul of over six thousand this time. But an alert teller at the next cage had spotted what was going on and slipped out to tell a couple of the men. She'd got out of the bank by then and they'd chased her.

"Just walking off on foot that way!" said one of them. "But, my God, even after we got her, she's so little and frail-looking we didn't like to, you know, use much force—and I guess she took us both by surprise when she jerked away—damn lucky you were there. I can't get over it—that old lady robbing banks—"

When they conferred with the Feds, it seemed her name was Wilma Moore. They had the money, and the gun, from her capacious handbag. The gun was an old Colt .32 revolver. "She doesn't like our faces," said Valenti. "Wouldn't say anything. Maybe she'll like you better."

Mendoza and Palliser went into the manager's office. She was sitting primly in the chair beside the desk, feet crossed and hands in her lap. She looked like a very nice old lady, her white hair in its bun, her trim little figure clad in a dark suit, a frilly white blouse. Her blue eyes were faded, her complexion delicately withered.

"Now, Mrs. Moore—is it Mrs.?" asked Mendoza.

"Oh, yes. Yes, of course." Her eyes were a little frightened.

"Would you like to tell us just why you held up the banks?" Palliser sat down in the desk chair, pulling it closer to her. "We really would like to know. Nobody's going to hurt you, you needn't be frightened."

"You look like a nice young man," she said. She didn't seem to like Mendoza any better than the Feds; he lit a philosophical cigarette and strolled away to look out the window. "What's your name? . . . Oh, that's a nice name. My husband was John too, but when our son was born he wouldn't have a Junior, so we called him Jerry. For Gerald, you know. Are you married? Do you have any children?"

"Well, my wife's expecting a baby in a couple of weeks."

"Isn't that nice!" She beamed at him. "Then I'm sure you'll understand how it was. You see, Jerry's had such bad luck, he couldn't work for months after that accident and it took all their savings. They'd been saving such a long time to buy a nice little house in the suburbs somewhere, Glendale, they thought. My son Jerry, and such a sweet girl he married, dear Norah, and the two darling children—Dickie's four and Anne's two."

"Yes, Mrs. Moore."

"It's so bad for the children, living in that tiny apartment, no place to play, no fenced yard—and dangerous too, you

daren't take your eye off them on the street. And I did so want
—I *did* want—to help Jerry and Norah get a nice little house
with a yard for the children. A substantial down payment,
you know."

"And you thought about the banks?"

"Well, they have a lot of money, and it's not like taking
it from a *person*. My goodness, I couldn't have done that."

"And where'd you get the gun?"

"Oh, it was John's. For protection. I didn't have the least
idea how to put any bullets in it, I don't think there were any
left, anyway." The gun, in fact, had been empty. "I thought
it was such a good idea!" she said brightly.

"But you didn't tell Jerry or Norah about it?"

"Oh, no!" said Mrs. Moore. "That would have spoiled the
surprise!"

Down at R. and I., Piggott had given Phil O'Neill the description of last night's heist-man, and presently the computer
picked out a list of men from Records who might fit it. This
would be just a first cast, of course.

At least Patrolman Steiner was recuperating nicely, which
was gratifying.

Piggott had been telling Glasser about the little tetras.
"Say," said Glasser after a moment's rapid figuring, "that's
quite a racket, Matt. The fish do all the work—well, you
have to feed them, but—and you get a nice little profit.
That's quite a thing."

"Well, see how it turns out, but we thought it sounded
interesting."

The list had twenty-eight names on it. They split them up
and went out hunting, back at the routine.

Hackett and Higgins came back to the office at eleven-
thirty, heard about Grandmother—Mendoza had called in,
said he and Palliser were going to find the family—and went
down to R. and I.

"You're busy up there," said Phil.

"And keeping fingers crossed that the I.A. hearing doesn't keep Conway from the double date," said Hackett, grinning. Phil looked annoyed.

"Of all things—Margot was furious. We've all looked forward to seeing this show, and then those witch-hunters—oh, well, fingers crossed. What can I do for you?"

"Theodore Cutter," said Higgins. They'd finally got a first name for him from an envelope in a wastebasket in the apartment; it had once held a welfare check. "Have we got him on file?"

She went away to find out, and five minutes later handed them the package: not a very extensive one. He was Caucasian, fifty-one, five-nine, a hundred and forty, gray and blue, no marks. The most serious charge on him was burglary, two counts, but he'd served his last time on that ten years ago. The rest said felonious drunk driving, three counts, D.-and-D., a long list of those.

"No good to ask the D.M.V. about a car, he won't have a license," said Hackett, "after those three felony counts."

"Which isn't to say he's not driving a car registered to her," said Higgins.

"True. We'd better ask. Had she a record? I know it looks like Cutter, plain and simple, but just conceivably it could have been somebody else, one of her prior men."

"Also true." They gave the name to Phil: Thelma Norgood. They had the name from the girl. Phil busied herself with that miraculous automatic teletype which brought answers back from the D.M.V. in Sacramento within minutes, and went to look in their files. Before she came back with another package, Sacramento had told them about a car registered to Thelma Norgood: a seven-year-old Ford two-door, plate-number such and such.

The package on Thelma was slim. It was very doubtful that she'd been married to Cutter; there wasn't any record of a marriage after the first husband had divorced her. She had a little pedigree of D.-and-D., soliciting, and she'd been picked up on a Vice raid of one of those massage parlors. She'd spent little stretches in the county jail, shoplifting, petty theft. No mention of any associates, except for that massage parlor bit, and that was five years back.

"I think we want Cutter," said Higgins.

Hackett thought so too. They put out a city-wide A.P.B. on him and the car.

Mendoza and Palliser were the ones to have a late lunch today. They had found Mrs. Jerry Moore at the apartment on Burlington Avenue, and she'd called her husband home from work. He had a job as a lathe-operator at a local plant, but he'd only been on the job a month. He eyed them, introduced as police, in annoyance. "This damn drunk rams me on the freeway, put me in the hospital for three months, and we've got no medical insurance, and the drunk doesn't have any period. So you put him in jail, that's a big help to me." He was a belligerent dark fellow. His wife was trying to shut him up, pulling at his arm; he ignored her. "So this is some more about that, you've got to have some more answers for your records? I thought all the red tape was—"

"Jerry, no—listen! It's something awful—I don't believe it, but—"

When they finally got it across to him, he was struck dumb. And then he said, "My God, my God—but she couldn't be thinking straight—that stroke she had last year—but what'll happen to her, what are you going to—"

Mendoza explained the formal procedure to them. "If the stroke has affected her mind, that'll be taken into consideration, you know. We've got her down at the facility on Alameda, she's quite comfortable, but if you'd like to see her, take her some clothes, that's quite all right."

They looked at each other. "Mother in jail!" said Moore, "My God!"

"Oh, we'd better go see her, Jerry! She'll be frightened and all alone—a cell—"

Mendoza and Palliser got up to Federico's for a late lunch at two-fifteen.

About one o'clock, as Sergeant Lake was thinking glumly of the carrot sticks and cottage cheese he'd had for lunch, a call came up from the lab.

"Say," said Duke, "we've got some dandy latents off a billfold you sent down. If we've got 'em on file, it'll be an easy make."

"Billfold?" said Lake. "Just a minute. Wanda, who sent a billfold down to be printed, on what?"

"I don't rememb—oh, I know. Jase was growling about it. That body in an alley—a Richard Bliss. They sent the billfold down to the lab and then they found out it was a bunch of known j.d.'s laying for the fags, so it wouldn't be any good—"

"Yeah, I heard something about that," said Lake. "Sorry to tell you your work's gone for nothing, Duke. It was a bunch of j.d.'s and nobody'll have them listed."

"Oh, hell," said Duke.

Piggott and Glasser came back to the office at one o'clock, one after the other; they each had a man in tow to question. "At least it's something new after all those men on P.A.," said Glasser. "That's a funny one, Jowett. That note. I know what Mendoza means when he says he doesn't like the feel of it. Neither do I."

But meanwhile they had these two to lean on, and they took them one by one. Both of them could prove they were elsewhere when the heist was pulled, so they let them go. They heard about Grandmother with interest, and about the prints on Bliss's billfold with annoyance; but that was how things went. In the fullness of time the j.d.'s would turn into legal adults, and as they would probably go right on committing the misdemeanors and felonies, their prints would eventually get on file somewhere.

They went out to look at some more possibles.

And once in a while, just once in a while, the routine paid off with surprising swiftness and efficiency. One of the names the computer had handed them was that of Ray Drummond, a record of robbery from the person, mugging, a number of counts as well as the simple D.-and-D.'s. He had got out of Chino the last time three years ago and wasn't on P.A., so there wasn't any firm address for him. But the I.D. card had the notation, *See Addison, Marion.* Her file, which was concerned with petty theft, shoplifting and various small-time bunco schemes, told them that Drummond was her common-law husband.

So now Piggott went to find Marion, and they had a more recent address for her because she'd been picked up only ten days ago on a bunco count; she hadn't been held because the victim wouldn't press charges. It was an old apartment house on Dundas in Boyle Heights. She wasn't home, but Drummond was, just blearily awake after sleeping off a drunk.

Piggott started talking to him, and decided he might have something hot here; Drummond couldn't tell him where he was at midnight last night. Conveniently, he aimed a clumsy blow at Piggott, so there was legal excuse to look around for any evidence visible, and very visible on the dresser in the bedroom was a gun, with a little pile of loot beside it, some cash, and the diamond ring Mr. Baker had described to the night watch. Piggott arrested Drummond formally, told him about his rights, collected the evidence, and brought his captive back to the office. Glasser was just back, empty-handed.

It wasn't any use to talk to Drummond until he was fully sober; they took him over to the jail, and Piggott dictated a report to Wanda.

"What's keeping the boss busy all this while?" Glasser asked Lake.

"No idea, he hasn't called in."

"Now if we could just find that sailor's pants—"

"Oh, I see what you're driving at," said Palliser over the belated lunch. "It's all up in the air, but—"

"It's the only reason I can think of for his running out

without stopping to grab up something," said Mendoza. Rather unprecedentedly he had had a shot of rye before lunch. "He didn't intend to fire the gun, but once he had, he might also figure that with the rain drumming down it wouldn't have been heard. Why didn't he go on and hold up Shaughnessy? I tell you, that wild shot is an—an earmark, John. A signpost, do I mean? He knew Shaughnessy, or the girl, from somewhere—and he hadn't expected to see any-body he knew. That's what could have triggered it, to leave the exact situation we've got."

"Oh, I follow you," said Palliser. "But where do we go looking, to turn up a lead?"

It was getting on for three o'clock. "The girl ought to be home from school by the time we get there. And possibly Walter Shaughnessy's still there."

They stopped first at the Shaughnessy house to see. He was there. He asked them if they'd found out anything. "Not much yet," said Palliser.

"I—we thought it was best to take the few valuables here," said Shaughnessy. "I suppose the house will be sold. John had some silver dollars, and— They called—and said we could—claim the bodies now."

"That's right," said Mendoza. "The school your niece went to, Mr. Shaughnessy—a parochial high school—is it coedu-cational?"

"I think they all are now. But Sue wasn't allowed to date much and—why do you want to know that?" He looked be-wildered.

"One thing," said Palliser as they started down the street from that house, "does strike me. We said, that very innocent sixteen-year-old. But innocent or not, teen-age girls do gloat over little secrets, don't they? Like to flout mama and papa a little, even in an innocent way. Confide in each other."

"*De veras*—things they wouldn't mention to mama and papa. That is a thought," said Mendoza. "I rather think, if there's anything in this at all, Diane Parrish might give us a hint."

She answered the door: the pretty dark girl, her skirt a

modest length. When Mendoza said they had a few questions for her, she came out on the porch instead of asking them in. There was a patio lounger and two chairs there; they sat down.

"But I wouldn't know anything to tell you," she said. She was, however, Palliser noted with amusement, unlike Grandmother: she was responding to the conscious charm in Mendoza's voice.

"Just a little background," he said. "I know you said Sue wasn't allowed to date—"

"Alone with a boy. We all went places in—in a crowd, paired off kind of. Beach parties and—"

"Mmh. And you know the boys at school, those in the same classes." Mendoza paused suddenly. If there was any lead here, he didn't see how Diane could give it to him. If his imagination hadn't been working overtime on this, that was it right there: the mere presence of boys at school. It could have been any boy she'd known casually, or not known except for his name. "Is it a very big school?" he asked absently, thinking of the possible routine on that: and looking at juveniles too, which was always awkward because of the laws.

"Oh, not nearly as big as a public school, I think the student body's about six hundred." She was looking at him curiously, but interested.

"Many of the boys drive cars to school?"

"Oh, hardly any. I know in places like Hollywood High, a lot of kids have their own cars. But mostly the ones in a school like Holy Family, well, it costs to go there, most families have sort of sacrificed to send their kids there, and can't afford—I know Daddy wouldn't let Donnie until he was out of high and going to Loyola, and then not until he earned the money himself. Which I think is O.K., the right way to do it. I—Lieutenant, I—I didn't like to call Sue's uncle to ask —about the funeral. Do you—"

"He's up at the house now, he can probably tell you." Mendoza, having exercised his imagination at this, was suddenly seeing all the legwork that could lie ahead, the probing at the juveniles. He opened his mouth to ask another random question.

"Oh, Donnie's home early," she said.

Automatically Mendoza followed her glance out to the street. A little bright red Corvair had just pulled into the curb. A big young fellow got out of it and started up the walk, carrying an armful of papers and books. And Mendoza said with a little gasp, *"¡Caramba! ¿Qué es esto? De buenas a primeras"*—He stood up; and at the same moment the young fellow noticed him and Palliser there, and stopped in his tracks.

Mendoza went down the walk toward him. Her light feet pattered behind. "These are the policemen, Donnie—about the Shaughnessys. I don't know why they thought I could tell them anything, but—"

And Mendoza said almost conversationally, looking up at Don Parrish who topped his five-ten by a few inches, "Could you tell us anything about it, Parrish?"

He was perhaps twenty or a bit more, but he had a vaguely immature face, round and showing only a faint down of beard. He was wearing slacks, a sports shirt, a little black beret. And he looked from Mendoza, suave and dapper, to tall dark Palliser, and he said stupidly, "Police? But I—but I—"

"What about it, Parrish?" said Palliser, suddenly alert.

"But I—don't see—how you knew it was me," he said. The chief emotion in his voice was surprise.

"Would you like to tell us about it?" said Mendoza gently.

"I'll tell you—if I have to. I'll tell you." Suddenly he dropped all the books and papers on the ground, as if renouncing them very finally. He said dully, "I—was—sorry. I was sorry. It—just—happened."

That was when the girl began to scream.

He was twenty-one, legally adult. They took him back to headquarters, after they'd talked to the mother. Mrs. Parrish was a plump, rather stupid-looking woman who didn't clearly understand what was going on at all; she said obediently she'd call her husband. When the Ferrari pulled away from the curb she had her arms around a sobbing Diane, mechanically patting her, bewilderment in her eyes.

He told them all about it, in a dull voice. He said he understood the rights they read to him, but he told them anyway. "The car," he said. "The damn car. Dad said—not till I was out of high. And I had to pay for it myself. I had to have a car—dates, and driving to college. *College.* I had to go to college—do better than him, he said. I didn't want to go to college—I'm no brain. I'm pretty good with my hands, something like that I'd like—working on cars, or— But that didn't count, what I wanted. The car—"

"What about the car?" asked Mendoza.

Don Parrish brought one fist down on his knee in sudden frustration. "I got the jobs in summer, I saved money for it—but there's dates, and everything so high—I got a job now in the cafeteria on campus, I thought I could keep up the payments on the damn car with that—twenty bucks a month, and twelve months to go—but there are things you've got to buy! Things—

"I was scared, I first thought of it. But the more I thought about it, it seemed the easy way to do. Real easy. A lot of hold-ups happening—and businesses insured, nobody'd really lose—I thought about it so long, way to get money, I—I—I got *used* to the idea. You know? You know? And then—the very first time I tried—"

"But why did you pick the Shaughnessys' pharmacy?" asked Palliser.

"Goddamn it, how did *I* know it was his place? *I* didn't know the Shaughnessys! It was Diane was Sue's pal—I just knew Sue, Diane's girl friend, hanging around our house! I didn't know her mother and father, how would I, she was just Diane's—I didn't know him, he was just a man there, at the counter. And nobody else in the store then, it was a good deal. I went up to him, I got out the gun—"

"The gun," said Mendoza.

He gave a half-sob. "It was Dad's, he got it last year—the crime rate up. He made me practice with it—this range out in Pasadena somewhere. I didn't even *say* it, This is a stickup, give me the money— Just all of a sudden she was there at the back, Sue, she said Hello Donnie, and I didn't believe it, but the gun went off and—it—was—all—on—account—of—the—damn—car payments. Everybody'd know—Dad'd know—and I—I did it before I knew what I was doing—I had to—"

"You shot them both," said Mendoza. "And then as you ran out, you saw the woman."

"She just—all of a sudden was there, behind that counter, and I—I was *sorry,*" he said desperately. "I was *sorry.*"

They would have to get a search warrant to pick up the gun. "You and your imagination," said Palliser. "You were a little off base, but basically you read it." And that was at five o'clock, just after they'd transferred him to jail.

Hackett and Higgins came in, wanting to hear all about it. "We've been wandering around all day on this damn Cutter. How'd you break it?"

Mendoza sat back and contemplated his cigarette, after they were told. "They do say, things go by threes. Having broken two today—"

"Three," said Piggott from the door. "We dropped on last night's heist-man. I understand we've got there on that multiple shooting."

"Proverbs," said Hackett.

And Kelleher walked in looking interested, Kelleher from Questioned Documents down in S.I.D. He said, "Good, you're still here, Mendoza. We finally got around to your second little love-note, and it's a lot more interesting than the first. I've got it mounted under ultra-violet to show the various points, but the main thing is, you've got somebody here imitating the illiterate scrawl, who isn't illiterate at all. It's ballpoint, of course—useless for pressure or shading—but that's clear enough. The pseudo-ignorant spelling, the—"

They stared at him. *"¿Qué demonio?* The note on Jowett— *¡Diez millón demonios desde infierno!"* said Mendoza violently. "I said it was the wrong shape—but what the hell, the note faked? But that says—*¡Por Dios*—Flavian! Flavian and the funeral—"

Thirteen

"Now where are you jumping to?" demanded Hackett.

Mendoza had sat up and was looking at Kelleher. "Scout's honor—a fake? But if that's so—"

"It's gospel, Lieutenant," said Kelleher. "And very interesting if you ask me."

"But, Luis, how could it—an imitation of the one on Reynolds—that was top security," said Higgins. "We didn't give that out anywhere."

"I know we didn't," said Mendoza. "I suppose we all told our wives—it was a little joke. A joke—*¡Por Dios!*"

"Oh, now, Luis," said Hackett. "You know police wives don't go opening their mouths. Angel would never have—any more than Alison."

"Or Mary," said Higgins. "But who else knew?"

Mendoza stabbed out his cigarette and immediately lit another. "When you stop to think, quite a few people in the LAPD knew about it. And I'd like to know where the leak was—mmh, yes. That we'll find out. But right now I'm thinking about what this tells us, about Jowett. And the most obvious thing it tells us—Jowett was set up to look like the outside job. The impersonal kill. Now we hear this—*pues no.* There must have been a personal motive, and so now I think we want to know a lot more about Jowett and his wife and friends and acquaintances and enemies. And the couple of rather odd little things Flavian told us about that funeral."

He looked at his watch and stood up. "Want to do a little overtime, Art?"

"I'll hear what you turn up tomorrow," said Higgins. "I've had a day, and this damned impossibility puts the topping on it. A faked note! A leak! Oh, I see it, I see what you're talking about, but I don't like it any better than I did before. It's still a freak case."

"I might agree with that," said Palliser, yawning. "So we start to work it all over. Hell. And good luck on the overtime."

Mendoza said to Lake on the way out, "Call both our wives and say we'll be late, Jimmy. We'll pick up something to eat."

"That much overtime?" said Hackett. "You know, one thing, Luis. It can't have been the wife. She was alibied. He wasn't cold when he was found, and she was at some neighbor's helping her with some sewing. I saw the report. But, my God—if Kelleher's right—this turns it all upside down!"

"*Pues sí*. And I am now wondering," said Mendoza, "whether that was planned too. Whether somebody told her to provide herself with an alibi."

"Where are we going?"

"First, to talk to her." But at the apartment on Commonwealth Avenue they got no answer to their knocks. Mendoza finally tried the door across the hall, and plump little Mrs. Walling opened it to them.

"You're different police than came before. Mrs. Jowett? Well, I don't know where she'd be, out with friends, I suppose. No, I haven't seen her today."

"Do you know Mrs. Jowett pretty well, Mrs. Walling?" asked Mendoza.

"Why, she seems like a nice person. The little I've seen of her. She helped me out with that hem. I'd just mentioned how it was awkward to do alone—oh, dear, that was the same night her poor husband got killed. We hardly knew him, of course, they only moved in here in January."

Mendoza raised his brows at Hackett. "I see. Do you know if they moved from somewhere in this area, or—"

"I don't know, I'm sure. I think I heard her mention Huntington Park. But what do the police want of her now, it's all—"

"Well, a few things came up," said Mendoza vaguely. "She's not planning to move, is she?"

"I'm sure I don't know, she hasn't said so, but it's her own business." When he thanked her she shut the door a little emphatically.

"And now where?" asked Hackett as they went downstairs. Mendoza stopped in the front hall, eyeing the front door vaguely. "Waiting for the fairies to tell you?"

"An inside case," said Mendoza. "Yes. That note—and I'd like to know where the leak occurred, so that he knew enough about that note to fake another— To cover up. To make it look— Mmh, yes. And of course, whatever or however, the obvious thing is the other man."

"You said she's a dreep."

"There are other men for all sorts of females," said Mendoza. After a moment he added, "And if so, ten to one Jowett did some talking to somebody—best pal, mother, whoever—if, of course, he knew about it. Which he might not have. But—it isn't a hard and fast rule, but most people have relatives." Suddenly he went into the public phone booth in the lobby and began hunting in the book.

"Going to go and see every Jowett listed?" said Hackett. "It's not like Smith, but there'll be a few."

"*Imbécil.*" Mendoza shut the book, came out, took him by the arm and led him back to the Ferrari. "Crenshaw Boulevard."

"What?"

"The Everett Funeral Home."

"It'll be closed," said Hackett.

"Not at all. Some prettied-up corpse will be lying in state for mourners." And Mendoza was quite right; the double front doors were open and a few people just going up the steps. There was a good-sized parking lot. When they got past the doors, two discreet signs greeted them: *Mr. Bryson Paul-*

son, Slumber Room 1, and *Mrs. Laura Frye, Slumber Room 2.* Mendoza regarded them with distaste and asked a too-well-dressed attendant if Mr. Everett was on the premises.

"Well, young Mr. Everett, sir, but it's not business hours—" He stared at the badge. "Oh, I'll tell him, sir. If you'll just come back here—"

Out of the cloying scent of too many flowers, in the hushed rear premises, Hackett looked around uneasily. "This reminds me," he said, "of that other funny business, and all the bodies. Undertakers. What the hell are you looking for here, Luis?"

"Coffin Corner. Mmh, yes," said Mendoza. "Let's wait and see."

The attendant came back. "Mr. Everett says you're to come right in. This door."

It was a small but businesslike and comfortable office. Young Mr. Everett was in his thirties, good-looking, and he said, "Now what in the world do the police want here?"

"You had a funeral here last Saturday," said Mendoza. "Kenneth Jowett."

"Oh," said Everett. The interest in his eyes sharpened to avid curiosity. "Oh, yes, indeed. The one who was murdered. There'd been an autopsy. What about it?"

"You generally have some way of—mmh—recording who attended funerals? For the benefit of the family?"

"That's right. We ask people to sign the little cards, and deliver them to the—in this case, the widow, of course. We—that is, my father—told Mrs. Jowett we'd have them here for her to pick up the next day, but as a matter of fact she hasn't done so yet."

"*¿Y despues?*" said Mendoza. "Just fancy that. Have you still got them here?"

Everett looked from him to Hackett. "Well, yes. We thought perhaps we'd mail them to her—"

"*Bueno.* I'd like to see them. If you want to abide by the letter of the law, I can get a search warrant, but in the interests of saving time—"

"No, no," said Everett hastily, "anything we can do to oblige the police—" He went away and came back with a neat stack of small envelopes, held together by a tasteful black silk ribbon; the effect was somewhat spoiled by the cardboard tag tied to it, with a scrawled *Jowett* across it. "We distribute these as people come in, ask them to leave them in their seats—they're collected afterward."

"I see." But with the little stack in his hand, Mendoza looked at Everett meditatively and added, "By the way, who paid for the funeral? Mrs. Jowett?"

"Well, no. Actually, no. Funerals often occur—er—unexpectedly."

"*Naturalmente.*"

"And the family helps out, or we make some time arrangement. But in this case, the bill was paid in full."

"By whom?"

"As a matter of fact, the man's brother. A Mr. Joseph Jowett. He attended the funeral, of course, and he came up to my father afterward and asked—quite abruptly, Dad said—about the bill. The widow had made the arrangements, of course, and signed the contract to pay on time. But Dad had told him the figure, when he pressed for it—it came to seven hundred and eighty-five dollars—and we had a check two days later."

"*Sé. Extraño.*" Mendoza at last untied the ribbon, and shuffled through the envelopes rapidly, looking at the little cards. "And here we are, Arturo. Mr. and Mrs. Joseph Jowett, an address in Hollywood." He started to hand the rest back and then thrust them into his inside breast pocket. "On second thought, I'll keep these. We might find some witnesses in this lot. To something. Thanks so much, Mr. Everett."

Everett followed them down to the front door; he was obviously dying to ask questions. At the last moment he said, "Lieutenant—all you've been asking—for God's sake, *did she kill him?*"

Mendoza laughed. "No," he said, "she didn't, Mr. Everett. That we know at least."

It was seven-thirty. In the car he said, "I'll buy you a steak. And even a drink beforehand."

"Calories," said Hackett. "And then we go to see Mr. and Mrs. Jowett. This is a very funny one, boy. And that damned note worries me—how the hell could anybody have—"

"It doesn't worry me that much," said Mendoza, "I don't think the leak was at home, Art. But that we'll think about later."

Piggott came home and looked at the tank before he kissed Prudence. "I only just put him in," she said. They'd set the new tank up last night and after a good many frustrating attempts with the little net—an inquisitive serpa tetra kept getting into it instead—they had succeeded in transferring the female with eggs into it. She had been swimming about lazily ever since, more and more bloated with eggs. "I had an awful time catching him, and it's not the biggest one, but anyway he's *in*. This is quite exciting, Matt."

What Piggott found a little exciting was the thought of that extra money. Money for nothing, really. They watched the fish for some time, but nothing happened, so they went to have dinner. "Oh, by the way," said Piggott. "You remember the Reynolds case, Prue. I told you about that funny note—the first one. You didn't pass it on, did you? To your mother or—"

"Matt, you know I wouldn't. Anything you say not to talk about, and you said that was top secret. Of course I didn't. Why?" She looked at him curiously.

"Well—" said Piggott.

The Hollywood address was Sierra Bonita Street, and it was a single house, not an apartment: a small white frame house. It was impossible to say, in the dark, whether its front lawn was green, but it had a neat look about it. There were lights inside and a four-year-old Chevy in the carport. Mendoza and Hackett went up to the porch and Hackett pushed the bell. The inevitable chimes sounded, and after a moment the porch-light flicked on and the door opened.

"Mr. Jowett? Lieutenant Mendoza, Sergeant Hackett, LAPD. We'd like to talk to you about your brother, if it's convenient."

The tall man inside the screen door said, "Convenient! We were a little surprised the police didn't—but then why should you, it was some mugger down there and— Oh, come in. I didn't catch your names. Oh, yes." He looked at them, at dapper Mendoza, a little doubtfully; burly Hackett, looming, seemed to satisfy him better as a cop. "Jean, it's the police."

She came forward slowly, and Mendoza felt the small glow of warm satisfaction that reassured him he was on a right track toward something. Here, unless he was blind, was Flavian's pretty dark girl who had looked daggers at Rose Jowett at the funeral. Jowett introduced them and she said, "About Ken? But why now—I mean, us? We don't know anything about how he—"

"Things come up in homicide investigations sometimes," said Mendoza. "We have to ask questions that seem irrelevant, now and then."

"Well, sit down," she said. She was a pretty girl, younger than her husband; he looked to have been older than the brother. "What questions?"

Jowett offered cigarettes and Mendoza lit one of his own. "God, to think of Ken getting it like that!" said Jowett bitterly.

"You've got a job that pays pretty well, Mr. Jowett?" asked Mendoza. "You wrote a check to pay for the funeral in one fell swoop."

Jowett looked at him, and at his wife. "I'm an engineer at Lockheed. Yes, well, I knew they hadn't been able to save much. Least we could do. After all the—" he stopped.

"After all the other trouble?" said Mendoza.

"I don't know what you mean. There wasn't any trouble."

Mendoza looked at the wife. "Not between you and Rose Jowett?"

Jean Jowett flushed. "I don't know what you—"

"You didn't seem to be loving her much at the funeral."

"I didn't see you at the funeral," she said sharply.

"No. A minion. What about it?"

"Well, we can't all like everybody in the world."

Hackett asked suddenly, "Had there been trouble between them? And you sided with Ken?"

Husband and wife looked at each other. "Look," said Jowett in a low voice, "it's all over and done with. Ken's gone. It doesn't matter any more. What concern is it of yours?"

"It might be, Mr. Jowett. You said, a mugging. A little new evidence has just shown up that there could have been a personal motive. Just could have been."

Jean gasped. "You don't mean *she—Rose—*"

"No," said Mendoza. "We know your sister-in-law is in the clear, Mrs. Jowett. But we really would like to hear if there'd been—trouble. Another man. Arguments, what about."

"Trouble!" she said. "Trouble!"

"I don't see how that could be," said Jowett uneasily. "Over just—I mean, we all know the crime rate's up, and Ken going to work late—that dark drive— Look, it's not— not very pleasant to—after someone's dead—"

"We really don't enjoy—er—looking at other people's dirty linen," said Mendoza, "but sometimes we have to. You needn't worry that it'd get any publicity—unless it turns out to be relevant."

"Trouble," said Jean. "Relevant! Joe, do we have to tell them? I hate it—I hated it all so! It was so—it makes Ken look like such a fool, and he wasn't. I liked Ken—and a thing like that—"

"I know, hon," he said. "I know." He looked very troubled. Mendoza waited. Presently Jowett sighed and got out a cigarette and lit it. "All right. When it—got under way—

Ken used to come and talk to us. Blowing off steam. Only natural, and he knew we wouldn't talk about it. My God, keep the dirty gossip in the family. But it can't have anything to do with his getting killed, I don't see that."

"There'd been trouble between them?" said Hackett. "Another man?"

Jean gasped again and uttered a hysterical little laugh. "Hardly! That would have been bad enough, but—"

"I'm telling them," Jowett said. He looked at Mendoza and Hackett. "It was this woman," he said simply. "I know it sounds crazy. At first Ken said he didn't think much about it—a new girl friend, Rose talking about going out with Naomi, this and that about Naomi—well, my God, who would think anything? But then Rose moved out on him and moved in with her—that was last August—and he woke up to—to what was going on."

"You don't mean—" Hackett was incredulous but also amused; and Jean saw the incipient grin and flushed with anger.

"You *see?* You *see* why— It made him look like a weak fool—his wife leaving him for a—a—I don't know what you call those horrible women—"

"A butch," supplied Mendoza. "Well, I will be damned. I will be damned. Do you know her name? Where did Mrs. Jowett meet her? Know where she lives?"

"She met her at one of those ridiculous Women's Lib meetings," said Jean, "and Rose is such a nitwit, I don't suppose she knew what it was all about—trailed off with some neighbor they had then, just to be going somewhere. They were living in Huntington Park then. And when Ken *realized,* he knew how weak and silly Rose can be, and beside everything else he thought she'd be getting into trouble, with—with *that* kind. No, we don't know where she lives or anything else about her, and heaven knows I don't want to know. Her name's Naomi Buckler."

"Ken kept after Rose," said Jowett, "and he finally argued her round, made her see how wrong it was, and they went back together again, around Christmas. That's when they moved to that apartment."

"I'm sorry," said Jean, "but I just couldn't ever feel the same about her. Knowing she'd— Even if she had come back to Ken, and stopped seeing that—that—"

"Butch," said Mendoza. "That's a funny tale, all right." And the gossip would have got round the neighborhood then, when she left him—that explained the behavior of people at the funeral.

"But she had gone back to him," said Jowett. "You can see it couldn't have anything to do with—"

Mendoza stabbed out his cigarette, got up and yanked down his cuffs automatically. *"No se,"* he said absently. "If it isn't —relevant—we'll forget it. But thanks for telling us."

"Raking it up after he's gone," said Jean. "Relevant!"

Before he got into the Ferrari, Mendoza stood dangling the keys in his hand and said, *"Qué caso tan singular.* That's a very queer tale, isn't it? It makes you wonder about Jowett. A very forgiving husband, Art—a magnanimous husband, still concerned about the erring wife's reputation."

"Well, you can see the position he was in. He seems to have been a good man—the way his brother struck me too. Most men would be mad enough, put in a silly position like that, to've said good riddance."

"Exacto." Mendoza lit a cigarette. "And maybe typical. The strong character. Rose Jowett is a—dreep. Not bad-looking, but the very weak character, who'd always fall for the strong one—" He laughed. "Male or female! I wonder if anybody else she knows could tell us more about Buckler. Mmh. And what Flavian said otherwise, about that funeral —keep the gossip at home, said Jowett, but I'd take a bet that some kind of word had got around, among the people who knew Ken and Rose—at least that she was straying from home. And people seem to have liked him better than her. Attended the funeral out of respect, but didn't linger to sympathize with her. I wonder how to get some lead on Buckler."

Hackett cocked his head at him. "You have any hunches in that direction?"

"*Nada.* What I do have a hunch about—because I know my own men—is something else. And that we'll see about in the morning. Come on, I'll take you back to your car."

But he did ask Alison about it, being thorough, and she looked at him reproachfully and said, "Of course not, Luis! You know I don't talk your top secrets abroad. Máiri and I laughed about it—oh, as an oddity—but you know she wouldn't tell it around either, not even to sister Janet."

"I wasn't really thinking you had, *amada.*" To prove it he brought her up to date on Jowett. She was sitting up in bed over a book, looking very fetching in a green nylon gown; all four cats were asleep in a tangle on Mendoza's pillow, and Cedric was snoring on the foot of the bed.

"But of all the fantastic stories!" said Alison. "And sordid."

"The sordid we deal with more often," said Mendoza. "That is a fact. And if I'm going to sleep in this bed to-night— Livestock! At least we seem to be rid of that damned bird."

Alison woke up the cats, and they were annoyed.

Hackett asked Angel, just to be thorough, and she told him not to be silly. "You said it wasn't to be talked about, and you know I never do, Art." She was busy frosting a cake. It didn't help Hackett on his perennial diet that his Angel was a very gifted cook. "And you might look in on Sheila, she's been having nightmares again—"

But his darling Sheila was peacefully asleep at the moment, and in the room next door Mark had drifted off over Dr. Seuss.

On Wednesday morning Mendoza was idly scanning a report when Hackett and Higgins looked in. Glasser was off, and Grace back. "So how do we start all over on Jowett, Luis?

I've just been telling George what we turned last night. What's that?"

"Clean-up," said Mendoza, dropping the report. "Medical evaluation of Kevin McLeod. We are all going over to see Sergeant Ballard."

"Overnight, I had the same thought," said Hackett.

"My God, and talk about outlandish," said Higgins.

They found Sergeant Ballard in Welfare and Rehabilitation peacefully at the paperwork, puffing on a pipe and looking efficient. When they came in he said, "Don't tell me—"

"No, we don't tell you," said Mendoza, sitting down. "We've come to lay a little security leak in your lap, Ballard." He told him what Kelleher had said about the faked note. "Now, my men I know. Most police wives learn to keep their mouths shut—if they can't, their husbands know it and don't pass on secrets. But somebody—somebody outside, a civilian—heard about that first note, on Reynolds. And somebody used it in a very canny way to send us off on a wild-goose chase, making Jowett look like a random kill in the course of robbery. Now just how did that happen?"

Ballard looked angry. "Are you accusing me of—"

"Not accusing you. We don't know how it happened. But I'll vouch for the men in my office. The note being what it was, we came to you for the names of men on P.A., so you knew about it. Your office. Can you give a guess as to how it leaked—contents and style of that note—to somebody outside?"

Ballard put his pipe down. He looked, now, astonished and bewildered. "It couldn't have," he said flatly. "I'll swear on a stack of Bibles I never talked about that to anybody in this office. And that just happened, because ordinarily I would have mentioned it—as a little joke, the queer thing. But we had the hell of a lot of paperwork to get out about then, and I got tied up in other things, and— Nobody else in this office knew about it. The note itself, or what it said."

They looked at each other. "Somebody must have," said

Mendoza sharply. *"Obvio,* somebody did know about it, enough to fake an imitation."

"What about the lab men?" asked Ballard. "Questioned Documents—"

"Claro qué no. They're all working cops too, conscious of the top secrets. I think it's got to come back to this office, Ballard, because you men are—cops at one remove, shall we say. Not so conscious of the —"

"I deny that. We're just as aware as you are—" Ballard massaged the top of his head, disarranging his thick dark hair. "Damn it, I don't see how it could have leaked, Mendoza! It's just impossible."

"It did, so it's not impossible," said Mendoza. "Did you tell your wife about it?"

"Yes," said Ballard. "I did. She's the one person I did mention it to. But Angela wouldn't—she knows better than that."

"Could anybody have overheard you?"

"No," said Ballard absently. "Well, that shows you, because I remember I'd just come in the back door, she was in the kitchen. And ordinarily I wouldn't have told her a thing like that right out there, I'd have waited until we were in our room or— But Ellen and Mike were out that night, at a rehearsal of the class play—they're the teen-agers. And—" He stopped. After a silence he said, "But that's impossible, Mendoza. That couldn't be—"

"What couldn't be?"

"My God," said Ballard quietly. "Greg might have heard me. He was in the dining room with the dog—but that's crazy. A seven-year-old wouldn't have taken it in, been interested enough to remember—"

"It's surprising what a bright seven-year-old might take in," said Higgins. "He might have. And I think maybe we'd better ask him if he did, and if he remembers now, Ballard. About who he might have told about it."

"It's crazy!" said Ballard. "It couldn't be. But if you're

[231]

bound to check it out all the way—" He shrugged. "He'll be at school. Do we all go?"

"I think we do," said Mendoza.

Ballard lived in West Hollywood, and the boy went to an elementary school there. Mendoza was unhappy on the way; he detested being driven, but the Ferrari couldn't accommodate all of them and they took Higgins' Pontiac. At the school, they found the principal's office and Ballard asked for Greg to be fetched out of class. "This is silly," he said. "A seven-year-old."

In five minutes the boy came in, a nice-looking dark-haired boy. "Hi, Daddy," he said in surprise. "What's up, why'd you come to see me in school?"

"Listen, Greg—" They were in the anteroom of the principal's office, only an indifferent secretary busy at a typewriter behind the counter. Ballard sat down on the long built-in bench along the wall and pulled the boy between his knees. "I want you to think about something. It's kind of important. Do you remember, a couple of months ago, when I came home and was telling Mother something about a note the Homicide office was asking about? On one of their cases. A funny note. I didn't think you could hear me, or would pay any attention, but maybe you did. I didn't suppose you'd be interested, or remember it—but did you?"

The boy looked a little more surprised. He was curious about the other men, eyeing the two big ones covertly. He sensed that he might be in some trouble about this, and he hesitated, on the defensive. "What about it?" said Ballard.

"Yeah, I did hear it," he admitted. "I—I know sometimes you say to Mother, not to talk about something, but I didn't hear you say that then."

"All right," said Ballard. "All right. Now, did you tell anybody—anybody at all—about that note? What it said?"

Greg wriggled. "Well—well, I didn't know what 'illiterate' meant. And when she said why did I want to know, I—I told her about that. That's all. It was only—"

"Told who?"

"Only teacher," said Greg. "Only Miss Buckler."

A new one had gone down just after Mendoza and his two senior sergeants left, and Palliser and Grace went out on it. And after a thorough look around, and a talk with the uniformed men who'd got the call first, Grace said gently, "You know, John, I don't think our spate of queer ones has quite come to an end."

"You may be right," said Palliser. "It's offbeat, all right." When they got back to the office he wanted to call Robin; the baby'd been acting up again, she said, all night, kicking her like a kangaroo. It might decide to come early.

This one did indeed look a little queer. It was a two-room apartment in an old building on Cortez Street. The dead woman had been found by a girl friend who had a key, said she sometimes stayed there with her. They were both Negro. The Traffic men said they were both known prostitutes.

And it wasn't unusual for the prostitute, picking up with any man, to meet a violent end at a client's hand. What was unusual was that this one, whose name had been Sadie Simpson, had died suddenly of a dose of cyanide in a glass of gin and tonic. They had noticed the odor of almond at once; let the doctors confirm it. She was lying quietly on her back in bed, naked as a jaybird, and there wasn't, at first glance, any useful clue in the room—her clothes, a litter of cosmetics on a table, nothing extraneous.

Of course the lab might turn up some scientific evidence as a lead.

They took the girl friend back to the office to question, and Palliser called Roberta, who said it had quieted down. "But I'll be very happy to have this over, John."

"So will I," said Palliser fervently.

The A.P.B. hadn't yet turned up Theodore Cutter.

They had brought Naomi Buckler back to headquarters, and Hackett and Higgins went out to find Rose Jowett. They found her in the manageress's apartment explaining that she'd be moving on the first. She just looked frightened when they asked her to come back downtown, and when she came into Mendoza's office and saw Naomi Buckler she went white and began to cry.

They were eyeing Naomi with interest. There wasn't any hard and fast rule about what the male fags looked like, but with the Lesbians you could nearly always pick out the butch on looks. Naomi was a big woman, and a handsome one, with a rather heavy square face, brilliant dark eyes, black wavy hair cut short and severe as a man's—or as most men's used to be, shingled at the neck. She was lean and trim and plainly dressed in an oxford-gray suit with a stark white blouse. Her square hands were blunt-fingered, ringless, and she had a flat contralto voice.

"Oh," wailed Rose Jowett, "I don't know anything—I didn't know anything!"

"You shut up," said Naomi tersely. "I'd like to know just why I've been brought here."

"Surely," said Mendoza. "The scientific evidence is very helpful sometimes, Miss Buckler. You had a very cunning little idea there, about that note. You'd heard Greg Ballard's little story about that first note. You knew his father was a police officer, and you could put two and two together and surmise that that was a tale out of school—not a thing the police would let out. And when you needed a—mmh—gimmick, there it was tucked away at the back of your mind. I think you were very much annoyed when Ken Jowett persuaded his wife to come back to him. Yes—the two strong characters, pull devil, pull baker, with the weak one caught between. You were trying to get her back, weren't you?"

Her cold bright eyes met his. "Prove it," she said briefly.

"I *wanted* to—but I *didn't* want to—and Naomi said he was d-dominating my life and Ken—"

"You be quiet, Rosie. They can't do anything," she said roughly.

"You hated him for that, didn't you?" said Mendoza with intellectual curiosity. "For coaxing Rose back to him. And

[234]

you knew if he was—removed—you'd have no more trouble with her. And, lo, into your head came that little tale told out of school you'd heard from your second-grade pupil, Greg Ballard. You could, as I said, surmise that the contents of that little note wouldn't be very common property. The illiterate note, God bless the parole board. Another one, found on another body, would certainly misdirect us, look like the impersonal kill.

"And you knew from Rose, of course, what time he left for work. I think you told her to make sure she was with a neighbor at that time—to show all the clearer it was an outside thing—"

"I didn't know, I did go across to the Wallings but I didn't *know*—"

"And the Jowetts hadn't lived there long, nobody there knew there'd ever been trouble between them. You were waiting for him there outside the garage, with the knife. And the note already prepared. What exactly did you know about that note, how did Greg describe it? Obviously, enough. What it said, and that it looked illiterate. You made a neat little job of it—until," said Mendoza sardonically, "the scientific boys had a look at it. They could tell us—and they'll be testifying in court—that it's a fake. An imitation of illiteracy. Quite possibly they can tie it to you from your normal writing."

A little spasm passed over her face, but she was silent.

"You're a very efficient woman, Miss Buckler, and as strong as a man. You got him from behind as he was going into the garage, and I don't suppose he knew what hit him. And you tucked that note into his breast pocket, rifled all the others —hey presto, the violent random kill. The near-illiterate on parole." Suddenly Mendoza laughed. "If it's any consolation to you—¡Dios, did you send us on a wild goose chase! All those parolees— But we do usually catch up in the end. Even on the offbeat ones. Where will we find the knife?"

"Prove it," she said.

"Maybe we'll find it right back in the bread-drawer at

your apartment? The scientific boys will tell us, even after it's been washed."

"Go to hell," she said. "You've got no evidence."

Mendoza smiled at her slowly. "That," he said, "is just where you are so wrong, Miss Buckler. Some very nice clear-cut evidence that you're the only person outside of police personnel who knew about that note in the Reynolds case. Greg's a very bright little boy, the court will admit his testimony. And that really ties you in nice and tight, doesn't it?"

Her hands moved convulsively. "You never really told me," wailed Rose. "You just said, be with somebody after he left—I never wanted anybody hurt, Ken was always nice to me, but I did what you *said*, Naomi, only I didn't know—"

She began to swear obscenely, in a low flat voice. But she was entirely rational when she aimed a punch at Higgins as he took her arm, a blow delivered like a man. He dodged, and got out the cuffs. "If you want it that way—"

"I'll get the machinery going on the warrant," said Hackett. "Murder one. On her and—?" He looked at Rose.

Mendoza looked at his cigarette. "I think two warrants on murder one, Art. She knew. She shut her eyes, but she knew." They took them both out.

Mendoza put out the cigarette and said to himself, "People. The things we see—" He stretched and got up, went out to the communal office. "Any new ones down?" Grace and Palliser were both there, with a scared-looking Negro girl.

"A kind of queer thing," said Grace. "I think we'd like to hear your ideas on it."

Fourteen

Mercifully, the I.A. hearing had closed down at four o'clock on Tuesday afternoon, so Conway and Landers and their two girls had enjoyed the double date uninterrupted, and were enthusiastic about the musical. When the night watch came in on Wednesday night, they told the other two they really ought to see it, it was damn good.

"I've heard it's worth seeing," said Galeano. The initial attempt to stop smoking, and his sudden gain of ten unwanted pounds, had shaken him; he was back to Camels, and lit one moodily.

But Schenke had found a note from Hackett, and exploded, "My good God! You will never believe how that Jowett case turned out! You won't believe it—my God, talk about queer things—"

They kicked that around awhile, surprised and amused and wishing they had more details, before the first call came in: heist at a liquor store on Grand. Conway and Landers went out on it. "The same old round," said Landers, thinking of last week and the heists, of the monotonously similar heistmen. "I know we cuss the offbeat ones, but at least they aren't so boring."

Of course the manager, clerk, and customers at the liquor store weren't bored. "It was a real big gun!" said the female customer. "He was a great big guy, maybe six feet, and he came in—"

"He was a white man," said the manager, "young, about twenty-five maybe, and he sure acted like he knew how to use that gun. I looked at the register tape, he got away with about three hundred—"

"He didn't take your wallet, or—"

"No, sir, it was the register money he was interested in! As soon as I handed it over, he stuck it in his pocket and ran out—I didn't see a car, no, but all the traffic out there, he could've got in one—well, I don't know about a description, I'd say he was about six foot, like the lady said, and not fat, but stocky, you know—big. He had a hat on, I didn't see his hair, except it's not real long or it'd'a showed. Well, I guess his coloring was sort of medium—"

"He was only here a minute," said the male customer, "and we wasn't exactly in the mood for noticing did he have a long nose or big ears."

"No, sir, I know," said Landers. "Anybody remember anything else about him? His clothes?"

"He had on dark pants and a turtleneck and a jacket, all dark," said the manager. "It's the first time I been held up this year. Last year I started right out on January second gettin' held up, nine times altogether up to December. I got a good business here but I'm thinkin' of gettin' into something not so vulnerable like they say."

They all said he hadn't touched anything. There wasn't any point doing any dusting. Landers and Conway went back to the office and flipped for who'd write the report; Landers lost and uncovered his typewriter resignedly. He'd be just as happy to go off the night watch and back on days, to start using the services of Robbery-Homicide's secretary on typing reports.

On Thursday Higgins got started on the darkroom. Their March heat wave had come along as expected, and it went up to the nineties, but it was the day he had, and he used it. He went out early to get the lumber and by noon he'd got the studs up and most of the plywood partitions.

Mary had the baby in the back yard, on a blanket under the big umbrella, while she weeded the flower beds behind the house. Margaret Emily cooed to herself and moved her toes and fingers like little starfish, and Brucie the good watchdog lay beside her.

By the time Steve Dwyer got home from school, Higgins was sitting in a deck chair in the back yard with a bottle of iced Coke. "Hi—how'd it go?" asked Steve eagerly, riding up on his bike.

"Just have to put the door up—I waited for you, you can hold it while I get the screws in. Running in the water, well, we'll have to figure how much pipe we'll need—"

"Gosh, this is going to be great!" Steve looked around the bare five-foot-square space ecstatically, already seeing sink, faucet, counter and lights installed. "Come on, let's get that door up, George—"

On Friday morning Grace and Palliser went out on a new call, and came back talking bitterly about offbeat ones. A second Negro girl, known prostitute, had been found dead when her erstwhile husband got let out of the drunk tank this morning and went home. It looked like the cyanide again, this time in a glass of bourbon and water. Again, nothing extraneous around. They hadn't had a lab report on the first one yet.

"Don't tell me we're in for a series of poisonings now!" said Palliser. "What do you think?" They'd found Mendoza shuffling the cards, cigarettes in one corner of his mouth.

"We don't get the poisonings just so often," said Mendoza. "But seeing we've got two, I don't see any reason we won't get three. *Condenación*—have we got one of these lunatics taking off whores? Shades of Jack the Ripper."

"This one was Florrie Stone. Usual record with us. Thirty-three, served little stretches for petty theft. The husband—common-law—has a felony record. Burglary. But he was in the tank until eight o'clock, and she was killed last night."

Sadie Simpson, her girl friend said emphatically, would

never have gone suiciding herself, and besides there wasn't any cyanide in the place, or anything that had held any. Ditto for Florrie Stone's two rooms. "Bainbridge ought to be able to say something about it by now," said Mendoza, and called him. Bainbridge said irascibly that he'd just got to the Simpson body, and it was the first time he'd run across this in a while. Seen it used by suicides sometimes. The cyanide had been in a mixture used in amateur photography, anybody could buy it in any photographic supply shop, and they could probably pinpoint the brand if that was necessary.

"Photography!" said Palliser. And of course the only way to work this was the way they'd started on Simpson, back-track her and try to find somebody who'd noticed who she might have picked up on Tuesday night. Both the women had frequented bars along Temple, First, Second.

About the middle of Friday afternoon, Grace, asking patient questions at an usavory bar far down on Temple, struck a little pay dirt. A girl named Rosanna Peters told him she'd seen Sadie last Tuesday night. The girls like these knew what had happened to Sadie, and were eager and willing to talk to cops.

"All right," said Grace, "was she with anybody when you saw her? Where?"

"It was in at Harry's place over on Second, sir. No, sir, she was by herself, I sit at the table awhile, an' she tole me she hadda date for later on, see—you suppose that coulda been *him,* one give her poison?"

"What did she say about him? What time was this?"

" 'Bout nine o'clock. She dint say no more, just she hadda date, an' he was gonna pay her twenny bucks. Honest, thass all she said, but did you ast Gertie?"

"Gertie who?"

"Geesis, Gertie was her best friend, sir! Gertie Mack. I dunno where she lives now, I ain't seen her around in a while, but her and Sadie was allus goin' round together, maybe Sadie tole her more about the guy."

When he got back to the office, Grace asked R. and I. about

Gertie and eventually discovered that she was doing three months in the county jail for a fifth count of purse-snatching.

It went like that, and it was the usual slogging routine, with nothing in the way of a lead. There'd been two more heists on Thursday night, committed nearly simultaneously nine blocks apart, with different descriptions given of the heisters, so they now had the routine on that, R. and I. having given them two lists of men who fit those descriptions.

The autopsy on Sadie Simpson came in on Saturday, with Sergeant Lake off reading a new paperback on dieting he'd borrowed from Hackett, and Farrell sitting on the board. The only new thing the report told them was that Sadie had been drunk.

"And all the easier to spike her drink," said Hackett reasonably. "She wouldn't be noticing. And you know this is another nut, George, with some hangup about whores."

And of course Sadie and Florrie weren't going to be missed much; but anyone who has killed is apt to pick on any citizen next, so they wanted to find him.

On Saturday too, Piggott and Glasser dropped on one of the possibles for the heist on Wednesday night, and he got tangled up trying to answer questions and admitted he'd done that. "Say, how are your fish coming?" asked Glasser after they'd stashed him in jail and gone back to apply for the warrant.

Piggott said, "I tell you, Henry, it seems there's a little more to this fish breeding than the book says."

They had done all the things the book said, and after they were sure the two parents had done their part of the job, the female shrunken back to slenderness with all her eggs dropped, they'd carefully fished for them with the net and returned them to the other aquarium. A day later, if they looked close, they could faintly make out the masses of eggs adhering to the green nylon mop in the tank. Some seemed to be bigger than others.

Forty-eight hours later some of the bigger ones had turned

into minute creatures free-swimming about in small areas of the tank. And that morning Piggott, examining those before he left for work, had to his horror seen one dive down to absorb several of the eggs still adhering to the mop. But at least some of them were hatched and growing. When he left, Prudence was boiling more eggs. The yolks had to be strained through muslin, said the book, and formed into very small particles—

Well, time would tell how many young tetras they would have in three months.

Mendoza came into the office on Sunday, but he didn't know why. There was nothing of any particular interest going on—unless the nut after the whores had been busy again.

He hadn't, unless the body hadn't been found yet. But Palliser had come across a girl who claimed to have seen Florrie last Thursday night with a man. Palliser was still yawning; he'd been out on overtime last night, because that was the best time to find these girls, sitting around bars.

"She said he was a dude," said Palliser. "Dressed to the nines. 'Nobody from around here,' she said. A white man with a beard and moustache. What do we do with that?"

Mendoza was stacking the deck of cards. He grunted, "You know without asking. Ask the whores around if they recognize the description."

"They won't," said Palliser. "He's a nut, out for the first time with his hangup, whatever. Him and his photographic cyanide." But Grace was bringing in another Negro girl to talk to, and Palliser went to hear what she had to say.

Mendoza was still sitting there practicing the crooked deals at twelve-thirty when the phone buzzed at him. He picked it up. "Mendoza."

"Say, I just had a call from Mrs. Donahue," said Carey. "Lucky thing I happened to be here. She was on her way to meet a girl friend for lunch and a movie just now, she says, and all of a sudden she saw this blond hussy who came for Mrs. Borchers' suitcases. Said she recognized her right off, and so she followed her, and the blonde's sitting in the Brown Derby right now, and will I come catch her. She's standing guard at the door. I thought you might be interested."

"*¡Cómo!*" said Mendoza. His initial mild interest in the disappearance of Mina Borchers had fanned into heat over the very curious matter of those old silver certificates. The really frustrating thing about that was that, greed being an inevitable part of human nature, it would be practically impossible to trace them. If that had been the motive for taking her off, as he was inclined to suspect, whoever had done it would quietly sell them to a numismatist as a hoard found in Grandpa's attic, and that was that. And how very typical of that particular kind of petty miser that she hadn't, apparently, known what she had. Money was money. He looked at the deck of cards. Until, he thought, it became evident that it was only pretty engraved paper, with nothing of intrinsic value behind it, and it was a damn good thing he was still in practice at the crooked deals, with the hostages to fortune. "I'm interested," he said. "Meet me in the lot—we'll use my siren."

In front of the Brown Derby out on Wilshire, the Ferrari swooped into the loading zone, and they both got out. Mrs. Donahue, dowdy in a brown suit and a very unbecoming beige hat, looked very relieved to see Carey.

"She's still there," she greeted him, waving her purse as if she was calling a taxi. "I'd know her anywhere! I was just getting off the bus when I saw her, she's with another woman. I didn't dare go right in, but I sort of lurked around just inside the door, and you can see her—they're at a table in the middle of the room."

"O.K.," said Carey. "What's she got on?"

"A bright red sleeveless dress and black patent leather sandals and no stockings," said Mrs. Donahue disapprovingly.

"Good. You wait here." He and Mendoza went in, stopped

a moment to let their eyes adjust to the dim light, and spotted her. Mendoza recognized the type instantly, a fairly common type maybe the world over. A what-the-hell girl, free and easy and largely friendly and generous. She had a good deal of tawny ash-blond hair, frosted, and a round face, eyes made up with everything from fake eyelashes to green eyeshadow, and too dark a shade of lipstick. She was sipping a drink; the girl across from her was much the same kind, dark and prettier.

They stopped at the table, and both produced badges. "We'd like to talk to you, miss," said Carey genially.

"What the hell?" she said, startled. She craned her neck up at them. "What about?"

"Mind if we sit down? Mind telling us your name?"

"Yes, I mind," she said, annoyed. "I haven't done anything wrong, what do cops want of me anyway?"

"Well, you've been identified," said Mendoza, "as the woman who went to an address on Bonnie Brae Street last—"

"November seventh," supplied Carey.

"—And said you'd come for Mrs. Borchers' suitcases. You had the key to her room and you took the suitcases away with you."

She didn't say anything, and then she said, "That's no crime."

"No, it wasn't. But we'd like to know about it."

"What's there to know?" She shrugged.

"Well, for instance," said Mendoza, "did Mrs. Borchers ask you to do that?"

She regarded him warily. "So what if she did?" But some other emotion was under the wariness. The other girl had been listening uneasily; now she shoved her chair back.

"Listen, dear, I guess I won't stay for lunch after all, these guys got business with you, huh? Give me a ring sometime." She went off in a hurry.

"Damn it, what's this all about?"

"You might tell us your name," said Mendoza mildly.

"My name's Sandra Bush," she said hotly, "and I've never done anything to make me ashamed of it! I'd like to know what *business* cops think they got with me!"

"These suitcases," said Mendoza. "Why did you go to pick them up and what did you do with them?"

"And what the hell does it matter?"

"Well, you see," said Mendoza, "Mrs. Borchers has disappeared, and we think she may be dead. And by going to pick up her suitcases, you were a party to—er—conniving at her disappearance."

"Disappearance!" said Sandra Bush. She blinked at them. "That's crazy. She went back east to live with some relatives. And I didn't steal those suitcases, you can't— What do you mean, disappeared?"

"She hasn't got any relatives except for a son," said Carey, "and she wouldn't have wanted to live with him, and he wouldn't have wanted her either. She hasn't been seen by anyone who knew her since last November sixth, at The Broadway department store. She didn't tell anyone she was moving, though it seems she may have meant to, those suitcases all packed."

She looked from him to Mendoza. "She—was going back east," she said slowly.

"Who said so, Miss Bush?"

"Look," said Carey harshly, "we're pretty sure this woman is dead, and that she may have been murdered. You're going to tell us what you know, if not here then down at my office. Who told you that? Who—"

"Murdered!" She let out an involuntary little shriek and then clapped a hand over her mouth. "Oh, my God!" she said. "Listen, he's a nice guy and all and I was glad to do him a favor, but I'm not getting mixed up in a murder! Look, he told me the old lady decided to go back east, but he didn't want to upset his wife, his wife was real fond of her and might, you know, sort of take offense, so they fixed it up she'd leave while his wife was off on vacation. Only she came back

[245]

a day early, before he got to send her luggage after her. He said I was just to say I come for the luggage, and he'd pick it up later, send it on. He didn't want his wife to think he'd had anything to do with the old lady leaving, 's all."

"Who?" said Mendoza and Carey together.

"But at that—*murder?* He always seemed like a nice guy," said Sandra. "Not the kind that'd do anything like that. He used to drop into the Gem Bar when I worked there, I hadn't seen him in a while till he happened to see me where I work now, the Three Trees—I'm in the bar there—he was on the crew built the new wing."

"Who?"

She blinked at them. "Why, Jack Donahue," she said.

The Ferrari being the size it was, they called up a black-and-white to take Sandra and Mrs. Donahue back to the house on Bonnie Brae. Mendoza wondered if they found anything to say to each other on the way.

He wasn't there. Fat old Mrs. Pruitt, crocheting on the front porch, and considerably alarmed at the patrol car, said he'd only gone out for cigarettes, he'd be back because there was a TV show he wanted to see.

They sat in the living room, too full of old-fashioned furniture, and Mrs. Donahue kept saying, "I don't believe it! She's just covering up for somebody else, Jack wouldn't know any floozy like her."

"Listen, lady, I'll have you know I'm no tramp and I'm not going to listen to you calling me names! I told the cops straight how it was. There wasn't anything between Jack and me, he's old enough to be my father, but he always seemed like a nice guy—beats me how he came to get hitched to a prune-faced old maid like you!"

"Now, ladies," said Carey, "calm down."

When he came in ten minutes later, the first one he saw was Sandra, perched in her red dress in the big chair beside the television. Then he saw Carey, and Mendoza, and his heavy face crumpled like a baby's and he said, "Aw, Sandra. Aw, Sandra, why'd you have to go and—"

"Listen, I couldn't help it, I'm sorry but they said about murder and I'm not getting mixed up in any murder, Jack. Not little Sandra." But she looked at him doubtfully, and he certainly didn't look very dangerous at the moment, a big man carrying a growing paunch, his shoulders sagging.

"Oh, Jack, how could you—go behind my back—that awful girl—" Mrs. Donahue began to cry weakly.

"Listen," said Sandra angrily, "I'm not—"

"Oh, hell," said Donahue. "Oh, hell, get me away from these damn females and I'll tell you. It was an accident— I never meant to do it, it was just an accident! And ask me, it was part her own fault—"

He told them about it in Mendoza's office, with a police-woman from Carey's office taking it down. "I tell you, she was the orneriest, crankiest old bitch I ever knew in my life. Couldn't please her no matter what. I felt damn sorry for Mary, she did her best, but that Borchers woman, all she knew how to do was bitch, bitch, complain, grouch, morning to night! The other two old folks, they're nice people, and it's a way to have extra money coming in, I don't mind, but that Borchers woman!" He passed a big hand over his face.

"We've heard that before," said Mendoza. "I believe you. How did you happen to find out about the cash, Donahue?"

"Cash!" said Donahue. "I didn't know nothing about that, for God's sake! I tell you just how it happened. I was outta work, that time, and the Borchers woman was going to see the doctor. And she was bitching about the cab-fare, she couldn't get all the way on the bus, and Mary has to speak up and say why don't I drive her. So I did. With her tellin' me all the way what a lousy driver I am and I should be out huntin' a job. So I put her off at the doctor's office, and she says she'll be about an hour, I should come back. Like I'm her private chauffeur or somethin'. I tell you, that woman was a real pain in the— Well, so I park the car and I go into a bar down the street and I have three beers. Three lousy beers, and if you think I'm anywheres near tight on that—!" He lit a cigarette and Mendoza shoved over the ashtray.

"So I drive back to where that doctor's office is—it was about noon. I didn't have a watch on me, and I'd got talking to a guy in the bar about football teams, and so the old biddy's bitchin', bitchin' about I'm late, go off get drunk in a bar and leave her stand around in the cold. She got in the front seat, goin' on like that, and I think of all the trouble she's been to Mary, and before I knew what I was doin', I just give her a backhand and said, 'Shut up, you old witch!' "

"*Entendido*," said Mendoza, and his lips twitched.

"Well, my God," said Donahue, "I didn't mean any such thing—but, Jesus, she just fell over and when I looked she was dead. She was an old lady and not in too good shape, I guess—she'd fell against the top of the door, and I don't know if her neck was busted or her head hurt some way, but"—he swallowed—"she was dead! I was scared as hell, I never meant nothing like that! But—there she was, I was stuck, and I sat there tryin' to think what to do, and Jesus, a patrol car come by and honked I should get out of the loading zone, and I just—drove off. With her. She just looked like she was asleep, sort of."

"And what," asked Carey rather grimly, "did you do with her?"

"Jesus, I didn't know what to do!" said Donahue. "But I got down to the Stack, my mind's not exactly on my drivin', and first thing I know I'm on the Pasadena freeway. And by the time I got up past the Dodgers Stadium, I'd got to thinkin' about all the wild country there still is, out the other end o' the valley—way out past Chatsworth. So I got off on the Golden State freeway, I went all the way out to past where it starts to get all wild, all empty land out there. And I got off the freeway and drove up Kagel Canyon. It was all damn rough country, and I finally figured it was far enough away from everything, and I just carried her out and put her under some bushes, kind of hidden away. I—"

"Can't you be any more specific?" asked Carey. "There's the hell of a lot of Kagel Canyon."

Donahue thought. "Well, on the way back I noticed a sign said Indian Canyon Mountain. And I'd been thinkin' about all her stuff. How to explain her goin' off—make it look like she just went somewhere. She always kept her room locked, had a special Yale lock on it, but I had her keys then. So that night—oh, I told Mary the story about leavin' her at The Broadway, and when she didn't come home Mary had to call the cops, but it was O.K., in all the traffic nobody could say I didn't drop her there. And I made Mary take a sleeping pill. The other two old folks, they're kind of deaf. And I got in that room. Jesus!" said Donahue simply.

"And found the money." Mendoza laughed.

"I didn't believe it. I don't. Fifty-seven thousand bucks! Fifty-seven—"

"*¡Porvida! ¡Parece mentira!*" said Mendoza. "That much left—what a woman. What did you do with it? And did you notice anything different about it?"

"Different?" said Donahue. "What do you mean? I didn't believe it, that much money, and my God, I'm not a thief! I don't want to steal the old witch's money! I got it hid in an old tool-kit in the back o' my car, where Mary won't be lookin'. I been tryin' to figure out some way to send it to that son of hers, without nobody knowin' I'm the one, but mail can get lost— And see, later on we heard that this other old lady was sick and goin' to die, that Mrs. Eldon, only one ever came to see the Borchers woman, so I think it'll die down, nobody'll come looking, not for a long time anyway. And then she didn't die after all—" He looked at them forlornly. "I never meant to kill her."

"An accident," said Mendoza. Suddenly he laughed. "And I was building all the complex tales about some cunning X who was after that hoard! But human nature never has been very complicated."

"Hell and damnation," said Carey. "It's going to be a job to locate that corpse."

The suitcases, Donahue said, he'd thrown over a cliff along the beach down toward San Diego. They'd look; probably the bank book was among her effects.

They turned the sheriff's men out on that; there was a lot of rough country to search. Two weeks later they found part of a skeleton, including a skull; coyotes had been at it. Eventually dental records established that it was Mina Borchers' corpse, and after some legal red tape and a bite to the state, Charles Borchers got what was left of the hoard.

The D.A. decided to call it manslaughter. When he came to trial, Donahue might get a three-to-five.

The Pallisers' baby arrived, with little fuss, on March twenty-first, turning out to be David Andrew.

At the end of two weeks, there were about seventy tiny fragile baby fish sailing around the rented tank, and Piggott said there was more to this game than he'd expected. The surviving baby tetras had eaten all the other eggs. But Prudence was fascinated, straining more hardboiled egg yolk. "I wonder when they start to show any color, Matt. They're transparent as glass!"

In the original aquarium, one of the two pretty little rosy tetras had a dark ominous spot on its belly. "We'd better try that salt cure again," said Piggott. After a frustrating half hour he managed to catch it in the net and transferred it to the asparagus steamer and the salt solution.

There was really quite a lot to do, keeping the pretty little fish.

Glasser rallied around and helped Higgins get the water line and electricity run into the new darkroom. "Gosh, this is really great!" said Steve, eyes shining. "You wait and see what I can turn out here, George! And I'm going to save like anything—that camera shop up on Glendale Boulevard's got a real good secondhand enlarger for only forty bucks—"

They still hadn't found Theodore Cutter.

They now had four Negro prostitutes dead of the photographic cyanide, and Mendoza was talking to himself about lunatics and obsessions. And why he stayed at the thankless job.

"You wouldn't know what to do with yourself," said Alison.

But he shelved the endless routine, coming home to the twins. The twins suddenly starting to grow up.

"Goats!" said Terry imperatively, showing him the picture in the McGuffey primer. "See, Daddy, I can read what it says. 'The goats love Bess, for she feed them and is kind to.' I'd like a goat. We'd be kind to a goat, ¿cómo no, Johnny?"

"Heaven forbid," said Mendoza. "Yes, that's fine, querida."

"I know the next lesson!" shouted Johnny. "Mamacita didn't help—I did it myself! It says the house is on fire! The roof all burned up!"

"That's right," said Mendoza, looking at the next lesson. At least the primer seemed to be guiding the twins toward a more exclusive use of English.

After they'd been settled down, he sat somewhat somnolently over Kipling, half-thinking about this lunatic with his hangup on harlots. The funny things came along sometimes, the queer ones: not often. Mostly, it was the monotonous routine, and why he stayed at this job—

All four cats were in a complicated tangle, asleep, on his side of the bed. El Señor had his tongue out and was twitching spasmodically, jungle-hunting in a dream. Alison was poring over a book he'd given her for Christmas, *Paintings of the Old West*.

"Livestock!" said Mendoza. "If I'm going to sleep in this bed tonight—"

"*Si, amado,*" said Alison. She woke up the cats and El Señor hissed at her.

And five seconds after he switched out the bedside lamp, a voice sounded out there in the yard, faint but distinct. *Coroo-coroo,* it said. Yawk. *Too-whoo.*

Alison sat bolt upright. "It's him! *El pajaro*—our mockingbird!"

Mendoza muttered, "I might have known nothing would happen to that damned creature—there's no peace for the wicked!" He pulled the covers over his head.